THE
GRAIL
MURDERS

Being the Third Journal of Sir Roger Shallot
Concerning Certain Wicked Conspiracies
and Horrible Murders Perpetrated
in the Reign of King Henry VIII

Michael Clynes

OTTO PENZLER BOOKS
New York

OTTO PENZLER BOOKS

Otto Penzler Books
129 West 56th Street
New York, NY 10019
(Editorial Offices only)

Simon & Schuster Inc.
Rockefeller Center
1230 Avenue of the Americas
New York, NY 10020

First United States Edition

Manufactured in the United States of America

10   9   8   7   6   5   4   3   2

Library of Congress Cataloging-in-Publication Data
Clynes, Michael.
    The grail murders: being the third journal of Sir Roger Shallot concerning certain wicked conspiracies and horrible murders perpetrated in the reign of King Henry VIII/Michael Clynes.
        p.   cm.
    1. Great Britain—History—Henry VIII, 1509–1547—Fiction.
I. Title.
PR6053.L93G73   1994
823'.914—dc20   94–8932
                                                        CIP

ISBN 1-883402-49-2

Niall Harrington — in memory of the many conversations we had about whodunnits.

THE GRAIL MURDERS

Prologue

Murder has marked us all as Cain's children: Cain who when the earth was young slew his brother with the jawbone of an ass and hid in the forest until God hunted him out, grasped his head and gave him the assassin's mark. We must be his children, mustn't we? If Cain, the son of Adam, is father to us all, then we must all bear his mark.

I see my chaplain sniffing as if he has smelt something foul: his prim lips are pursed, that cherry nose wrinkled. The trouble with him is his nose is too near his codpiece! Never trust short-legged men – the gap between their brain and their buttocks is too close for comfort.

Ah, well, so we are all Cain's children. In fairness, I must confess that's not an original thought. Michael Nostradamus, Catherine de Medici's fortune-teller, once told me that whilst I was hiding in Paris from a group of assassins who wanted to take my head but, as I keep saying, that's another story.

A strange man, Nostradamus! In his secret chamber at the Castle Blois he had a famous mirror. If you looked into it, you could see the future. Catherine de Medici, voluptuous, murderous Catherine – Madame Serpent as I call her – used to spend days staring into it.

Nostradamus also claimed he had dreams which foretold the future: demons who appeared to him at night, their black eyes filled with blood, huge scrolls in their fists, the written records of the sins of men from the first day to the last. Nostradamus said they kept unrolling these scrolls and there was no end to them. No end to the terrible and bloody murders of men.

I agree with him for Murder has haunted my life and still plagues my dreams. Oh no, I am not an assassin myself but I have spent my life tracking them down. Now I, too, have the same dreams as Nostradamus: strange, merciless devils, faces twisted with rage, teeth showing over their lips. They belong to the blackest darkness for they are the lost souls of murderers.

The other night these spirits woke me just after the last snowfall which cloaked the fields in thick white clouds. I sat up in my fourposter bed, pulled back the curtains and gazed through the great oriel window which stares out over the lawns in front of my house. The moon shone ghostly white, the stars gleamed like silver wings in the heavens. On either side of me Phoebe and her sister Margot snored in their soft, warm plumpness. (A marvellous way to keep warm in the depths of winter!) I stared over the lawns, thinking of my past, and saw the black shadow move like some great bat. I knew it was the Lord Satan's precursor.

(My chaplain is laughing. The little sod had better be careful! 'More like wine fumes,' he sniggers. If he is not careful, I'll grab the cushions from beneath his bum. Oh, yes, I will and my homunculus, my little dwarf of a chaplain, shall feel hard wood under his buttocks.)

I did see the shadows come, the nightmare men, ghosts from my past.

The next morning the stranger arrived, travelling through the deep snow bearing letters and warrants allowing him access to Sir Roger Shallot, Privy Councillor, Knight of the Bath, Knight of the Garter, Justice of the Peace, Commissioner of Array, Marshall of the Order of St Michael. (A gentleman who styled himself Tsar of all the Russias, a homicidal bastard if ever there was one, gave me that.)

I met the stranger in my secret chamber behind the arras in the great hall. The captain of my guard stood beside me, his sword drawn, for though I am now well past my ninetieth year, old Shallot still has his enemies. The secret agents of many a crowned head still seek a reward for cutting my throat and letting my life-juice spill out. So you have to be careful when you approach me.

This man was: he stopped at the great gates leading to my estates. If he had entered without permission, my great Irish wolfhounds would have torn him to pieces and, if they hadn't, the jolly boys who serve in my troop of mercenaries would have strung him up from the nearest branch.

Anyway, I met him in my secret chamber, the only light coming from the braziers of glowing charcoal and the pure wax candles whose flames darted long and strong against the darkness. Enough light glowed for me to see him but not enough to reveal the coffers, chests, sealed packets and padlocked boxes full of old Shallot's papers, the legacy of a murderous past, which stand around the walls.

The fellow looked nondescript, old and balding, his skin the colour of darkened leather, but I liked his eyes, clear and bright. They reminded me of my old master, Benjamin Daunbey, nephew to that fat slob Cardinal Wolsey, in whose service we both toiled for many a year.

My visitor sat for a while and stared at me.

'You don't remember me?' he said.

His English was perfect though tinged with a slight accent.

'Sweet Lord!' I answered. 'Must I remember everybody?'

I looked at the warrants he'd brought, lying on the desk in front of me, bearing the seals of that lovely lass Elizabeth of England. Green-eyed Elizabeth, Boleyn's daughter. (I don't say Henry VIII's. That fat bastard. The Great Killer couldn't create any life. I know who Elizabeth's father really was but I'm not telling you. Well, at least not now. Perhaps some other time.)

'Why should the Queen,' I asked, 'give you these warrants?'

The man shrugged and leaned closer. The captain of my guard put his sword gently on the fellow's shoulder as a warning that he was close enough.

'Who are you?' I demanded.

The man unhitched his cloak, revealing the blood-red gown and white six-pointed cross of the Knights of St John, commonly known as the Hospitallers. I sighed and smiled.

'As I said,' my guest continued, 'you do not remember me, Sir Roger. I am John de Coligny, knight hospitaller, bailiff in that Order, but I was born on the manor of Templecombe in Somerset.'

Oh, sweet Lord! I just sat and stared at him as the memories came rushing back: overcast skies and the snow-laden trees and meadows of Somerset. Flames roaring round a bed. A maddened horse dragging its rider, pounding him to death. And the icy cold water of that lake as Benjamin and I fought against a most cruel assassin. I let the tears roll down my face.

'Sir Roger.' Coligny paused. 'I did not mean to upset you. Her Majesty the Queen said you would understand the need for secrecy. I am a Catholic and, by all rights, should suffer the supreme penalty for even setting foot in England. I have come to repay a debt, to fulfil a vow.'

He loosened his doublet and brought out a small stained leather pouch tied by a cord round his neck.

Oh, bitter-sweet memories! I knew what was coming but could only stare with tear-filled eyes at the small amethyst ring the fellow pushed across the desk.

'I was a child,' Coligny continued, 'only a babe-in-arms when you gave that to my mother. She always spoke of your kindness and courage.'

Do you know, I didn't know whether to laugh or cry. Here was someone paying homage to my courage! Me, Roger Shallot, who in his time was the swiftest runner in Christendom – and, believe me, I always proved it. When

4

swords were drawn and blood was spilt, old Shallot, to quote my friend Will Shakespeare, was 'like a greyhound in the slips', ready to charge – always the other way. I picked up the ring and gazed at its brilliant sparkle.

'So long ago,' I murmured. 'So many horrible deaths. Such terrible murders.'

I lapsed into a reverie and de Coligny withdrew.

I later feasted him for a day, revelling in his praise and adulation, then I rewarded him well, furnished him with safe conducts to Dover and watched him leave. His coming was a sign. A grim reminder of the past. He could praise my courage but old Shallot knows the truth: the past is a pack of lies. My dreams would taunt me. The nightmare men would come.

At first I ignored them but last night when I awoke, one hand on Phoebe's tits, the other on Margot's, I stared through the oriel window at the shadows crawling across the thick-capped snow and knew I would have to continue my memoirs. If I didn't the dreams would grow worse. It was time to start again.

I had drunk three cups of rich red claret and snuggled up between Phoebe and Margot. (Lovely lasses but violently jealous of each other.) We played a little game and I fell asleep. I don't know whether it was a dream or a vision but I found myself, face pressed against the oriel window, staring out into the darkness.

An animal skull appeared, moving through the air, hovering just beyond the glass. Then a knight dressed in the robes of a Templar, black-faced with a scarlet helm, on its crown writhing snakes tearing into the rotting belly of a chicken. In the knight's hands was a decapitated grey head with bandaged eyes, covered with a seething mass of insects.

Other visions came. They crowded round, so intense, so pressing, I screamed myself awake. I couldn't go back to sleep until Phoebe and Margot had brought me a cup of sack and performed the dance they had learnt at last May Day's mummer's play.

So here we are. Because it's winter I am not sitting at the centre of my maze but in my secret chamber, wrapped in rugs in my high-backed throne. On one side a jug of claret and a deep-bowled cup, on the other my black ash rod just in case my chaplain mocks too much. You see, this little sod thinks that I dream it all up. He thinks I drink too much wine and that I am a consummate liar. If I am, I am no different from people of his ilk, as he knows to his cost. Oh, yes, I know my chaplain's little sins. I see him steal glances at young Phoebe's rounded thighs or Margot's generous tits. I have heard the stories about how he likes to take young ladies into the hay loft of one of my barns. He must think I am as stupid as he looks! After all, a hay loft on a warm summer's evening is not the ideal place to instruct some buxom wench. Or, on second thoughts, perhaps it depends on what the instruction's about!

I think my chaplain is jealous of me. He prides himself on being a fine orator, able to give a pithy sermon. Two years ago he was invited up to court to dispute certain theological matters before Her Majesty the Queen. I forget the details – something about the existence of angels.

A venerable bishop began the debate and did quite well. He kept me awake for at least five minutes. Apparently, the old boy chattered on for an hour. I awoke just as he left the pulpit then it was my chaplain's turn.

I was sitting next to Elizabeth. I nudged her and declared in a loud stage whisper for all to hear, 'Here comes counsel for the other side.' A subtle joke, only the Queen and I realised its true significance, and she couldn't stop laughing. My chaplain gave his oration whilst the rest of his brother clerics just glared at me. When it was all finished, some elderly, snivelling bishop came over to me.

'It's easy to mock, Sir Roger,' he cried. 'But could you give a sermon?'

Well, you know old Shallot, in for a penny in for a pound!
'Of course I could!' I cried.

Her Majesty caught my eye, nodded, and the court reassembled. I was helped into the high pulpit. (I had drunk a little too much claret.) I leaned against the wooden rail and gazed blearily around.

'My text,' I began, 'is: Don't do to others as ye would have others do to you. After all, they may not like what you do to yourself.'

Well, gales of laughter greeted this. Up springs the red-nosed bishop who had sunk as much claret as I had.

'A proper sermon!' he screamed. 'Do not mock us, Sir Roger!'

Elizabeth nodded her red-wigged head and commanded me to continue.

'One with a moral!' a bishop shouted out.

'Yes,' another of his colleagues roared. 'Practise what you preach, Shallot! Something uplifting.'

I leaned drunkenly against the pulpit and looked at these two hypocrites, two cheeks on the same arse.

'All right,' I bellowed back, my mind racing through the possibilities.

The Queen, lovely girl, was biting her lower lip. Her face had gone puce-red and even her wig had slipped slightly askew as she tried to control herself. She clapped her hands and glared sternly at me.

'Sir Roger, you are commanded. Make your sermon short and give your gentle listeners at least three themes to reflect upon!' She winked quickly at me.

'Once upon a time,' I began, 'there was a little sparrow who started to fly south rather late in the winter.'

I stopped and stared round at my congregation gathered in the tapestry-hung chapel of Hampton Court. The clergy were glaring at me. Elizabeth had lowered her head, hiding her face behind her hand. I think she knew what was coming. Little Cecil, her secretary, stared fixedly at the ceiling.

'In a short time,' I continued, 'ice formed on this little sparrow's wings and he fell to earth in a barnyard. A cow passed by and crapped on this little sparrow. The sparrow thought he would die but the manure warmed him and thawed out his wings. Snug and happy, the little sparrow began to breathe and then to sing. A passing cat heard this, cleared away the manure, found the sparrow and promptly ate him.

'Your Majesty, brothers and sisters in Christ, that is my sermon!'

'What is the moral of this tale?' the bishop shrieked, jumping to his feet. 'Her Majesty commanded that there be three themes for us to reflect upon.'

'Can't you see them?' I bellowed back. 'First, my lord, any one who shits on you is not necessarily your enemy. Secondly, anyone who gets you out of the shit is not necessarily your friend. Thirdly, if you are warm and happy, even in a pile of shit, keep your mouth firmly shut!'

Well, that was it. The Queen swept out of the chapel and I was placed under house arrest at my London home until I wrote the bishop a fulsome apology. I did so and was promptly fined a further hundred crowns for saying he was one of the nicest old ladies I had ever met.

Ah, well, if you can't take a joke you shouldn't be a Christian!

(I see my chaplain's shoulders shaking. He'd better not be laughing at me, I'd wring his neck if he bothered to wash it! Good, he has sobered up. He taps his quill on the edge of the manuscript and it's time to begin.)

We must go back into the past. Think of it as a corridor with many rooms and each chamber thronged with murderers. I must go back to those golden days when I was in the service of Benjamin Daunbey, nephew to the great Cardinal Wolsey. We were both the Cardinal's special agents working for his good and that of the crown. The good of the crown! Fat, murderous, syphilitic Henry VIII, The Dark Prince, The Mouldwarp who drenched his kingdom in torrents of blood and sent the best and noblest of his court to the scaffold . . .

I am ready. I have opened the leather casket with the year '1522' inscribed in faded gold letters. We have taken out the relics of that bygone, murderous age. They lie before me upon the desk. Some are tinged with purple where a wine cup spilt, others bear a deeper scarlet, the traces of some poor bastard's life blood. The ring given back to me is not important. My eyes are drawn to the scarlet threads, strips of tough silk, so light, so pathetic, yet in their time they concealed mysteries which stretch back to the time of Arthur.

I half-close my eyes, summoning up the past. I can almost catch Benjamin's voice and, in my mind's eye, glimpse his dark sardonic face, gentle eyes and lanky, stooped figure which masked so many subtle skills. Ah, I was so different then. No great lord but a mere commoner, a jumped-up jackanapes rescued by Wolsey's nephew to plumb the dark treacheries of Henry's court.

I look at a picture framed in gold which hangs on the wall on the other side of my room. A fair replica of me in my golden youth. Will Shakespeare once asked me to describe myself.

'I was a hungry, lean-faced villain,' I replied. 'A mountebank, a threadbare juggler, a hollow-eyed, sharp-looking wretch.'

Will thanked me for it and, as always, used it in one of his plays. You'll find the same description in his *Comedy of Errors*, a subtle humorous piece which I sponsored with my gold.

Ah, well, no more dalliance or asides. The curtains are drawn so let the bloody drama begin. I will exorcise the ghosts in my mind. Purge the demons from my soul and

9

order them to go back to hell and tell the Lord Satan I sent them there. (Oh, by the way, you'll find this same phrase in one of Will Shakespeare's plays. He borrowed that as well!)

Chapter 1

After we returned from France in the summer of 1521, my master Benjamin Daunbey was left untroubled by his uncle, the great Cardinal Thomas Wolsey. Old Tom had other things on his mind as we later discovered. You see, the fat Cardinal had one great nightmare: how to control the King. He used a magic ring, so they say, to call up demons, and hired the chief of witches, a harlot known as Mabel Brigge, to go on a Satanic fast in order to keep the King's mind firmly in his grasp.

Old Wolsey was a fool. I told him so when he lay dying in Leicester Abbey, cursing all princes and Henry in particular.

Now Henry VIII, that limb of Satan, had his brains firmly in his codpiece whilst his soul was a storm of emotions. He was a great Catholic yet he attacked the Mass. A learned scholar but he killed poor Tom More. A fervent friend until he tired of you. And, above all, a loving husband until someone more young and buxom caught his eye.

You may have read how Henry wanted a male heir and rejected both his daughters. First, poor Mary. (That was her problem, you know. Mary was always looking for her father in other men, including me. And that shows you how desperate she was!) Secondly, of course, the great Elizabeth, Boleyn's daughter. And wasn't that funny? Satan must be laughing in hell. Old Henry searching for a boy whilst his poor, rejected daughter, Elizabeth, turns out to

11

be the greatest monarch England has ever seen. Mind you, that's not the full truth. Elizabeth was his heir, ostensibly his daughter, only I know the truth . . . but that's a story for another time and another place.

What is important is to realise that Henry was ruled by his lusts. Oh, he had his passing fancies: Bessie Blount, Lucy Rose, but in the summer of 1522 he was reverting to type. He liked the Howard women: Elizabeth Howard, Anne Boleyn's mother, had already graced his bed. So had Anne's eldest sister, Mary. Now Anne herself, that dark sensuous witch, had returned from France full of coquetry, with her satin dresses, thick lace petticoats, crimson high-heeled shoes, dark sloe eyes, and those beautiful hands which fluttered like the wings of a butterfly.

Henry lusted for her but this time it was different. Anne had been trained at the court of the greatest lecher the world had ever seen, Francis I of France, where seduction, love-making and affairs of the heart were treated with as much attention as matters of state. Anne had seen her elder sister pursued, wooed, seduced – only to be rejected as the 'English mare', a hackney whom anyone could ride. Anne was different. She wanted one thing and one thing only: to be Henry's wife.

Wolsey, lost in his intricate game of human chess against Boleyn, left us alone. So we trotted back to our manor house outside Ipswich.

Now Benjamin was a strange fellow. We had gone to school together. Afterwards he had become a lawyer's clerk and, in doing so, saved me from an undeserved hanging. He was astute, cunning, an expert swordsman, but at times could be infuriatingly naive; not childish but very childlike. He was not your usual landowner who exploits the peasants and seduces their daughters. Oh, no! Benjamin really believed in the milk of human kindness. Despite my protests, he cancelled all levies, tolls and dues owing to him as the Lord of the Manor. His tenants became freeholders, allowed to till their own soil and grow their own crops. He set up a small hospital in the village and hired an old physician, a gentle, caring man who knew the art of physic.

(A rarity indeed! I wouldn't trust any doctor as far as I can spit. They call me a rogue, but you watch any quack! He will grab your wrist, stare at your urine, poke about your stools, shake his head and stroke his beard. Do you think he's concerned about you? Like hell he is! All he is doing is calculating the bill.

I discovered this recently when the rogue who calls himself a doctor came up to visit me. He brought a jar of physic distilled from the dry skin of a newt and the head of a frog with a touch of batwing. I drew my dagger and said that he must drink it first. Do you know what the bastard did? He coughed, looked narrowly at me, and said on second thoughts perhaps a little more claret and a good night's sleep would put me right. Take old Shallot's advice, never trust a doctor or a lawyer! Well, the only good one I have seen was hanging by his neck from a scaffold.)

Ah, well. Benjamin had set up his small hospital as well as a school in the manor hall where all the scruffy little villains from the nearby villages could attend free of charge. Benjamin hired a schoolmaster – a proper teacher, not one of those sadistic bastards who enter the profession so they can inflict as much damage as possible on every child who comes into their care. No, this man was a scholar who had studied with Colet and Erasmus. He could teach Mathematics, Geography, and was fluent in Latin, Classical Greek, French and Italian. Soft as dough was old Benjamin. He never had a business head. Mind you, out of respect to his memory, I have started similar schemes on my own estates.

The administration of the manor was left to a thrifty steward called Barker, the grandfather of my present captain of the guard. (Oh, yes, I believe in keeping everything in the family. Even my little turd of a chaplain, on whom I lavish so much love and affection, is the great-nephew of the teacher Benjamin hired.) Suffice to say that with my master looking after his fellow man and others more capable looking after the estate, I grew bored. I drifted back to London, ostensibly to take lessons with a duelling master, a Portuguese who had taught Benjamin, having left his country one step ahead of the Inquisition.

'You have a good eye and a quick wrist,' the fellow remarked one day. 'You are swift in your parry, cunning in your lunge – but there's something lacking.'

'Too bloody straight there is!' I answered. 'I don't like being killed and I have no desire to kill anyone!'

The sword-master, leaning elegantly on his fencing foil, stroked his short goatee beard.

'Good!' he murmured. 'The mark of a true swordsman.' He wagged a finger at me. 'One day you will understand. When the blood runs hot, you'll know it. A wild unselfish desire, something which comes from the very marrow of your soul: to kill or be killed. All your life, all your existence, channelled to that one end.'

Of course I thought this was nonsense and the fellow short of a king's full shilling. Yet he was right. Years later, on a golden sea-shore, Benjamin and I fought sword against sword, dagger against dagger, over a woman with a face as beautiful as Helen of Troy and a heart and soul as black as the deepest pit in hell. However, that's another story and doesn't concern us here.

Soon I had learnt enough of duelling and began to drift around the capital. London is such a wonderful place! It harbours every type of villain under the sun: gamblers, foists, footpads, cut-throats and cut-purses, sturdy beggars, palliards and counterfeit men . . . I really felt at home. Naturally, Benjamin kept a wary eye on me and insisted that I spend no longer than three nights in succession in

London. He would sit behind his desk in the great solar of our country manor and waggle his bony finger at me.

'Roger, you're my friend but you have the same penchant for mischief as a cat does for cream. You will either come home or I'll come for you. Do you understand?'

I did. To be perfectly honest Benjamin was the only person I was really frightened of and the only person I never lied to. Well, within reason. Yet, cats like cream and Shallot likes mischief.

I fell into bad company: some gentlemen of the road who skulked in the graveyard of St Paul's well beyond the sheriff's writ. They were led by a former cleric, a defrocked priest. I forget his name, we just called him Rat's Arse. He had the innocent face of an angel and one of the most eloquent mouths which ever drew breath. He could convince you black was white and night was day!

Rat's Arse persuaded me to raise money from our tight-fisted banker Waller so he could set up a molly house in an alleyway off Cock Lane. An exclusive brothel where gentlemen of leisure could take their ease. Of course he took the gold and I never saw him again. Well, alive that is. Two years later, whilst crossing Hampstead Heath, I passed the gallows and saw poor Rat's Arse tarred and gibbeted hanging by his neck. I said a little prayer. He was a villain but his heart was in the right place.

Anyway, old Waller came for me like a whippet after a rabbit. On the very afternoon I was fleeing the city he grabbed me by the arm in Paternoster Row.

'Shallot!' he screamed. 'Where's my money?'

(Have you noticed that about bankers? If you've got money, they'll lend it. If you haven't, they purse their lips and shake their heads.)

I was desperate. I gazed round looking for a way out and suddenly glimpsed old Tunstall, Bishop of London, who was riding down to St Paul's for his daily verbal assault on the

Almighty. Now I had met Tunstall when I had been with Benjamin at court so I seized Waller by the wrist.

'You see over there?' I cried.

'Who?' the wretch replied.

'His Grace the Bishop of London. He agreed to stand surety for the money I have used to send the sick and the poor on a pilgrimage to St James Compostella!'

Waller drew his sour face back like a viper about to strike.

'I don't believe you!' he snapped.

'Look.' I drew off my boots. 'Hold these and I'll go across and prove it to you.'

Waller held my boots and I tiptoed across the cobbles towards the bishop.

'My Lord Bishop!' I gasped. 'Your Grace!'

The bishop, surrounded by his flunkeys, reined in and looked down at me.

'Yes, my son?'

'A petition, My Lord Bishop. A petition. Your holiness may remember me?'

The old hypocrite stared sourly back, gathering his reins as if to move on.

'I am the manservant to Benjamin Daunbey, nephew to the great Cardinal.'

Well, that stopped the old bugger in his tracks. He forced a smile. (Have you noticed how priests do that? As if they were God Almighty and everyone else some poor benighted wretch?)

'What is it, my son?'

I pointed back to where Waller stood like an idiot, holding my boots.

'My Lord Bishop, I was in violent disputation with that man over the nature of the Trinity when you passed by. My Lord,' I lied, 'your reputation as a theologian is known to all. I offered you as an arbiter in our debate. My friend said he did not believe me so I left him with my boots as an assurance that you will grant him an audience and clarify the error of his ways.'

Tunstall drew himself up and nodded wisely.

'My Lord, I know you are busy,' I continued breathlessly, 'but if you will just agree to fix a time and place where you can see him . . . ?'

Again the holy nod and Tunstall beckoned Waller over.

He, the old fool, approached bobbing and curtseying.

Tunstall looked at him reprovingly. 'Give your friend his boots back,' he commanded. 'And be at my chambers tomorrow morning at ten o'clock and I will settle matters then.'

Waller was almost prostrate in his thanks. The bishop sketched a blessing in the air and moved on. I grabbed my boots and left London within the hour.

I returned to Ipswich sober-faced and assured Benjamin that my good work amongst the London poor had now reached an end and perhaps it was best if I helped him on the estates. He looked strangely at me, smiled with those innocent grey eyes and went back to the list of accounts he was studying.

I looked at that dark intelligent face, framed by long black hair, and desperately wondered if my master was the most cunning man I had ever met or the nearest thing to innocence in human flesh.

The days passed and then, just before All Saints, one of those last, beautiful golden days of the year when the sun burns hot and you think summer has returned, I was on top of a hayrick with some young girl from the village – a joyous, happy lass, pleasant-faced and warm-bodied. I was trying to persuade her that her bodice was too tightly tied and she, laughing, gently tapped away my probing fingers. Her resistance weakened as her laughter grew when suddenly I heard Benjamin shouting for me.

'Roger, Roger. Quickly, come here!'

I looked over the hayrick. My master stood in hose and a white shirt open at the neck, hopping from one foot to another as he tried to push his feet into his boots.

'Here I am, Master!'

'Roger, what are you doing?'

I hissed at the wench to be quiet whilst I clambered down and boldly declared I was trying to track the path of the sun.

'You are too curious, Roger,' he murmured. 'Your mind never ceases its probing.'

My master pushed me up the grassy knoll on which the manor house stood.

'What is it?' I asked.

Benjamin pointed along the dusty trackway which led down to the main gates.

'Riders, Roger. And I think they are from dear Uncle.'

I shaded my eyes with my hand and saw the puffs of white dust, a small pennant snapping in the breeze, the bright jerkins of the horsemen and the rider in front clothed all in black. My heart sank. Dear Uncle was making his hand felt. If he was sending his personal secretary and adviser, the magician Doctor Agrippa, some bloody business was afoot.

We met the visitors in our large hall, freshly painted and wood-panelled with shields bearing the arms of Shallot and Daunbey along the wall. The riders, a group of Wolsey's mercenaries, dressed in the scarlet livery of the Cardinal, were taken off to the buttery to quench their thirst and ogle the maids.

Doctor Agrippa, dressed from head to toe in black leather, tapped his broad-brimmed hat against his leg, waiting for the servants to serve chilled white wine and sweetmeats. All the time he smiled and indulged in tittle-tattle, studying me with those cold, colourless eyes.

A strange man, Agrippa. I have mentioned him before. He was always cold and, whatever the heat, I never saw him perspire. He was a true magus. Yet, superficially, he looked like some benevolent village parson with his round cheery face sweet as a cherub's, neatly cut black hair, and that smile which failed to reach his eyes. He never grew old and, after Wolsey died, had the gift of appearing in the strangest places.

Raleigh once told me – yes, that freebooter is still at sea, financed by my gold – that he had seen Agrippa near Jamestown in Virginia. How he got to the New World God only knows! A spy reported he was in Madrid and, years later, when I was fleeing from Suleiman's stranglers, I caught a glimpse of his face in the crowd as I was being pursued through the filthy streets and alleys of Constantinople. I saw him at court once and, only fifteen years ago, he turned up at Burpham looking as young and fresh as he had in my youth. I asked him what the matter was. He only smiled and gave me warning that Mary, Queen of Scots, imprisoned at Fotheringay, was plotting Elizabeth's death. Then he disappeared.

Agrippa was a magus with a gift for seeing the future and once told me I would die in a most unexpected way, which is one of the reasons I keep my eye on this little turd of a chaplain. A strange man. Perhaps Agrippa was the wandering Jew, condemned to wander the face of the earth for ever? I once asked a few Rabbis about this legend. They just looked askance and shook their heads.

(By the way, I like Jews. They remind me very much of the Irish. They love debate, honour, the family, and have a wicked sense of humour. Indeed, I have published a learned treatise in which I argue that the Irish are really the lost tribe of Israel. My main conclusion was as follows: when Moses and Aaron left Egypt, they put all the rogues together at the back of the column. After the Israelites crossed the Red Sea, the lot at the back took a wrong turn and ended up in Ireland. Very interesting, you should read it.)

On that far golden day, however, Agrippa was concerned with more pressing matters. He waited until Benjamin had cleared the hall of servants then slumped down on a high-backed chair before the empty fireplace. As he passed me I caught a whiff of that strange perfume of his – as if some precious ointment had been poured on a burning pan. His eyes changed colour, giving them a black, marble look, and the smile faded from his lips. He stared at Benjamin and myself, sipped the wine and nibbled at a piece of diced marchpane.

'For goodness' sake, sit down!' he said softly, indicating the empty chairs. He stretched and eased his neck to combat the stiffness after his long ride. 'It's begun,' he murmured.

'What has?' Benjamin asked testily.

'The killing,' Agrippa replied. 'The Mouldwarp's emerged.' He held out his hand and splayed his fingers. 'Each man has a choice of different paths. King Henry is no different. He could have been the greatest monarch England has seen, but has chosen instead to be The Mould-warp, The Dark Prince who will drench his kingdom in blood.'

'Doctor Agrippa,' I retorted, 'be more precise.'

'I shall be. In two days' time, Edward Stafford, Duke of Buckingham, will lose his head on Tower Hill.'

Benjamin just stared aghast and even I, with my ignorance of court politics, could only gape in amazement. Stafford was the direct descendant of Edward III, one of the greatest landowners in England, the son of the Duke of Buckingham who had plotted against Richard III and lost his head just before Henry Tudor landed to kill the usurper at Bosworth.

'What happened?' Benjamin asked.

Agrippa shrugged. 'Stafford was always a thorn in the side of your uncle.' He smiled apologetically at Benjamin. 'He was for ever calling him an upstart jackanapes from Ipswich, a common mountebank hiding behind the robes of a Cardinal.' He pulled a face. 'Well, a few weeks ago Stafford was at court. He was standing near Henry and, as is customary, offered the King a silver basin to wash his hands in. When the King had finished, Wolsey dipped his own fingers into the water basin. Stafford, enraged, threw the water over the Cardinal's robes.'

Agrippa stopped talking, brushing flecks of dust from his black hose.

(Isn't it strange how great men can lose their heads over a drop of water?)

'Your uncle was furious,' the doctor continued, 'and, shouting that he would sit on Stafford's robes, strode off, sloshing water, making himself look an even greater fool.'

I just lowered my head and thanked God I hadn't been there. The sight of Cardinal Tom walking like some little boy who had pissed his breeches would have had me roaring with laughter.

'The rest of the court laughed?' Benjamin asked.

'Oh, yes, they roared. The palace rocked with their merriment. Stafford only made matters worse. The next day he turned up wearing a common jerkin and hose and when the King asked him why, replied it was to prevent the Cardinal from sitting on his robes.' Agrippa spread his hands. 'The mockery grew even louder.'

'But if a man is to lose his head for mocking a cardinal,' I replied, 'then Henry would lose all his subjects.'

Benjamin smiled wryly for, although he had great affection for his powerful uncle, he had no illusions about this commoner with a brilliant brain who had managed to rise to be Cardinal and Lord Chancellor of England.

'Ah!' Agrippa leaned forward as if he suspected there were spy-holes behind the panelling. 'You know your uncle, Master Daunbey. No man insults him, and Stafford he has always hated. My Lord Cardinal has always believed that revenge is a dish best served cold.

21

'Despite my advice, he began to play upon Henry's secret nightmares.' Agrippa studied his finger nails for a while. 'It's the same story,' he murmured, 'the same words, the same tune. Henry may be the son of Elizabeth of York but his father was Henry Tudor, nothing more than a Welsh farmer. The German reformer, Martin Luther, publicly derides him as Squire Harry. He has always feared that others such as Stafford have a better claim than he to the throne.

'Now,' Agrippa continued, 'the Tudors have a craving for a dynasty. The present King's father called his eldest son Arthur, trying to use his Welshness to build up legends linking his family to Arthur of the Round Table. Do you know these legends?'

I shook my head. 'Of course not. I'm no scholar.'

'Well', he stroked his chin, 'there is a legend that, after the great Arthur died, prophecies grew up in the West Country that one day he would return, come riding out of the setting sun to right all wrongs. The Great Miser wanted to depict his family as Arthur's line come again but his eldest son died and now Fat Henry is king. Nonetheless, the Tudor dream or nightmare continues.'

'Oh, come!' I interrupted. 'You are not saying our noble Henry is frightened of some mythical King riding down to Westminster with the Knights of the Round Table?'

Agrippa narrowed his eyes. 'Of course not, but he is frightened of the Yorkists, the Plantagenets, those who have better claims to the throne than he! And you know how superstitious he is. What would happen if Stafford or some other prince with Yorkist blood in his veins produced the sacred relics? Arthur's sword, Excalibur, or worse the Grail which sat on his table, the chalice which Jesus drank from at the Last Supper?'

(No, don't laugh. I know we live in the age of reason and commonsense but in my time I have seen the most incredible rebellions: people marching behind a piece of cloth or those who believe that pieces of the true cross will protect them from arrows or bullets. Isn't it wonderful what people will believe when they want to?)

'You are not saying,' I scoffed, 'that Buckingham obtained these relics?'

'Yes and no,' Agrippa replied. 'After Buckingham's insults, Wolsey's legion of spies went to work. The Cardinal concocted a story that Buckingham was plotting against the King and wished to gain possession of these sacred relics to rally forces to him.'

'Oh, that's ridiculous!' Benjamin interrupted. 'I understand that centuries ago Arthur's corpse was discovered at Glastonbury but, according to legend, Excalibur was tossed into a lake, whilst the whereabouts of the Grail is still a mystery.'

'Oh, but Wolsey has proof,' Agrippa replied. 'His agents arrested a Benedictine monk, Nicholas Hopkins, who is now lodged in the Tower. This Hopkins is from Glastonbury. He is also chaplain at the Santerre manor of Templecombe in Somerset.

'Hopkins claims he knows where both the Grail and the Sword are and that he offered them to Buckingham.

'According to Hopkins, the Duke planned to use them to lead a revolt, depose and execute Henry, and take the throne himself.'

'And Buckingham believed this junk was holy?' I laughed. 'Fell for the ramblings of some mouldy monk!'

'What about the Santerres?' Benjamin asked. 'Were they involved?'

'No. They are merely tenants of Buckingham. The good Duke went to Templecombe to meet Hopkins and tried to draw Sir John Santerre into the conspiracy. Santerre refused, which is just as well for Wolsey's agents had infiltrated both this household and Buckingham's retinue. The good Duke,' Agrippa concluded, 'certainly had an interest in the relics: he sent messages to his agent in London that once he obtained them he would lead a revolt.'

'There's more, isn't there?' asked Benjamin.

Agrippa rubbed his face with his hands. 'Yes. The Grail and the Sword are being sought by others.'

'Who?' my master asked.

'The Templars,' Agrippa snapped.

'Who?' I asked.

'The Templars,' he continued, 'were a military order formed in the twelfth century to defend the Holy Land. They acquired vast possessions in England and France – castles, land and manors. They also obtained secret knowledge and possessed all the great holy relics, such as the shroud in which Christ's body was wrapped, the Mandylion which cleaned his face on the way to Calvary, and, if legend is to be believed, the Grail and the Sword Excalibur.'

'So,' Benjamin asked, 'what have they to do with us?'

(Oh, my master was so innocent. I almost guessed what was coming next.)

'His Grace the King and my Lord Cardinal want you to go to Somerset, find the Grail and Excalibur, and if possible root out these Templars.'

'They still exist?' I asked.

'Oh, yes.' Agrippa rubbed the side of his face. 'I didn't finish my story. On Friday, the thirteenth of October 1307, the Templars were seized throughout Christendom, tortured and put to death on charges of idolatry, sodomy and black magic. Most of them died at the stake or on the gallows but a few escaped and organised themselves into secret conventicles. These Templars are determined that the Grail and the Sword should not fall into Henry's hands for they see him as the incarnation of evil.'

(Very perceptive, I thought.)

Agrippa cleared his throat. 'There is evidence that some

of the Yorkists were members of this secret order. Hopkins certainly was, and Buckingham may be.'

'And our noble King believes all this?'

Agrippa made a face. 'Hopkins confessed, Wolsey informed the King, and Stafford did little to help his cause. He was arrested at London Bridge and taken to the Tower. He would neither deny nor confirm Wolsey's allegations.'

The doctor steepled his fingers together. 'Buckingham had also been stupid enough, in the privacy of his own home, to make certain treasonable remarks to his own sister, the Lady Fitzwalter.'

Benjamin smiled thinly and I realised how clever the Cardinal had been: Henry had seduced Buckingham's sister and the Duke had been furious that the King should treat her like some common trollop. Wolsey would have struck – summoning the hapless woman before the Privy Council, placing her on oath and making her confess to words which he could so easily twist.

'Then what happened?' asked Benjamin.

'Buckingham was tried at Westminster Hall before a panel of his peers, led by the Duke of Norfolk. The sentence was a foregone conclusion: he was to be drawn on a hurdle to the place of execution there to be hanged, cut down alive, his private parts to be hacked off and cast in the fire, his bowels burnt before his eyes, his head smitten off and his body to be quartered and divided at the King's will.'

'Surely Henry will show mercy?'

'Queen Catherine went down on her knees and begged for the Duke's life. The King took to his bed for three days suffering from a fever, but the only mercy he will show is that Buckingham must lose his head. The rest of the indignities have been cancelled. He will die in two days.'

'When you came here, you said the killing was beginning, that Henry will be The Mouldwarp?' I prompted him.

Agrippa looked at me chillingly and I remembered his

diagnosis, many years earlier, of how sick the King's mind had turned.

'Can't you see, Roger,' he whispered, 'if Henry can kill the greatest peer in his realm, who will be safe? Already the courts of Europe have lodged their protests. The King of France has openly derided the Cardinal, claiming the butcher's dog has pulled down the fairest buck in Christendom.'

Of course, Agrippa was right. Henry was mad as a March hare: he was obsessed with plots against him and would brook no opposition. By the time he died, he was said to be responsible for at least sixty thousand executions. I can well believe it! I was with the fat bastard as he grew old. I'll never forget those puffy white cheeks and mad, piglike eyes. The open ulcer on his leg which smelt like a sewer and the syphilis in his brain which turned him into a devil incarnate . . .

Benjamin rose and refilled our cups. 'So the killing has begun?' he murmured. 'Buckingham will die and dear Uncle needs us.'

Agrippa folded his hands in his lap. Once again he underwent one of those remarkable character changes – no longer the sombre prophet but the amiable priest seeking counsel and help.

'You are right, Master Benjamin,' he said lightly, 'Buckingham will die and there's nothing we can do to prevent it. But, of course, there is also Master Nicholas Hopkins's confession. Your uncle needs you in London. He has given express orders that we are all to witness Buckingham's execution.'

(Oh, Lord, I thought, here we go again, blood and gore and poor Shallot in the middle of it!)

'And then what?' Benjamin asked sharply.

'We are to continue the interrogation of Master Hopkins and find out more about his mysterious revelations.'

'But you said the man was mad?'

'Oh, he undoubtedly is but that doesn't necessarily make his confession false.'

'Do you think Buckingham was involved in treason?' I asked.

Agrippa shook his head. 'No. But you see, Master Shallot, the problem has two sides. Buckingham is going to die and that is the end of that matter. Hopkins, however, was a bearer of messages. He must have received instructions. But from whom?'

'And Uncle is determined,' Benjamin concluded flatly, 'to seek out the truth?'

'Truth, Master Benjamin? What is the truth? Pilate asked me the same question and I could not answer him then.' Agrippa smiled as if we shared a joke and ran the edge of his cloak through his fingers.

'Enough,' he murmured. 'We must leave for London now.'

Chapter 2

Benjamin reluctantly agreed to our leaving immediately and brushed aside my objections. I went to my chamber feeling like a school boy being forced back to his studies and angrily began to throw clothing and other necessities into saddle bags. Benjamin slipped quietly into my room and stood with his back to the closed door.

'Roger, I am sorry but we have no choice. You remember the oath we took, to be the Cardinal's men during peace and war?' He waved a hand airily. 'Everything we have comes from him.'

'If the Duke of Buckingham can lose both his life and possessions,' I shouted, 'then what about the other fleas who do not live so high on the hog?'

Benjamin shrugged. 'We can only live each day as it comes.'

'Aye, and if the Cardinal has his way we'll have few days left to us!'

We finished packing; ostlers brought round saddled horses and sumpter ponies. Benjamin left strict instructions with Barker the steward and, by late-afternoon, we were galloping south. I remember it well. The sun died that day and winter came rushing in. Who says the seasons are not harbingers of what is to come?

Agrippa was now quiet, or rather talking to himself in a strange tongue I couldn't understand, whilst his entourage, the nicest group of gallow's birds you'd chance to encounter, kept to themselves. We stopped that night at a priory. Agrippa was still bad company, wrestling with his own problems. Only once did he pause, gaze round the deserted refectory and announce: 'There's more to it, you know.'

'What do you mean?' asked Benjamin.

Agrippa shook his head. 'There's more to it,' he repeated. 'Oh, how this world is given to lying!'

(You'll find that phrase too in old Will Shakespeare's plays.)

The weather continued to worsen but, early on the morning of our second day out of Ipswich, we left Waltham Abbey and reached the Mile End Road which wound through different hamlets into East Smithfield. The crowds on the road increased. Not just the usual tinkers and pedlars with their handcarts or wandering hedge-priests looking for a quick penny and a soft bed (I love to see my chaplain twitch!), but common folk, surging down to Tower Hill to watch one of the great ones spill his blood.

We turned north into Hog Street, past the church of St Mary Grace where we glimpsed the high grey turrets of the Tower, and into the dense crowd milling round Tower Hill. Believe me, all of London had turned out. There was not a place to be found between the Tower and Bridge Street.

I have often wondered why people like to view executions. What fun is there in seeing a man lose his head or his balls? I asked this of Agrippa.

'We are born killers,' he murmured. 'We have a love affair with death. And, if our Henry has his way, he will glut all our appetites for executions and the spilling of blood.'

We used our warrants and the swords of our entourage to force our way through, right up to the black-draped execution platform which stood on the brow of the hill ringed by yeomen of the guard. On the platform, arms folded, stood a red-masked executioner. Beside him his assistant, dressed from head to toe in black leather with a pair of antlers on his head, held the huge, two-headed axe near the execution block. A priest mumbled prayers whilst officials whispered to each other and gazed expectantly over the sea of faces around them.

At first quite a peaceful scene, but let old Shallot tell you: in later years (and, yes, it is another story), I had to place my head on that block, the axe was raised – and only a last-minute pardon saved me. I tell you, the waiting is worse than death itself. The great hunk of wood reeks of blood and all around you is the paraphernalia of violent death: a sheet to soak up the blood which spurts violently from the neck, the basket for the head, the elm-wood coffin for the torso, and the knife just in case they leave the odd sinew or muscle uncut. Quick it may be but it's still a terrible death. When Mary, Queen of Scots was decapitated, her eyelids kept fluttering and the lips moving for at least a minute after the head left the body. Mind you, matters were not helped by the executioner at Fotheringay not realising the Scottish queen was wearing a wig and letting the head drop and bounce like ball.

I had seen executions before but never anything so ceremonious as Buckingham's. Agrippa closed his eyes, I am sure he was asleep, whilst Benjamin, white-faced, stared under the platform. I followed his gaze and saw small, dark shapes moving about.

'Who are they?' I asked one of the guards.

'Dwarfs,' the fellow replied out of the corner of his mouth. 'They buy the right from the mayor. When the head is lopped off, the blood gushes out and seeps through the wood. They catch it in their rags and sell them as relics and mementos.' The man turned and spat over his shoulder. 'I understand there are always plenty of buyers.'

Our wait continued, the crowd growing restless. Pedlars moved amongst the throng selling sweetmeats, sliced apples and even ragged copies of Buckingham's so-called 'last confession'. Water tipplers with their stoups cursed and bawled for trade. Children cried and were hoisted up on their parents' shoulders. The great ones of the land, lords and ladies, both they and their horses covered in silken canopies, forced their way through for a clearer view. Everyone pushed and shoved and took their violence out on a cutpurse who was caught red-handed. He was nearly torn apart by the crowd until the sheriff's men hustled him away.

The sky darkened, great grey clouds sweeping up the Thames. People saw them as a divine omen, God's displeasure at Buckingham's death, and their curses against the Cardinal grew even more vocal when the cold rain soaked them to the skin.

The storm passed and, as the clouds broke, we heard a roar from the crowds near the Tower. A group of horsemen appeared, led by the sheriffs and mayor. They ringed a tall, auburn-haired man, his face as pale as the open-necked shirt he wore under a scarlet cloak. Agrippa whispered that this was Buckingham.

The horsemen approached the scaffold, dismounted, and Buckingham walked up the steps, cool and calm as if he was about to deliver a sermon rather than meet his maker. He knelt before the priest who sketched a hasty blessing, exchanged words with the sheriffs, then came and leaned over the scaffold above us. Yet, at the very moment he began speaking, a declamation of his innocence, a wind sprang up and wafted the words from his mouth.

Pressed in by people all around me, I looked along the line of yeomen. My attention was caught by a tall, swarthy-faced man, his hair black as night, nose beaked like an eagle. But what made him and his red-haired companion so singular were that both were garbed in black from head to toe.

My attention then turned to the young woman standing

next to these two crows. She had the hood of her cloak pushed back, revealing jet-black hair, a high forehead and a strikingly beautiful face. She must have sensed my interest and glanced towards me – and I was smitten to the heart by those dark luminous eyes. She moved her cloak slightly and I saw that she was wearing a gown of amber silk. One jewelled hand came up and I glimpsed the pure white froth of lace at neck and sleeve and the glint of a small spray of diamonds pinned to her bodice and another on the wide band of amber velvet which bound her beautiful hair. She smiled (though that may have been my imagination), then turned to speak to a tall, fair-haired man with the rubicund face and portly features of a wealthy landowner. He had his arm around a pale-faced, dark-haired woman and, as the crowd shifted, I saw that she was leaning against him, swooning in terror at what was about to happen.

'Who are they?' I nudged Benjamin who, like Agrippa, seemed to be asleep on his feet.

He shook his head but Agrippa followed my gaze.

'The fair-haired fellow is Sir John Santerre, Lord of the Manor of Templecombe in Somerset. The fainting lady is probably his wife.'

'And the young beauty?' I asked.

'Santerre's daughter, Rachel.'

'Why are they here?' I whispered.

'They are come to London to account and purge their innocence. Sir John and his family must, at the King's orders, witness Buckingham's death.'

'Why?'

'Never mind, you'll find out.'

Agrippa's face hardened as he shifted his gaze to the black-garbed men around the Santerres.

'Before you ask, Master Shallot, the man as dark as Satan is Sir Edmund Mandeville, his red-haired companion Master Geoffrey Southgate, and somewhere near them must be their two sinister clerks, Cosmas and Damien.'

Now even my master looked uneasy.

'Who the bloody hell are they?' I whispered hoarsely. 'What do they mean to you, Master?'

'They are the "*Agentes in Rebus*",' Agrippa continued.

My blood ran cold. I had heard of these unpleasant fellows, merciless bastards, the Cardinal's professional spies and assassins. You see, Benjamin and I were Wolsey's emissaries, given this task or that, but the '*Agentes in Rebus*', literally the 'Doers of Things', were the Cardinal's own special spies.

Even in my hanging around the court I had heard of Mandeville who worked like a spider, spinning webs to catch the King's enemies. And, if he didn't find the conclusive evidence, he just made it up. His agents could pop up anywhere, disguised as they wished: a pedlar, a mountebank, even one of the Moon People who wander the road in their gaudy painted wagons. Now every King has his spy service: the French have the 'Luciferi', or 'Lightbearers'; the Ottoman Turks 'The Gardeners'; the Doge of Venice 'The Secretissimi' and Henry of England his '*Agentes in Rebus*'. They were founded by Cardinal Morton, chief minister to the King's father, and still flourish to this very day, the most secret servants of the crown. Sometimes they can live for years as your servant, mistress, even your brother or sister. But when the time comes, if your head has to roll, they will produce the evidence.

'Were they involved in this affair?' I whispered.

Agrippa waved his hand at me. 'Yes, yes.' He stopped whispering as Buckingham stepped back from the executioner and suddenly did a very strange thing. He came across, leaned over the wooden balustrade and looked directly at me, then Agrippa, and finally Benjamin. His eyes were tearful but clear and bright.

'I am innocent,' he hoarsely whispered. I only caught his

words faintly. 'Before the hour is out, I shall meet my maker face to face, but I am innocent!' He pointed directly at Agrippa. 'Remember that!'

Somewhere a single drum began to beat. The yeoman began to push the crowd back, allowing us a better view of what was to happen. Buckingham once more knelt at the feet of the priest. The executioner then knelt to him, asking the Duke for the usual pardon as well as the customary fee. (I can never understand that! How can someone say they are sorry, then cut your bloody head off and, at the same time, ask to be paid for it? Many years later, when I was taken to the block, I told the bastard to piss off and do his worst!)

At last Buckingham knelt down before the block. A servant bound his hair up but the Duke shook his head when a blindfold was offered. He bowed and slightly turned his head, his hands spread out, moving them once like a stricken bird before it falls. The drum beat grew louder, the two-headed axe rose in a brilliant arc and fell with a thud which sounded like a clap of thunder. A bright spurt of blood shot up. The crowd, hitherto deathly silent, gave a collective sigh at the blood letting and the dwarfs beneath the scaffold became busy. The executioner held up Buckingham's head and came to the edge of the scaffold.

'So die all traitors!' he shouted.

I looked away. Benjamin had his back turned.

'So die all traitors!' the executioner repeated.

'Oh, piss off!' a voice shouted.

'You've got the wrong bloody head,' another bellowed. 'It should be the butcher's son's!'

Raucous jeers mounted as the scaffold began to be pelted with rotten fruit and offal. Soldiers began to move in and the crowd broke up.

'Come on, Agrippa!' Benjamin hissed.

The magician shook himself and looked around.

35

'Yes, yes, it's time we went.'

We forced our way down Tower Hill following the wall until we entered the fortress by the Water Gate. (Ah, my chaplain interrupts. Yes, yes, my little sweet is correct. Later generations call this 'Traitors' Gate' – and what a procession went through it! Anne Boleyn, defiant to the last; Thomas More cracking jokes; John Fisher praying; Catherine Howard jeering at Henry's sexual prowess. Oh, by the way, she was right, it wasn't much! I danced between the sheets with young Kate and we roared with laughter at Henry's antics. She was killed and I went to the block but that's another story.)

Inside the Tower soldiers and yeomen were now standing down, having manned the walls and gathered behind the sally ports just in case there was a riot. Led by Agrippa, we wound down between the different towers until we reached the Wakefield – what the popular voice now calls the 'Bloody Tower'.

'Come!' Agrippa ordered.

We opened an iron-studded door at the basement of the Bloody Tower and walked into a windowless chamber lit only by smoking cressets wedged between the bricks. At first I couldn't see clearly and all I could hear was the murmur of voices and the creaking of ropes, but then my eyes grew accustomed to the darkness. I heard my master gasp and, peering through the gloom, made out the sweat-soaked, half-naked figures of the torturers, grouped round the 'Duke of Exeter's Daughter', a popular name for the rack ever since the Duke of Exeter introduced it into England as a means of loosening tongues and getting to the truth – as politicians so aptly put it.

The poor man stretched there was naked except for a loin cloth. I glimpsed wispy white hair and a thin, emaciated figure stretched out on this bed of pain, a foot and a hand being tied at each corner. The torturers manned a wheel and, when they turned this, the bed stretched, cracking bone, muscle and sinew.

Agrippa, hidden in the shadows, beckoned the master torturer across. The fellow, greasy-haired and with a straggly beard, lumbered over like some great bear. His naked torso glistening with sweat, his threadbare hose pushed into boots were similarly soaked. Nevertheless, he was a man who obviously loved his job for he smiled cheerily through his tangle of beard.

'No news yet, Master.'

'Nothing new?' Agrippa asked.

'Only what he said before.'

'How long will he last?' Agrippa asked, still keeping well in the shadows whilst Benjamin and I stared fearfully at this dreadful scene. Believe me, if you wish to see hell on earth then watch a man being racked till his arms and legs pop out of their sockets, the torso grows longer and the privy parts become ruptured. Once I was forced to watch the torture of Nicholas Owen, the poor Jesuit lay brother who built the priest's hole in my house and others up and down the kingdom. A crafty, subtle carpenter was poor Owen. He was racked until his body fell apart; they had to hold it together with steel plates so that they could take him out and hang him. Lord, what a cruel world we live in! I fainted at the torture inflicted on Owen but, when I saw Master Hopkins, I stood like a rabbit terrified by a stoat.

'Do you think,' Agrippa asked quietly, 'Master Hopkins knows anything?'

'Yes and no,' the torturer replied. 'But he won't tell us. He is near death, Master. There's not much time left now.'

Agrippa led us back into the daylight.

'Stay here!' he ordered.

He went up the main steps of the Bloody Tower and came back with a bundle of clothes in his hand, afterwards re-entering the torture chamber. Benjamin and I stood like two school boys dismissed from their classroom.

'What now, Master?' I asked.

'Hush!' he whispered. 'All we are being shown, Roger, are the opening scenes. I am sure sweetest Uncle will tell us the plot of the play.' He waved a hand at the door to the torture chamber. 'I cannot abide such cruelty! Hopkins may well be a traitor but there's no need for this.'

The grass was still wet after the rainstorm so he led me across to a wooden bench next to a small paved square.

'Do you know, Roger,' he muttered when we took our seats, 'common law in England forbids such torture?'

(Well, I could have burst out laughing, and still do at the memory, for Fat Henry, the evil bastard, believed in torturing everyone. When he wanted to send his second queen to the scaffold, the musician Mark Smeaton was tortured until he confessed to adultery with her, being promised a swift death if he implicated poor Anne.)

I looked at the square pavement beside me and noticed a small dull stain in the centre.

'What is this, Master?'

Benjamin shuffled his feet. 'This is where princes die, Roger,' he murmured. 'When the person is too important to be a spectacle for the mob, a scaffold's set up here and the head lopped off.'

Strange, isn't it? There was I sitting next to the place where Anne Boleyn, who hired her own executioner from Calais, later put her neck on the block, as did poor Catherine Howard who spent the night before her death practising her poise for the execution stroke. Here died poor Tom More, old Fisher, Margaret, Countess of Salisbury and her three sons. Ah, well!

Benjamin was lost in his own thoughts so I gazed round, half-wondering what might happen to us, when a cart entered the inner bailey bearing a plain wooden coffin. The two waggoners were cursing and laughing between themselves.

'What do you carry, friends?' I asked.

The men smiled at each other, got down and hobbled the horses.

'Half the Earl of Stafford!' one of them quipped. He saw the look of stupefaction on my face. 'Well, the head's on London Bridge!' the fellow continued. 'And the rest—' He gestured towards the small, grey stone church of St Peter ad Vincula, the Tower chapel. 'The rest will go beneath the stones like all the others.'

He turned away as an officer and a group of soldiers hurried up to carry the loose-lidded coffin out of the cart and along the gravel path into the darkening chapel. A strange place, St Peter's! All the corpses of men and women executed on Tower Hill or Tower Green lie buried there. Now few people know this but, beneath the chapel, runs a secret passageway or gallery and, years later, I had to hide there. What a dreadful sight! The floor under the chapel awash with headless bodies, all dressed in the glittering rags in which they died. The coffins were simple and soon fell apart so I crawled across the skeletons of Lord Hastings, Anne Boleyn, the de la Poles, Catherine Howard and Thomas Cromwell. (A cunning bastard! I was one of those who arrested him after he had dinner in the Tower.)

Can you imagine it? Wedged between the foundations and the floor of the chapel, a sea of headless corpses? Good Lord, even today at the very thought of it I awake sweating, bawling for a cup of claret, Phoebe's fat buttocks and the plump tits of young Margot. No wonder they say the Tower is infested with ghosts!

I tell you, one time I was there at night, secretly visiting young Elizabeth when her sister Bloody Mary had imprisoned her. The gates were locked and I was shut inside so hid behind a rose bush which grows alongside the chapel of St Peter ad Vincula. At one o'clock in the morning I awoke, the hairs on my neck prickling. Deep fear seized me, freezing my heart and twisting my bowels. Looking up I saw a faint bluish glow at one of the chapel windows and heard strange music. I tell you this and I don't lie! I, Roger Shallot, who have seen the will o' the wisps glow above the marsh and witnessed the terrors that stalk the lonely moors, scaled the walls of St Peter ad Vincula and stared through the window. There, in ghostly procession, a long line of figures, including all those who had died at the Tower, swept in stately procession towards the high altar. Oh Lord, I half-fainted in fear. And if you don't believe me, go there, just sit in that chapel for half an hour, and you'll feel the ghosts gather round you.

Mind you, on that distant autumn's day I was more terrified of the living and wondered what the mysterious Agrippa was involving us in. We must have sat there for a full hour, subdued and rather morose, until the doctor suddenly reappeared, coming up the steps dressed in the garb of a priest.

'Hopkins has told me everything,' he murmured, sitting down between us like a benevolent uncle.

'What do you mean, sir?' snapped Benjamin. 'And why are you dressed like that?'

'Well, I heard his last confession.'

Benjamin stood up in surprise. 'Sir, you tricked the man! What is revealed in confession is sacred, and you are no priest!'

Agrippa smiled benignly. 'Who said I wasn't a priest, Benjamin?' He looked at my master squarely. 'And I am not interested in Master Hopkins's sins but in the information he provided. I know Canon Law, that's not covered by the seal of confession.'

Benjamin blew out his cheeks and sat down. 'In which case, what did Master Hopkins reveal?'

'Well,' Agrippa stretched out his short legs, 'according to Hopkins, the Grail and the Sword Excalibur still lie in Glastonbury.'

'Where?' I asked.

'Ah!' Agrippa smacked his lips. 'Do you have a wineskin, Shallot?'

'Yes, but it's empty.'

He smiled. 'Ah, well, it will have to wait.' He looked quizzically at Benjamin. 'Hopkins confessed, he does not care now. Other Templars will resolve the riddle.'

'What riddle?'

Agrippa leaned back and closed his eyes, murmuring:

'Beneath Jordan's water Christ's cup does rest,
And above Moses' Ark the sword that's best.'

'What in God's name does that mean?' I asked.

'I don't know. Hopkins found it in a secret chronicle at Glastonbury Abbey so I suppose we will all have to go there.' He stamped his feet against the cold and looked up at the lowering sky. 'It's going to snow,' he murmured. 'Thick and fast. We should leave London with the Santerres as quickly as possible. The snow will make the roads impassable.'

'We?' I cried.

'Oh, yes. Well,' Agrippa smiled, 'you two at least.'

'Why not go back and ask Hopkins what he meant?' I asked.

'I can't ask Hopkins anything.'

'Why?'

'He's dead, I cut his throat.' Agrippa shrugged. 'It was a mercy. What more could I do? The man would have died before the day was out and suffered even more terrible agony so I slit his throat.' He stood up, stamping his feet, and as he turned, his black robes wafting, I caught that strange exotic perfume once more. 'I must drink,' he whispered hoarsely. 'There's a fine tavern beyond the Tower gate, The Golden Turk.'

41

We walked back across the green. Agrippa disappeared into the royal lodgings to rid himself of the priestly robes and returned looking as cheerful as ever, clapping his hands and saying how a cup of fine blood-red claret would suit him. I studied the cunning little bastard with his smiling lips and soulless eyes and made a vow that I'd never turn my back on Doctor Agrippa.

Once we were in The Golden Turk he continued his role of genial friend, ordering trenchers of meat, capon soaked in lemon and a jug of the best Bordeaux.

After he had whetted his appetite and slaked his thirst, he leaned back, fingers locked above his stomach like some genial gnome. He stared at my master who had been quiet and withdrawn during the meal.

'You are suspicious, Master Benjamin?'

'Aye, sir, I am.'

Agrippa made a dismissive gesture with his fingers. 'So you should be, so you should be. But you have my drift? All you have seen so far are the opening lines of a play and what we see touches the fate of Kings, the power of the crown, mystery, treachery, intrigue – and, as you will later discover, bloody murder!' He sipped from his wine cup and smacked his lips. 'Oh, yes, you'll see wickedness,' he breathed, 'the like of which you have never witnessed before!'

Benjamin slammed his own wine cup down, disturbing the other customers, a group of tinkers who were sorting out their sundry relics and other wares to be sold at the nearby market of Smithfield.

'Why not tell us all? And why are you involved?' I stuttered.

Agrippa held out his hand, splaying his fingers. 'There are many routes to heaven,' he murmured. 'But, as long as we get there, who cares! The Cardinal controls the game, Master Shallot, and although I'll deny these words later, I control the Cardinal. Events must pattern out as they are intended and I am here to see that they do.' He wagged a stubby finger at the two of us, and smiled. 'And both of you are here to help me and, in doing so, will win fame and fortune.'

The last words held a sardonic tinge and I caught the wicked look on his face. Puppets, I thought, puppets on a string. But you know old Shallot – once locked in a game I'll play it out.

'Well,' Agrippa continued, 'poor deserted Hopkins's riddle:

"Beneath Jordan's water Christ's cup does rest,
And above Moses' Ark the sword that's best." '

'The River Jordan is in Palestine,' mused Benjamin, 'and I suppose the Ark of Moses refers to the Ark of the Covenant, the chest which carried the ten commandments. Though God knows where that is!' He sipped from his wine cup. 'Of one thing I am certain, my good Agrippa, you'll find neither of these at Glastonbury, so why should we go there?'

My master was out of moods, sickened by Buckingham's death and Agrippa's cool despatch of poor Hopkins. So this was one of the rare occasions I did his thinking for him.

'They must be in Glastonbury,' I insisted. 'Somehow or other the River Jordan and Moses' Ark refer to something there.'

'How do you reach that conclusion?' Benjamin asked.

'Well, the writing is from a secret chronicle at Glastonbury, the scribe must have been a monk there. He must have been writing a riddle known only to a few others, perhaps Templars in refuge. The River Jordan and Moses' Ark probably refer to places in or around Glastonbury.'

Agrippa leaned forward and squeezed my hand. 'Shallot, Shallot!' he murmured. 'There may be a slight cast in your

43

eye'— and in truth there was, an affliction since birth — 'but beneath that cunning face a subtle wit thrives and grows. The Lord Cardinal will be pleased.'

'Oh,' I mocked, 'my happiness is now complete. And what about this treachery and bloody murder?'

'In a while,' Agrippa smirked. 'Give the shadows more time to gather.'

Chapter 3

We left The Golden Turk and went down to the riverside. The day was beginning to fade as the barge we hired pulled to mid-stream and took us downriver to Richmond Palace. Benjamin crouched in the bows, rather dull and listless. Agrippa, pleased and contented with himself, kept leaning over and tapping me on the hand for my perspicacity in dealing with Hopkins's riddle.

The oarsmen swept round the bend of the Thames and down past Westminster. The quayside was obscured by the different ships moored there: carracks from Venice, fat sturdy cogs from the Baltic, and fishing smacks getting ready for a night's work. A pleasant enough sight for a trip down the river on a late-autumn evening.

Agrippa, basking in the calmness of the scene, smiled reassuringly at us. Believe me, if I'd known then what lay ahead – mysterious fires, the severed hand of glory, a haunted chapel, witch's curses and decapitated heads dripping blood – I would have slipped over the side of that wherry and swam for dear life to the nearest shore.

My master, however, had more immediate concerns. He looked sleepily back at the disappearing turrets of Westminster Abbey and shook himself alert.

'Why?' he asked abruptly.

'Why what?' Agrippa retorted.

'Why did we have to witness that execution? And was it

necessary for us to see Hopkins stretched out on that rack?'

Such thoughts had occurred to me so I stared curiously at Agrippa. He chewed on his lip as he tore his gaze away from the bank. The colour had returned to his eyes. Now they looked dark blue rather than that clear, glass-like appearance they always assumed when Agrippa witnessed any violence or bloodshed.

'In a few days,' the good doctor whispered, 'we will know all. But I tell you this: Buckingham, albeit a fool, died an innocent man.'

I stared at him in amazement.

'Oh, yes,' Agrippa continued. 'He may have been a secret Templar. He may even have been searching for the Grail and Arthur's Sword. But, according to Hopkins, that's all Buckingham was interested in.'

'So what proof of treason did the King produce at Buckingham's trial?'

'The testimony of Taplow, Buckingham's agent in London. Mind you,' Agrippa peered into the gathering mist, 'Buckingham is not the only one to lose his life over this matter.' He looked squarely at Benjamin. 'Did you know Calcraft?'

'A little.'

'Well, he was one of Mandeville's most trusted agents: a good man, a subtle scurrier who could worm out secrets and trap those plotting against the crown.'

'Yes, yes, I know,' Benjamin replied, 'I met Master Calcraft on one occasion. He had a face as sour as wormwood and was skilled in putting treasonable words into other men's mouths. Why, what mischief is he up to now?'

'Probably dancing with the devil,' Agrippa replied with a smile. 'Calcraft's dead! He was garrotted only a stone's throw from Richmond.'

'So these secret Templars may be striking back against Mandeville's men?'

'Perhaps. Calcraft was instrumental in sending Buckingham to the block. Anyway, he's gone.'

'Which is why dear Uncle sent for us?'

'Of course; Mandeville still has another agent, Warnham, investigating Buckingham's cover but Uncle wants you!'

'And our attendance at Buckingham's execution was to concentrate our minds.'

Agrippa smiled and nodded. 'The Lord Cardinal knows human nature well,' he replied. 'Master Benjamin, you have been lost in the calm and peace of Ipswich. Buckingham's death was a fitting prelude to the horrors which may await.'

Benjamin leaned back in his seat and closed his eyes whilst Agrippa diverted the conversation to the gossip and petty scandals of the court.

We arrived at Richmond just before dusk. A strange place even though it was relatively new, being rebuilt by the Great Mister, Fat Harry's father in 1490, Richmond was really a series of towers and halls built round a number of courtyards, each containing small orchards or gardens. The walls were covered with trellises of roses, red and white mixed together, to remind everyone that the Tudors united what was best in both the houses of York and Lancaster. The brickwork was ornamented with carvings and strange markings, gargoyles and statues, and each tower was capped by a large onion-shaped cupola. From the highest of these flew the banners of England and the pennants of Wolsey, proclaiming that both the King and his principal minister were now in residence.

Agrippa handed us over to a servant and we were taken to a rather narrow chamber in one of the towers, bleakly furnished with a bed and a few sticks of furniture. A battered painting hung on the wall depicting Noah's departure from the Ark. Benjamin looked around and smiled.

'My good uncle,' he announced sarcastically, 'appears to have the same high opinion of us as always.'

We unpacked our saddle bags then wandered along the corridors, a routine I always insisted on whenever we arrived in any strange place. One of Shallot's golden rules: when you find yourself somewhere strange or new, immediately find the quickest way out for you may well need it. (Only on one occasion did I forget this axiom. A young noble-woman was entertaining me in her bedchamber. I was that interested in seeing her gold-clocked stockings and scarlet garters, I forgot to check the window. When her brother returned unexpectedly, I found myself trapped. I don't recommend standing in a musty wardrobe for three hours whilst furry black rats scurry across your naked feet then return for a swift hungry nibble. Ah well, that's another story!)

We arrived at the buttery where a one-eyed cook refused us food so I knocked a brazier over and, when his back was turned, slipped the spit boy a penny and stole a nicely roasted capon and a loaf of bread. We were in one of the gardens eating our ill-gotten gains when Agrippa hurried up to us.

'Come! Come!' he ordered and, hardly stopping, hurried on, Benjamin and I behind him, greedily finishing our stolen meal. Agrippa took us out of the palace into an overgrown garden which, I realised, also served as a small cemetery. At the back, near the wall, stood a dilapidated charnel house, a small chamber where the corpses of servants who died in the palace would be taken out of the communal coffin and stitched into a cheap canvas sheet.

Agrippa thrust the door open, muttering to himself as he took a tinder and lit a candle. On a low stone slab in the centre of the room lay the corpse of a man, dressed in cheap brown fustian, now soaked and slimed with river water. His boots had been removed and several toes jutted through ragged stockings. He had died young, with a full head of auburn hair, but his face was disgusting and almost unrecognisable: the skin had turned black, tongue protruding out of one side of his mouth, eyes rolled back in their sockets. There were bite marks on his cheeks, probably caused by pike and other river fish. However, what really caught our attention was a cord wrapped tightly round his throat, the little rod the garrotter had used to tighten it still caught in its clever knot. I took one look, turned away and vomited up most of the capon.

'Who is it?' my master whispered.

'John Warnham,' Agrippa replied. 'Calcraft was killed in the same way.'

Benjamin, who seemed to have a stomach made of steel, knelt down and carefully examined the scarlet cord.

'It's like piping,' he commented. 'From someone's cloak.'

He peered at the knot. I watched him, trying not to glimpse that grotesque, blackened face. Benjamin got up, wiping the dust from his knees, went out and stood in the darkening garden. Agrippa and I followed.

'When was he found?'

'Early this morning in one of the carp ponds down near the river.'

'How long has he been dead?'

'He disappeared about two days ago.'

'Whoever did that,' Benjamin replied, 'was proficient with the garrotte.' He gently touched his own throat and half-smiled at me. 'Beware of the garrotte, Roger, the most skilled assassin, and it could be a mere child, could have his cord round your neck and choke out your life's breath within seconds. Did you know that?'

(At the time I didn't, and shook my head. But now I do! In one of my journals I'll tell you about bribing the Black Eunuch who was master of the harem in Constantinople. A terrible place with its marble walls, golden cups, scented gardens and silent death. The Turks do not believe in public executions. Instead they have a group of deaf mutes nicknamed 'The Gardeners', who carry scarlet cords. If a man or woman displeases the Sultan, the sign is given, 'The Gardeners' appear and strangulation takes place within seconds.

Sometimes it can be on a mere whim. On one occasion a Vizier, one of the Sultan's principal officers, decided to get rid of his entire harem. All the girls were strangled, put in sacks loaded with stones and dumped in the Bosphorus. One afternoon, whilst escaping from the Sultan's palace, I had to leave the boat in which I was fleeing and swam down, deep amongst the shallows of the Bosphorus. Now, you mightn't believe this, but the sea bed was dotted with sacks, with their grisly burdens, tied at the neck, standing upright under the force of the currents. Can you imagine it? A sea of dead girls within a sea? I see my little chaplain snigger. He thinks I am making it up. Far from it. I can swim like a fish, and often had to, and if he doesn't believe me, I'll take him down to the nearest pond and show him how!

Ah, well, that's quietened him and, true, I do digress.)

'Warnham was one of the Cardinal's agents?' Benjamin asked.

Agrippa nodded. 'As was Calcraft,' he added.

'But why murder them?' Agrippa continued as if talking to himself. 'What is the use of killing agents?'

'They must have known something,' I replied.

Agrippa shook his head. 'No. I think we have already gleaned the information we need. Buckingham is dead, Hopkins too.' He pulled a face. 'Ah, well, only time will tell.'

He waddled off and we went back to our chambers.

For the next few days we were left to our own devices. Oh, we glimpsed Wolsey from afar in his scarlet silken robes and, now and again, whilst feasting in the hall at a series of sumptuous banquets. The Great Beast made his presence felt.

King Henry looked a little older but still enormous with his bright gold hair and beard and those blue, agate-hard eyes which seemed to take in everything. He dressed in a brilliant array of jewel-encrusted jerkins, silver hose and high-heeled, ribbon-rosed shoes which made him look even loftier than those around him. The Great Killer always liked to enjoy himself and, whatever dangers threatened, lost himself in a round of festivities.

Some idiot must have told him more stories about King Arthur for this seemed to tickle his fancy and on our third evening at Richmond he staged a marvellous masque. We, along with other guests (the Cardinal had still not acknowledged his nephew), were led into a vast hall lit by hundreds of pure wax candles. Around the walls the rich scarlets, yellows and golds of Venetian tapestries sparkled in the light, whilst at the far end of this cavernous chamber loomed a vision all in green. It was a fairy castle, its high battlements crowned with towers and its walls pierced with crenellations. Carpenters and artists had laboured for two weeks to build this Château Vert or Green Castle, covering the wooden frame with green paper, foil and verdigris paint. The effect was quite remarkable: the green castle shimmered in the candle-lit hall like some spectre in a vision.

Well, you have the drift of what was happening. Eight lovely women representing Beauty and Honour, etc, had to defend the castle against eight nobles, led, of course, by the stupid fat beast himself. These eight lords, who had taken the names of Love, Youth, Loyalty and so on pelted the defenders of the Château Vert with flowers and were showered with rose-water and sweetmeats in return. Everyone took it seriously. I could hardly stop laughing to see the great ones of the land engaged in such childish games.

My master sat still, rather quiet and withdrawn, pondering on what Agrippa had told him. I was more interested in the food; mutton in beer, duck in orange sauce, pastries and sweet cubes of jellied milk, as well as the cups of claret and chilled wine. I drank as if there was no tomorrow.

One thing I did notice during the masque and another similar farce when we all trooped out to Shooters Hill to see Fat Henry clothed in Lincoln green play Robin Hood, was The Great Killer's new love: a dark-haired, sloe-eyed girl who moved with a languorous grace and whom the King was for ever singling out for marks of special affection.

That was the first time I saw Anne Boleyn. She wasn't beautiful, not in the classical sense, but exuded a sexual power which drew men's gazes like a magnet. Beside her, the short, dumpy Spanish queen, Catherine of Aragon, resembled a chamber pot next to a beautiful vase.

Poor old Catherine! The bearer of so many children, only one of whom survived: the little, red-haired, pinched-faced girl Mary, who followed her mother everywhere. Good Lord, the things we do to our children! Mary grew up hating her father and, like her mother, spent her entire life pining for a living child. I know she did. When she died she gave me her prayer book. I still have it. One part of it, the prayer of a mother asking to be delivered of a healthy child, was so tear-stained the ink had run.

Mind you, they have all gone now. I sit here and reflect on Fat Henry prancing around pretending to be Robin Hood. As the years passed, he killed all those round him before being murdered himself. Yes, murdered. I confess to it now, I wasn't involved but I knew about it. His council served him white arsenic which created a fire ball in his belly. He lay for days on a stinking bed, with blood-streaked eyes and parchment-coloured complexion, unable to swallow. His skin began to peel off, the gross fat in his belly turned to liquid whilst his stomach and bowels dripped blood. When he died, foaming at the mouth, his tongue was so big it completely filled his mouth and kept it a-gape. They had to hoist his rotting corpse into the coffin, stuffing it in like you would a rotten bale of straw into a sack. Ah, how the glories of the world disappear.

After a few days of kicking our heels round Richmond, the court began to settle down. We became more conscious of the Santerres as well as of the sombre presence of the *Agentes*. The latter slipped like shadows along the passageways and I formed a secret dread of Sir Edmund Mandeville. He looked as dark as Lucifer, some beautiful angel fallen from grace. He was good-looking in an arrogant, Mediterranean way: olive skin, jet-black hair, neatly clipped beard and moustache, though his lips had a strange twist to them and his eyes were ever mocking. He looked like a man who didn't believe in himself, let alone anything else.

Geoffrey Southgate, his lieutenant, appeared more cheerful with a shock of red hair, beetling eyebrows and pallid skin. The fellow had a slight lisp and rather affected movements but was the dagger to his master's foil.

We met them all in the Fountain Court a few days after arriving at Richmond. Benjamin was reading some manuscript he had borrowed from the library whilst I sat, bored to death, wondering what mischief I could get up to.

The first to approach us were the Santerres. Sir John was a bluff yet shrewd landowner who knew which side of the table to sit. He was the sort of fellow who would buy you a drink in a tavern, regaling you with some funny story, yet whom you would be a fool to trust. His eyes reminded me of the King's, ice blue and piggy in aspect. Lady Beatrice, his wife, now she had regained her composure bore the remnants of great beauty though her pallid-skinned face had a spoilt, rather sensuous cast. She was for ever leaning on her husband's arm as if she was determined he would never wander far from her clutches. Rachel, their daughter, was ravishingly beautiful. She wore a simple veil of murrey covering her hair and a modest blue dress made from pure wool, gilt-edged at the neck and cuffs.

The Santerres came into the Fountain Court as if they were simply wandering round the palace. My master closed the book he was reading and shrewdly watched them approach.

'I wondered when they would come,' he whispered.

'Why?'

'We are too humble to introduce ourselves,' he hissed, 'so they have to come to us. After all, if Agrippa is to be believed, we will be travelling back with them. So, Roger, to your feet and behave yourself.'

We rose as the Santerres swept grandly towards us; the introductions were made, hands clasped or kissed. Sir John stepped back, clearing his throat.

'I am given to understand,' he boomed, his accent burred by a rustic twang, 'that you will be returning with us to Somerset. This business!' He flung his hands up in the air. 'Lackaday! Lackaday! What can I say?'

Aye, I thought, what can you? A man looking for the main chance was Sir John. I could just imagine poor Buckingham's confidences being betrayed by him.

'You saw the good Duke die,' I blurted out.

'Good?' Lady Beatrice snapped. 'Buckingham was a traitor to his King. A Judas in Henry's court. Why say you differently?'

'The man's dead,' I replied quickly. 'And his soul's before God. Why should we speak ill of him now?'

Santerre rubbed his eyes and looked at me warily.

'Aye, aye,' he whispered. 'He was a good lord but he went poaching in the wrong fields.'

'Master Shallot is noble to defend the Duke.' Rachel Santerre spoke, her voice soft and low.

I glanced at her and my heart leapt. She had raised her face and it was truly beautiful: her skin was like shot silk, pure gold. I would have loved to touch her cheek or gently caress that long, slender neck. I looked for humour, perhaps sarcasm, but her dark eyes were clear and those lips, slightly parted, bore no trace of sneer. I blushed, bowed and showed a leg.

'Mistress, you are too kind.'

Benjamin nudged me for he knew me. My brains were in my codpiece and, when it came to beautiful women, discretion was cast to the winds – and a lot more if I could help it!

'Come, Rachel,' Lady Beatrice snapped. 'Your father and I have other business.'

'You mean my step-father,' she said quietly.

Now I smiled at her. I could see a little of Lady Beatrice in Rachel, but I had wondered how a red-faced, wart-covered farmer like Sir John could sire such a beauty.

'I am your father,' he firmly replied.

Lady Beatrice caught her husband's wrist and looked at Benjamin. She'd dismissed me with a contemptuous flicker of her eyelids, of course. Old Shallot was used to that.

'Sir John is my second husband,' she explained. 'Rachel's father died when she was a child.'

'In which case, Mother,' Rachel replied, 'I was a child for a long time. Father has only been cold in his grave for five years.'

Oh, oh, I thought, here's a pretty tableau for there's nothing more interesting than a family quarrel. I stared once more at Rachel, revelling in the beautiful lines of her face, and my wicked heart jumped with pleasure. If the mother disliked me, perhaps I had some hope with the daughter? (I see my little clerk sniggering. He thinks I wanted to bed her there and then. No, no, that's not the way of old Shallot. Well, not really, I just wanted to be with her. Gaze at her, become lost in those lovely dark eyes. Not all of us have minds like sewers!)

Looking back I think a family quarrel would have broken out then, but the door leading to the Fountain Court opened and Sir Edmund Mandeville and Geoffrey Southgate emerged, followed by two bald-headed individuals who looked as similar as peas in a pod. Sir John swung round to look at them and his face paled.

'Come,' he whispered. 'We have business to do.'

They walked off, Lady Beatrice still leaning heavily on his arm. Rachel turned her face slightly and I am sure she was smiling.

Mandeville and Southgate made to pass us by as they had previously. I stood watching, fascinated by the two characters trailing behind them: they were twins and reminded me of eunuchs with their fat, doughy faces, cod-like mouths and heads shaven as bald as pigeon's eggs.

Suddenly Mandeville turned, came towards us and bowed. (By the way, have you noticed that? How the most sinister of characters are often the most courteous?)

'Master Daunbey, Master Shallot. I see the Santerres have introduced themselves, and perhaps it is time we all got to know each other a little better.' He followed my gaze. I was still watching his bald-headed retainers. 'Oh, may I introduce Geoffrey Southgate and my two clerks, Cosmas and Damien?'

The eunuchs bowed.

'Are they twins?' I asked.

'Of course,' Southgate languidly replied.

The two eunuchs, as I called them, now watched me; they had eyes like a frog's, glassy and soulless. I couldn't see a speck of hair on face or head.

'Can't they speak?' my master asked.

Mandeville half-turned. 'Cosmas, open your mouth!'

I couldn't believe it. At Mandeville's order, both these nightmare creatures opened their mouths. I saw the red rag of flesh where each tongue should have been and glanced away in disgust. My master, God bless him, just peered closer.

'What happened?' he asked, like some family physician making a diagnosis.

'Oh, they were born in England,' Mandeville replied. 'They were with their parents on a carrack in the Middle Sea when it was taken by Turkish corsairs. Cosmas and Damien, as I now call them, were taken to Constantinople, castrated and made mute eunuchs.' He patted one of them affectionately on his bald pate as one would tap the head of a good hunting dog. 'But they are well educated.'

He looked squarely at me but I knew he was studying both of us. Benjamin may have mystified him but I caught the sardonic glint in his eyes as he dismissed me for a rogue. He suddenly stared over his shoulder at the door as if expecting someone else to join us, then took a step closer. Southgate also leaned forward as if they were two school masters admonishing students.

'The *Agentes* welcome you,' Mandeville whispered, his voice becoming steely. 'We trapped Buckingham. We can weed out these Templars and discover what His Grace the Cardinal needs, but he is insistent that you join us.'

I stared at their hard faces and, despite Rachel Santerre's charms, the prospect of a journey to Glastonbury in the company of this eerie foursome lost any remaining attraction. They both stepped back, bowed and walked out of the court.

Benjamin watched them go. 'I wonder what all that was about?' he murmured. 'I just wish dear Uncle would reveal his mind to us.'

'Sirs!' a voice called. 'I heard you talking.'

We both turned. A young man had come up quietly behind us. Perhaps his approach had warned the *Agentes* off. He stood as proud and pert as a barnyard cock. I groaned quietly: the fellow looked a troublemaker with his russet leather jacket, tight hose, protuberant codpiece, high-heeled boots and, above all, the basket-hilted sword he kept drumming with his fingers.

He was a fighting boy, one of those hangers-on who plague every court and nobleman's house, puffed up with their own pride, ever ready to make a quarrel. (Master Shakespeare has borrowed my descriptions of such fellows for Thibault, the swordsman in his excellent play *Romeo and Juliet*.) The man came closer and doffed his broad-brimmed hat festooned with a cheap plume. His face was sallow with thin bloodless lips and eyes that were narrow and hooded. He thrust his chin forward.

'Sirs, I asked you a question. What was that conversation about? I come across to join you and your friends immediately leave. Was it at your request? Do you find my presence offensive?'

Benjamin seized my wrist. 'Be careful, Roger,' he whispered. 'The fellow's looking for a fight.'

My master was so innocent he was always stating the obvious. Of course I was careful. Old Shallot is a coward! I will run like a whippet at the slightest hint of danger and was preparing to do so then when the fellow blocked my path and poked me in the chest.

'Are you leaving as well, cockscomb?'

'Sod off!' I hissed.

The man stood back, throwing down his hat and half-drawing his sword. Benjamin stepped in front of me.

'We apologise,' he declared. 'Sir, we meant no offence.'

My would-be opponent's eyes didn't leave my face.

'My quarrel is not with you, Master Daunbey,' he replied softly. 'I have no dispute with the Cardinal's nephew, but this fellow has insulted me.'

'No, I haven't!' I pleaded. 'I just don't feel well. Sir, let me pass!'

Benjamin came between us again. 'Stand aside, sir!' he ordered. 'We have no quarrel with you.'

'No, *you* haven't, Master Daunbey,' the man repeated and my stomach curdled with fear for the fellow knew our names. This was no accident. The man had deliberately set out to challenge me and, when that happens, two thoughts always dominate my mind. First, can I run? Secondly, if I can't, will I be hurt?

The fellow drew his sword and rested its cruel point on the ground.

'Both of you may go,' he said, swaying his hips in a mocking fashion. 'And by supper everyone will be talking about the courage of "Mistress Shallot". Mistress Shallot! Mistress Shallot!' he continued in a sing-song fashion. 'What's the matter, girl?' he taunted and cocked his head sideways. 'With those funny eyes, one is never too sure what you are looking at.' He held up a finger. 'I know, if you bend over and let me smack your bottom with the flat of my sword, I'll let you go.'

Now Benjamin's hand went to the hilt of his sword.

'If you draw, Master Benjamin,' the bully-boy continued. 'I'll just walk away.'

'Please,' I muttered, gazing round the deserted courtyard.

'Please!' the fellow mimicked back.

'You have no choice,' Benjamin whispered.

So there was I, stomach churning, bowels twisting. I doffed my jerkin, drew my hangar and put as brave a face on it as possible. We took up position. The salute was given, our swords crossed and the duel began. I moved, twisting my sword, one eye closed. The fellow just played with me, moving backwards and forwards. He nicked my wrist. I closed my eyes. He slipped behind me and slapped me on the buttocks with the flat of his sword.

'Mistress Shallot!' he called out.

I stared at Benjamin but he had looked away. Then a strange thing happened. Old Shallot has always put a high price on his own skin but that blow on the buttocks stirred my pride (wherever it was hiding) and I recalled the words of my duelling master. I opened my eyes and stared at this braggart dancing before me. He represented everything that was wrong in old Shallot's life: the mocking dismissal of Wolsey, the patronising attitude of Agrippa, the sly taunting jibes that I hid behind my master's skirts. In other words, I lost my temper and found my courage.

My sword came down. I narrowed my eyes and took up a proper fighting stance and a different duel began. I wanted to kill that bastard and he knew it: red spots appeared high on his cheeks, his eyes became fearful, mouth half-open. His breath came in short gasps as we feinted and parried, cut and thrust. Poor sod! He was just a street brawler and, as God is my witness, I only meant to wound him. I thrust, aiming for his fighting arm, he moved with me, and my sword went in, deep into the soft flesh beneath the rib cage.

I let go the handle and stood back in horror.

The fellow stared at me, clutching the blade of my sword as blood spurted out of the wound. He dropped his own weapon, took one step towards me, his life blood shot out of his mouth and his eyes, still filled with astonishment, glazed over as he collapsed to the ground.

Benjamin turned him over.

'Dead as a stone,' he muttered. 'Sweet Lord, Roger, you had no choice.' He smiled faintly at me. 'I never thought you were a duellist.'

'Neither did I, Master!'

I sat down on the grass in a half-faint. I had just retrieved my sword when the gates of the courtyard were suddenly thrust open and a group of the Cardinal's halberdiers hurried across. Pikes lowered, they ringed both of us. The captain, fat-faced with a russet beard, plucked the sword out of my hand.

'Sir, by what name?'

He clicked his fingers and two of the soldiers dragged me to my feet.

'My servant's name is Roger Shallot,' Benjamin declared.

'This fellow challenged him to a duel and would not let him go.'

The captain made a face. 'That may well be.' He peered closer. 'You are Master Daunbey, the Cardinal's nephew?'

'I am.'

'Then, sir, you should know that duelling is expressly forbidden by His Majesty and to draw swords in anger in the King's own palace is high treason. Master Shallot, you are under arrest!'

I gazed speechlessly at Benjamin's white face. He shrugged helplessly.

'Go with them, Roger,' he whispered hoarsely. 'I will see my uncle.'

Ringed by the group of halberdiers, I was half-pushed out of the courtyard. We turned and went down a passageway. Mandeville and Southgate had been standing in the gallery watching the entire spectacle through a window. The two bastards seemed to be enjoying themselves but Southgate held up his hand and the guard stopped whilst Mandeville grabbed my wrist.

'You had no choice, Master Shallot,' he murmured. 'That is why we left so abruptly. We saw the bully-boy coming and thought he might be trouble.'

Oh, thank you very much, I thought. But that's the way of the world. If there's a mound of shit, old Shallot is always dropped in it!

Mandeville and Santerre stood aside and I was marched down to a small narrow cellar which also served as the palace dungeon. I was thrust in, given a candle, a cup of watered wine and a loaf of the hardest bread the kitchen could supply. It was tinged with green mould and, as I sat gnawing on it, reflecting on my fortunes, I realised that bastard of a one-eyed cook had apparently missed the capon I had stolen. I sat there for hours.

At first the blood ran hot in my veins and I loudly

61

protested my innocence to the cold grey walls and to two large rats which seemed to appear from nowhere. They listened to my declarations of innocence and, when I fell into a fitful sleep, gnawed the bread and drank what wine was left in the battered cup. When I awoke it was dark and cold and I became frightened. The bully-boy, God rest him whoever he was, had forced that fight deliberately. So who had sent him? Who had staged that little masque?

Then I thought of the King, with his piggy, sly eyes; the Lord Cardinal, his Master of Games – and my fear turned to heart-stopping terror.

Chapter 4

Mind you, old Shallot's not a dog to lie down for ever. Believe me, I have been in so many narrow spots: on the gallows at Montfaucon; hunted by wild animals through the slums of Paris or Francis I's maze; swimming for my life in the Bosphorus and cornered in the ruins of Rome by hordes of bloodthirsty Lutherans. So my stay in the dungeons of Richmond Palace only frightened me a little, rather than laying me prostrate with terror. I only vomited twice and my breeches soon dried. (Which is more than I can say for my chaplain's if he does not stop sniggering and put pen to paper. Do you know, I never see his face without thinking of hell fire?)

I eventually fell asleep and woke cold and hungry. I peered through the small grille high in the wall, saw that night had fallen and believed everyone had forgotten me. Of course, they hadn't. An hour later the cell door swung open and Benjamin walked in with a cup of warm posset in his hand. (God give him rest, he was a thoughtful man.) A group of the Cardinal's retainers followed, drawn swords in their hands, their faces grim under steel conical helmets.

'Come, Roger,' Benjamin murmured, 'His Eminence the Cardinal, not to mention His Majesty the King, seeks an audience with us.'

He watched me drain the cup of posset and sniffed.

'A strange smell in here,' he observed. 'Certainly no place for a man like you, Roger.'

(God bless him, he was so naive!)

Wolsey's liveried thugs took us back upstairs, along dark wainscoted galleries to a chamber high in one of the towers. The room was in shadow, only a line of wax candles on the smooth oval table affording light, as if His diabolic Eminence didn't want anyone to know that the meeting was taking place.

At the top of the table sprawled the King in a purple quilted sleeveless jerkin, his pure white silk shirt fringed at cuff and collar with Bruges lace. I say 'sprawled' for the King looked drunk. His fat face was flushed whilst those boorish hard eyes looked even more dangerous than ever. (I remember dark-eyed Anne Boleyn . . . what on earth did she see in him? She did confess to me, two days before she lost her head, that if she had her life all over again, she would prefer to be married to a Death's Head with a bone in its mouth than go within a mile of our fat King. I agreed.)

Henry looked dangerous even as he sat there, tapping stubby fingers on the table top, the click of his rings on the wood like that of a death beat on a drum. Beside him sat Wolsey, garbed as usual in purple silk, his dark black hair cropped and oiled, fleshy face inscrutable.

'Come in! Come in!' His Eminence murmured softly, gesturing to two chairs at the bottom of the table. 'Dearest nephew, at last we meet. I think you know everyone?' He waved his hand.

On the King's left sat the *Agentes*, Mandeville, Southgate, and those two ghastly-looking clerks. Across the table, seated next to Wolsey, were the Santerres who, the comely Rachel included, looked very apprehensive at such a midnight meeting.

'You have all met?'

'Dearest Uncle,' Benjamin replied, 'we have met everyone except you.'

Wolsey caught the rebuke and smiled. 'Affairs of state,

affairs of state, dearest Nephew.' He pushed back his chair and swept down the chamber. Leaning over, he grasped Benjamin by the shoulders and kissed him affectionately on each cheek. 'Be careful! Be careful, dear Nephew!' I heard him whisper. 'Do whatever the King commands.'

He stood away, smiled falsely, and returned to his seat next to the King. (Lord, he was a treacherous bastard! Wolsey's ambitious fingers poked in every man's pie. Do you know, he was so oily that at the end of the world, when everything else catches fire, he'll burn a week longer than anyone else).

'Master Daunbey,' Henry called out, 'you wish for some wine?'

He clicked his fingers and Agrippa stepped out of the shadows. (God knows where he had been hiding during the last few days.)

The good doctor put two cups down in front of us, filled them and went back to stand at the door. I caught his warning glance but he didn't have to tell Old Shallot anything. I may have the courage of a wild duck but I have more wits than a dog has fleas. Fat Henry had also been studying me.

'A rare honour for you, Master Shallot. We do not welcome traitors close to our bosoms – men who kill in our presence.'

'Your Majesty, I was provoked!' I blurted out.

Henry smirked as Wolsey leaned over and whispered in his ear. The King flicked his fingers contemptuously at me. Wolsey smiled unctuously, like some pompous priest talking to his dimmest parishioner.

'Master Shallot,' the Cardinal purred, 'so pleasant to see you again.'

I became more nervous and stared quickly round the room: the windows were all shuttered and none of the cresset torches had been lit. A dark shape lurked in the shadows and I knew Agrippa was standing listening to everything. Wolsey nodded at the King, clasped his hands and leaned forward. Oh Lord, I thought, here comes danger.

'Dear Nephew, you saw Buckingham die?'

The King sniffed and dabbed at his eyes with one laced cuff.

'A bosom friend,' he interrupted, 'a man close to my heart. How could he betray his friend and King?'

I just stared at the fat hypocrite as Wolsey patted him gently on the wrist. One of the finest actors I have ever met, old Henry. He could turn the tears on as easily as the tap on a beer keg. He always delivered a fine performance, almost believable – unless you knew how black his heart was.

'Buckingham was a traitor,' Wolsey declared sonorously, 'and deserved his death. Dearest Nephew, Hopkins was questioned in the Tower and you have the famous riddle. How does it go? Ah yes:

> "Beneath Jordan's water Christ's cup does rest,
> And above Moses' Ark the sword that's best."

'Yes,' he murmured. 'Very clever.'

'Agrippa discovered that,' Benjamin answered sharply.

'Yes, yes, he did,' Wolsey purred. 'But let us review matters. Buckingham's power lay in the South-West along the Welsh march and in the counties of Somerset, Devon and Dorset. He had Yorkist blood in his veins and a history of treason, for his father also went to the block. Now his treason began when he went to Templecombe . . .' Wolsey glanced sideways at Sir John Santerre. 'Perhaps, sir, you would like to continue?'

Santerre cleared his throat. 'My Lord of Buckingham,' he began, then coughed. 'I mean, the traitor Buckingham, came to my house on a Friday evening late last autumn. I

66

thought it strange for, although we corresponded on estate matters, he very rarely travelled so far south, even though I knew he had a special regard for Father Hopkins.'

'Now, Hopkins,' Santerre continued, 'was a London-born priest, a Benedictine monk from Glastonbury who had been dispensed from his monastic vows to serve as chaplain at Templecombe as well as a priest serving the outlying farms and granges belonging to Glastonbury Abbey.' Santerre looked down the table at us. 'Hopkins was a strange man, an antiquarian and historian. He knew all the legends of Somerset and Devon and could recount the tales of Arthur backwards.'

'Did he ever talk about the Grail or Excalibur?' Benjamin interrupted, ignoring his uncle's frown of annoyance.

'Sometimes at the table he would do so, but he spent most of his time either in his chamber or on what he called his travels, visiting the farms or ferreting out new secrets.'

'About what?' I asked.

'About Arthur, and the whereabouts of his Grail. His chamber was for ever full of manuscripts.'

'Where are these now?' Benjamin asked.

'Destroyed,' Southgate interrupted lazily. 'The mad priest burnt everything before coming up to London.'

'Continue, Sir John,' snapped Wolsey.

'Dearest Uncle, one more question?'

Wolsey nodded angrily.

'Sir John, was Hopkins friendly with you and your family?'

'No,' Santerre replied heatedly. 'I have explained that. He kept himself to himself. Oh, he performed his priestly functions, Mass and Confession, but you could see his heart was not in it. They were more duties then priestly celebrations.' Sir John glanced quickly at his wife and daughter. 'He didn't seem to like women. I rarely saw him, nor can my wife or daughter ever remember having a conversation with him, which lasted longer than ten minutes.'

'This is true,' Rachel added softly, and her dark sloe eyes smiled, making me momentarily forget I was sitting in the presence of a great murderer.

'Continue!' Henry rapped the table.

'I now know,' Santerre continued hurriedly, 'that Hopkins often visited my Lord of Buckingham and, when the Duke visited Templecombe, he asked to see me in my private chamber. The Duke was very excited, claiming that Hopkins had told him that the Grail and Arthur's Sword still existed, that he was most desirous of obtaining them, and that Hopkins believed that once he had solved a secret cipher, such precious relics would be in his possession.'

'This secret cipher,' Benjamin intervened, 'is the riddle heard from Hopkins's dying lips at the Tower and which my Lord Cardinal has just recited?'

'Yes, yes,' Santerre answered.

'And where did Hopkins find that?'

'Apparently in the fly-leaf of a book, an ancient chronicle, in Glastonbury library.'

'We do not know if that's true,' Mandeville spoke up, 'but it can be verified.'

'Anyway,' Santerre continued, aware of the King's fingers drumming on the table top. 'I asked my Lord of Buckingham why he needed such relics, to which he replied: "Who knows? Who knows to what heights a man could rise, if he held Arthur's sword and drank from the cup Christ himself used?" '

'Dear Uncle,' Benjamin said sweetly, 'is that treason? My Lord of Buckingham was like other great men. Indeed, His Grace the King and yourself are avid collectors of relics.'

'But not traitors,' Mandeville interrupted. 'You see, Master Daunbey, what Buckingham did not know is that two of my men, skilled ferreters out of treason, were members of his retinue.'

Benjamin smiled. 'You mean Calcraft and Warnham who have since been garrotted?'

Mandeville lost some of his composure. His grin fell away and he chewed angrily on the quick of his thumb.

'Yes.' He nodded. 'Yes, Master Daunbey, Calcraft and Warnham who have since been killed, but let that wait. Suffice to say that at Templecombe they approached Sir John Santerre and asked him what Buckingham had said. My Lord of Templecombe was astute and loyal enough to tell the truth.'

'And then what?' Benjamin asked.

'We established,' Mandeville continued, 'that Hopkins often carried messages to a certain Master Taplow in London. Taplow, a Lutheran tailor, used his links with certain noblemen to report back to my Lord of Buckingham the doings of the court and what was happening in the city. Master Taplow is now in the Fleet Prison. He has confessed that letters written to him by Buckingham and carried by Hopkins demonstrate how this traitorous Duke intended to find the sacred relics and use them to cause bloody rebellion against the King. We seized such letters. Buckingham has gone to the block, Taplow will go to the stake, whilst Hopkins has already answered for his crimes.'

'Very neat, very neat,' Benjamin muttered. 'But this business of the Templars?'

Wolsey, who had been watching his nephew, waved his hand for silence and whispered into the King's ear. Henry, who had been staring assiduously at Rachel Santerre, lifted his heavy-lidded eyes, smirked and nodded.

'Dearest nephew,' Wolsey continued, 'the Templars were fighting monks dedicated to defending the Holy Land. They amassed great wealth in this country and others. On Friday October the thirteenth 1307 all the Templars in France were arrested, their lands and wealth were seized by King Philip IV with the blessing of Pope Clement V. Similar arrests occurred in this country and elsewhere but some Templars survived. Their fleet disappeared from La Rochelle whilst those who escaped arrest went underground, particularly in Scotland, where they were protected by Robert the Bruce. The Templars vowed vengeance against every royal family who betrayed them, and that includes the Crown of England. The spiritual descendants of these Templars are now a secret brotherhood.' Wolsey paused and smirked. 'The word "brotherhood" must not be taken literally. The Templars themselves were celibate men but we know this society includes cleric and lay, young and old, married and celibate, male and female, English and French, high and low. Some people say the Yorkist princes, enemies of His Grace the King, may have been members of this brotherhood.'

Wolsey stopped speaking as Henry stirred in his chair. The Cardinal had rubbed an open wound for Henry, the Welsh squire, hated any reference to these Yorkist princes and (as I have demonstrated many times in my journals), by the time the old bastard died, he had destroyed that family root and branch.

'Now,' Wolsey pushed his cup away. 'Hopkins confessed to being a secret Templar. He also said comrades of this brotherhood were close to the King.'

Henry's piggy eyes flickered at us down the table and I felt a chill of fear.

'My Lord Cardinal is right,' he whispered though his voice carried. 'There may be members of this secret brotherhood, this nest of traitors, here at court. And if Master Hopkins can be believed, they too search for the Grail and the Sword Excalibur. Buckingham,' the word was spat out, 'was undoubtedly of their coven and our two faithful agents, Warnham and Calcraft, have paid for their loyalty with their lives.'

Henry hit the table top with his fist. 'But enough is enough!' He jabbed his finger at Benjamin and myself, 'You,

70

Master Daunbey, and that thing you call your servant, will journey to Glastonbury with my good servants Mandeville and Southgate. You will lodge at Templecombe. You will bring the work of these traitors to nothing and for me, your King, find both the Grail and the Sword of Arthur. Is that clear?'

'Your Grace, I have a number of questions?'

'Then ask them!'

'Dearest Uncle, what makes you think the Templars are so active in the South-West?' Benjamin asked.

'They are active everywhere,' Wolsey replied. 'In Madrid, in Rome, in Paris, in London, but particularly in the South-West. Old memories die slowly where the Templars formerly owned most of the land, such as the Santerre estates.'

I looked at Sir John and his wife, rigid and still as waxen figures, Rachel quiet as a nun beside them.

'Templecombe was a Templar stronghold?' I asked, speaking my master's thoughts.

Lady Santerre looked dolefully down at us. 'Yes, and we fear the Order as much as His Grace the King. My maiden name is Belamonte. My ancestor was the King's agent in Somerset and Dorset, responsible for arresting the Templars and seizing their lands.' She muttered something else.

'Speak up, My Lady!' Henry insisted. 'Tell us what you know.'

'They say,' Lady Santerre began, 'that the Belamontes are cursed and that no good will come to us for the seizure of the Templar manors. My first husband died in a riding accident.' She grasped her second husband's hand. 'I took the name Santerre. Perhaps that will wipe out the curse.'

'No curse, my Lady.' Mandeville spoke up. 'There is nothing under heaven which cannot be tracked down, trapped and killed. These are a treasonable coven.'

My master abruptly changed the conversation, 'You said that Hopkins was born in London?'

'Yes,' Mandeville replied.

'Does he have any kin here?'

'Yes, yes, an elder sister. A woman of faded beauty and slender means. And, no, Master Daunbey, before you ask, she was not party to her brother's treasonable activities.'

My master pulled a face.

'Why do you ask?' Wolsey demanded, his chin thrust forward aggressively.

Benjamin gazed unblinkingly back whilst I studied these men, their hearts filled with arrogance and pride: the King and Wolsey were devils in silk, Mandeville and Southgate looked venom-mouthed, whilst the Santerres just sat like a row of candlesticks.

What are you up to, I thought. Why was I provoked into that duel? And what will come of us? Does our fat King see us as mere crow pudding?

'Dear Nephew, I asked you a question?'

'I was just wondering,' Benjamin replied, 'you say Buckingham wrote to Taplow?'

'I did.'

'So Taplow must have carried messages to someone else?'

'As I said, dear Nephew,' Wolsey pulled back the silken sleeves of his gown, 'members of this secret Templar brotherhood could be here at court.'

'And could be responsible for the deaths of Calcraft and Warnham?'

'Perhaps.'

'It stands to reason they must be,' Benjamin continued remorselessly. 'Someone here in London killed your two agents, either as revenge or because they continued to meddle.'

Wolsey smiled. 'You are most perceptive,' he murmured. 'Yes, yes, Warnham and Calcraft did believe a Templar lurked high in His Grace's Council, but whom we do not know. Master Taplow, who has been ruthlessly questioned, could not assist us.'

'So why should we go to Templecombe?' Benjamin sharply asked. 'Dearest Uncle, you have your own agents.' He nodded at Mandeville and Southgate. 'And what guarantee do we have that we will not suffer the same fate as Warnham and Calcraft?'

The King's face turned thunderously angry.

'Because I want you to!' Wolsey intervened quickly, then closed the trap. 'Of course you will be rewarded – whilst the charge of treason, of duelling in the King's presence by Master Shallot will be dropped.' Wolsey spread his hands. 'Indeed, a pardon has already been drawn up.'

If the fat bastard had not been glaring down at me I would have burst into peals of mocking laughter. Benjamin, God bless him, just sighed at how sly Tom Wolsey had trapped us.

He smiled wanly. 'In which case, dear Uncle, we are as ever your most humble servants.'

The atmosphere in the room lightened. Mandeville, that crow bait, leaned forward.

'We shall be honoured by your presence, Master Daunbey. Your assistance will, I am sure, be invaluable.'

Wolsey tossed a red-ribboned scroll down the table towards his nephew. 'This is further information. You may study it at your leisure.'

Another thinner scroll followed.

'And that, Master Shallot, is your pardon for the killing of Robert Brognar.' Wolsey shrugged his shoulders. 'He was a city bully and will not be missed.' He smiled at me.

Oh, no, I thought, poor Brognar won't be missed, you bull's-pizzle of a Cardinal: once I had drawn my sword I was guilty of treason. I took cold comfort in that wily Wolsey had probably intended Brognar to make a fool of me as well as involve me in treason. Instead I'd killed him, a sure protection against mockery though it made my 'crime' all the worse.

Wolsey smiled and clapped his hands. 'These proceedings

73

are now finished, dearest Nephew. You may withdraw.'

Well, what more could I say? Benjamin and I trotted off back to our tower like well-trained lap dogs. I am sure that after the Santerres left, Henry and Wolsey must have rocked with laughter at us. Once we were in the security of our own chamber, I gave full vent to my anger.

'Doesn't your bloody uncle care?' I cried. 'Is that how he treats his kith and kin? Of course he doesn't give a mouldy fig about old Shallot!' I added bitterly. 'I am just a cross-eyed piece of turd to be discarded at will!'

Benjamin smiled. 'One of the many things I like about you, Roger, is how very rarely you complain. My uncle's treatment must have hurt you. I apologise.'

(Lord, wasn't he innocent?)

I refused to be mollified.

'Do you know,' I bawled, 'I once talked to a mariner who sailed north of Newfoundland. He claimed to have seen great islands of ice floating in the sea but, large as they were, there was more ice under water than showed on top. Your bloody uncle's like that,' I whispered hoarsely. 'A great, fat, floating dangerous rock!'

'True, true, Roger, and it also applies to the story he spun us this evening. Or, as the vicar said about the lady's bosom, "There's more to it than meets the eye".' Benjamin looked at me. 'Someone told me that as a joke. I never really did understand it.'

'Never mind, Master,' I muttered. 'Similes and metaphors will not get us out of this.'

Benjamin undid the red cords and loosened the two scrolls his uncle had tossed at him. He read the first and handed it over – my pardon for killing Brognar. The second was a memorandum from some anonymous clerk describing the ancient legends of Glastonbury: how, a few years after Christ's death, Joseph of Arimathea and other refugees from the Roman persecution of the early Christian Church had fled to England. Joseph had planted his staff at Weary Hill near Glastonbury which flowered as a white rose bush, a cutting from which was always sent to the Crown every Christmas.

Benjamin, standing beside me, tapped the parchment.

'Our noble King would not like that,' he murmured. 'Any reference to white roses, the emblem of the House of York, sends him into a state of frenzy.'

'Good!' I murmured and read on.

The legends, so the clerk maintained, also stated that Joseph brought with him the Grail, the cup used at the Last Supper, and this was supposed to be buried somewhere in the grounds of Glastonbury Abbey.

The second part of the document was an extract from the twelfth-century chronicler Gerald of Wales and described how, in 1184, the monks found the bodies of Arthur and Guinevere in a hollow oak coffin in the grounds of the abbey. A cross of lead placed over the coffin claimed: 'HERE LIES BURIED THE RENOWNED KING ARTHUR WITH GUINEVERE HIS SECOND WIFE IN THE ISLE OF AVALON'. Guinevere's skull still had traces of yellow hair attached to it and, when a certain monk tried to grab it, crumbled into dust. The clerk added that these remains were re-interred in 1278 under a marble slab before the high altar of Glastonbury Abbey.

'Do you believe all this?' I asked. 'Knights of the Round Table, magic swords and mystical cups?'

Benjamin lay down on his bed and pulled his cloak over him.

'There are more things in heaven and earth, my dear Roger, than are contained in our philosophy.'

A nice phrase, isn't it? I gave it to old Will Shakespeare to use in his play *Hamlet*.

Chapter 5

We both slept badly that night: on two occasions I woke when Benjamin cried out in his sleep. He was as anxious as I was about our journey to Glastonbury and the next morning we went down to the palace refectory feeling heavy-eyed and sluggish. A surly servitor thrust poorly baked bread and watery beer at us and we sat, lost in our own thoughts, until the door was flung open and Mandeville and Southgate entered. They looked as fresh as maids in May. (You take it from old Shallot, the wicked have little difficulty in sleeping!) They slid on to the bench opposite us, making pleasantries about how cold the weather had become and that we should soon be on the road for Somerset.

'Do you believe all this?' I abruptly asked them the same question I had of Benjamin.

'Do we believe what?' Southgate answered angrily.

'In Arthur's sword and a miraculous chalice?'

'If the King does,' Mandeville replied, 'I do. We also believe, Master Shallot, in the need for good order, strong rule, peace, and no stupid, futile rebellions.'

His two strange secretaries slid into the room and, without a flicker of a glance at us, went to sit at another table.

Mandeville, his mouth full of bread, nodded towards them. 'You consider us ruthless, Shallot? Then think of Cosmas and Damien. Or, even worse, of their elder brother

77

who tried to escape. Do you know what the Turks did? They stripped him naked, pegged him to the soil, tied a hollow pipe to his side and took a starving rat—' Mandeville slurped from his beer '—not one of your English sort. Those in Asia are two foot long from tip to tail. Anyway, they put this rat down the pipe with a fire at the open end. The rat could only go one way, burrowing its way out through the living flesh.'

I gagged and glanced at the two bald-pated twins: they didn't seem so terrible now but rather pathetic. I then stared at Mandeville and Southgate. Whatever they said, these were the real madmen. They had a passion for law and order which bordered on mania, living examples of Machiavelli's *The Prince*, for what Henry wanted, these men would do.

'Why do we have to go to Glastonbury?' I blurted out before my master could stop me.

Mandeville sneered as his strong teeth tore at the coarse rye bread.

'Master Shallot, you and your master have a growing reputation for quick eyes and subtle wits. Do you ever go hunting?'

'Not if I can help it!'

'You should do, Shallot. Especially with dogs, for that's what we are going to do in Somerset. Hunt down traitors and find what the King wants. We are the huntsmen and you are our dogs.'

I bit back a tart reply as my master tugged at my sleeve and we tactfully took our leave. Outside in the corridor I grabbed him by the elbow.

'I'm no man's dog, Master!'

Benjamin shook his head. 'Just leave it, Roger, leave it! We have other matters to tend to.'

'Such as?'

'Hopkins's sister, not to mention Tailor Taplow.'

'Master Shallot!'

We both spun round. Rachel Santerre stood there, looking as beautiful as a summer's dawn though her face was pale with dark rings round the eyes.

'Master Daunbey, Master Shallot.' She looked fearfully over her shoulder.

'Mistress, what's the matter?' I asked, watching that lovely bosom rise and fall in agitation.

'I don't know,' she stammered. 'But I am fearful. Buckingham's blood is on Sir John's hands, and Mandeville and Southgate frighten me. They are going to stick their noses into matters which do not concern them.'

We looked at her.

'You don't understand,' she whispered hoarsely. 'I live at Templecombe. God forgive me, I feel the ghosts there, the Templar knights.'

'Rachel! Rachel!'

The young woman cast one more despairing glance at us, shook her head and disappeared round the corner to answer her mother's plea.

Benjamin kicked at the rushes. 'Pray,' he muttered. 'Pray, Roger, that we return safe from Templecombe!'

(As if I needed such urging!)

We returned to our chamber for our cloaks and wallets though Benjamin appeared to dally.

'Master, we should go.'

'In a little while, Roger, I am waiting for someone.'

He became lost in one of his dour moods so I let him be and went to the window to stare out at a dairy maid carrying pitchers of milk between the barns and the kitchen. At last there was a knock on the door and a young man entered wearing a battered leather jacket and torn breeches. He bobbed his greasy head at Benjamin as if greeting some great lord.

'You have the address?' my master asked.

'Oh, aye, sir.'

In any other circumstances the young man's burr would have made me laugh.

'Well?'

'Hopkins's sister is a widow and has been for many a year,' the fellow replied. 'She lives in a small alleyway just past The Magpie and Crown off Watling Street.'

'Thank you.' Benjamin slipped the fellow a coin and closed the door behind him.

'Mistress Hopkins,' I asked, 'off Watling Street? What has she to do with this business, Master?'

'She may know something, a piece of tittle-tattle, which may help us.'

'So we are off to Watling Street?'

Benjamin smiled. 'And Newgate Prison.'

Naturally we had to obtain Doctor Agrippa's permission to leave but, within the hour, we were on a barge taking us upriver. It was a cold but beautiful day. The sun shone from blue skies, the water was glassy smooth and, on every side, I felt London press in: the green fields, the orchards, the cries of the boatmen and those of children playing with hoops along the river bank. Suddenly I felt homesick, even before I left, and quietly raged at the royal bastard's devious plans.

We landed at East Watergate and made our way up into Knight Rider Street. Our short walk through London soon cheered me up, especially the taverns – The Raven's Watch, The Bible and Swan, The Leg and Seven Stars – with drinkers outside, their flagons full of 'angel's food' or 'dragon's milk', whilst the air was sweet with the smell of soft raisin-filled saffron cakes baking in the cookshops.

It was mid-morning and many of the apprentices and stall-holders were taking a short rest, albeit some of them were already as drunk as March hares: one group of apprentices outside The Death's Head on the corner of Old Fish Street were indulging in a strident belching contest. I kept a wary eye open for any of my old friends, in particular the goldsmith Waller, even as I was distracted by the sight of the apprentices throwing their caps in the air as they shouted for custom, pompous city officials in their fur-lined robes and, of course, those beauties of the night, the high-class courtesans in their satin dresses and flowery head veils. These arrogantly wandered along the streets raising plucked eyebrows at the young bucks and gallants resplendent in tight hose, padded doublets and incredibly large codpieces.

We then took a short cut through some alleyways. Here the street-walkers were not too sophisticated: outside her tenement a harlot stood, skirts raised, over a chafing dish of coals on which she had sprinkled brimstone and perfume so as to fumigate herself. Further along, an apothecary was trying to sell the customers of such women a cure for the clap made out of boar's grease, sulphur, bark and quicksilver, all thickened by heavy treacle.

My master, of course, ambled along like a child and I had to keep him away from the rufflers, those former soldiers looking for easy pickings, the mad Abraham men who danced naked pretending to be insane, the cappers who begged for money and attached horse-locks to the outstretched arms of people stupid enough to give it. Once attached, the cappers would not let their victims go until they handed their purses across.

The din became even louder as we turned into Trinity where a gang of felons was being driven about London in a cart wearing a scrawled notice around their neck listing their offence. These were hookers – rogues who carried a tall staff with a hook at the end which they pushed through windows to pluck down everything of value – best blankets, nightshirts or pots. (It was because of these men that the legends spread that goblins and elves stole such stuff.) Anyway a gang of these had been caught and the crowd now vented their fury by pelting them with rotten eggs whilst householders tipped chamber pots from upper stories. A young man was chained to the back of the cart for pretending to be a priest. His back was lacerated, the tips of his ears bloody where they had been cropped whilst a fool's cap, fastened to his head, listed his lies and deceptions.

At last we reached the alleyway just past The Magpie and Crown. A beggar lad showed us the house in a dank, narrow alleyway where Mistress Hopkins lived. It was a lean, high tenement, three or four stories high. The windows were all shuttered and what paint was left was peeling off in huge flakes. The door was ill-fitting yet surprisingly open, off the latch. I knocked loudly and shouted. Even then I had a premonition of danger, of menace. Old Shallot's signs: a pricking at the back of the neck, a churning of the bowels, light sweat on the forehead and this incredible desire to run.

'Mistress Hopkins!' I bawled. 'Mistress Hopkins!'

The small passageway was shadowy and fetid and my words rang hollow. 'Mistress Hopkins!' I repeated.

Above us the old house creaked and groaned. Benjamin pushed me in and slammed the door behind us. We groped around in the darkness, found a fat tallow candle and I lit it with my tinder. Hands shaking, I walked deeper into the house, Benjamin behind me. We passed a small, ill-kept chamber, dusty rickety stairs, then entered a scullery or kitchen. This was a little cleaner. A battered pewter cup stood on the table and, at the other end, in a chair facing an ash-filled fire grate, sat a lady, head forward, shoulders hunched, her veil fallen over her face. The place stank of death.

I walked over, tipped the head back and bit back my scream. Mistress Hopkins, no beauty in life with her scrawny face and wispy hair, had been brutally killed: her eyes popped out of their sockets, her swollen tongue was clenched between gapped yellow stumps whilst her skin was blue-black, the breath throttled by the scarlet garrotte cord still tied round her neck. Benjamin lifted the old woman's hand.

'Not too cold,' he murmured. 'She probably died within the hour'.

'Why?' I asked. 'Why an old lady?'

Benjamin covered the woman's face with a cloth and sat at the table. 'Someone,' he declared, 'knew we were coming. But that was no great secret. After all, I hired a servant at Richmond to discover where Mistress Hopkins lived.' He rubbed his chin. 'I suppose it's useless asking him. He could have let others know where we were going without realising it. No,' he sighed, 'someone knew we were coming. Someone who knows the mind of priests. A monk, especially a recluse like Hopkins, would have few friends and would scarcely confide in his brothers at Glastonbury. So perhaps he discussed matters with his sister?'

Benjamin tapped the table top. 'The sensible conclusion is that our secret assassin decided to remove the danger just in case.' He waved a hand round the silent, smelly room. 'And I suspect it was someone powerful, perhaps the secret Templar my uncle is hunting. After all, Mistress Hopkins would scarcely open the door to anyone. There is little sign of a struggle so I conclude our murderer arrived as a welcome visitor.' Benjamin pointed at the pewter cup. 'Mistress Hopkins probably served him wine.' He looked under the table and picked up another cup. 'She even joined him. The assassin would assure her all was well, slip behind her chair, then fasten the garrotte string round her neck.'

'He may have also been searching for some of Hopkins's papers?' I added. 'Perhaps something the mad monk entrusted to his sister?'

We inspected the rooms on the lower floor. Their contents were pathetic though the assassin had made his presence felt; two battered coffers had been prised open, tawdry jewellery cast aside along with scraps of parchment and a thumb-marked Book of Hours, but none of these proved of any value. We went upstairs and searched amongst her paltry possessions in those dusty, shadowy chambers.

'Nothing,' Benjamin murmured.

'Perhaps there was nothing to begin with,' I replied. 'Perhaps Mistress Hopkins was murdered simply because of what she might know.'

We left the house and walked up Budge Row into Cheapside. We forced our way through the bustling market which was packed from one end to the other with stalls, carts, horses and people of every station; the poor in their rags, the rich in their costly silks. A group of powerful noblemen pressed their way through, preceded by men-at-arms three abreast, mounted on great destriers and hoisting gilded spears. The standard bearers followed, banners of bright red and yellow depicting strange devices: black griffins, scarlet dragons and silver stags.

We continued on past the stink and stench of the Shambles where the lowing of the cattle waiting to be slaughtered jangled our nerves and hurt our ears. At last we reached Newgate, that loathsome pit of hell, the city prison built around the gatehouse of the old city wall. We went through Dick Whittington's archway and banged on the metal-studded door for access.

A greasy tub of lard with filthy hair and a red, unshaven face introduced himself as the keeper and became almost fawning when Benjamin informed him who he was.

The keeper wiped dirty fingers on a stained leather jacket and jangled a huge bunch of keys.

'Come, come, my lords!' he murmured, bowing and scraping before us. He smiled ingratiatingly. 'After all, Master Taplow hasn't much time left, he's to die at two this afternoon.

He led us across the antechamber to show us a tar-drenched jacket lined with sulphur which hung from a hook on the wall. The gaoler stopped and gazed at it admiringly.

'Master Taplow's winding sheet,' the evil sod murmured as if he was examining a painting by da Vinci or Raphael.

'He'll wear that!' I exclaimed.

'Of course,' the keeper replied. 'It will be slipped round him and he'll burn all the quicker.'

'Why not just hang the poor sod?' I muttered.

'Oh, no.' The gaoler stepped back, eyes widening. 'Oh, no, we can't have that! The law is the law. Taplow is a common traitor and the law says he should burn.'

(Do you know, I am a wicked old man, I love soft tits and a good cup of claret. I must have lived, oh, well over ninety-five years, but when I eventually meet God I want to ask him a question which has haunted me all my life. Why do we human beings love to kill each other? And why do we do it in the cruellest possible ways? Excuse me, I must lift my cane and give my chaplain a good thwack across the knuckles. 'You'll not go to heaven and meet God,' the snivelling little hypocrite mumbles. 'Yes, I will, I'll tell St Peter a joke and, when he's busy laughing, I'll nick his keys.' Lackaday, I digress!)

The little grease-ball of a gaoler waddled off, taking us along passages and galleries as black as midnight, down steps coated with slime and human dirt where rats swarmed thick as fleas on a mangy dog. The smell was nauseous, the cobbled floor ankle-deep in slops. At last we came to the Corridor of the Damned, the cells housing those waiting to be executed.

'Hello there, my beauties!' A smiling, mad face pressed itself against the grille. 'Don't feel sorry for me,' the madman shouted. 'All Tyburn is is a wry neck and wet breeches!'

The gaoler spat a stream of yellow phlegm and the mad face disappeared. At last we stopped at a door. The gaoler opened it, took a cresset torch from the passageway and pushed it into a small crevice in the cell wall. The dungeon pit flared into life as the door slammed behind us. It stank like a midden and the straw underfoot had lain so long it was a black, oozy mess. A heap of rags in the corner suddenly stirred and came to life and Taplow, loaded with chains, got to his feet. He had dark hair and his plump body was covered in filth. He grinned at us through the darkness.

'Welcome to my palace, sirs. And who are you? Those who like to see a man before he dies? Do you like to ask me how I feel? What I am thinking?' He peered closer at us. 'No, you're not that sort.'

'We are from the Lord Cardinal,' Benjamin announced. 'No, no,' he added quickly. 'We bring no pardon. But, who knows,' he added desperately, 'perhaps a mercy, a bag of gunpowder tied round the neck. Master Taplow,' he continued softly, 'later this day you will be burnt at Smithfield, convicted of treason.'

Taplow crouched down. 'Aye,' he muttered, 'a bad end to a good tailor.'

Benjamin crouched down with him. I just leaned against the wall, trying to control my panic for I hate prisons, Newgate in particular. (Oh, yes, and before you ask, I have been there many a time. If you want to see hell on earth go to the condemned hole the night before execution day. The singing, the crying and the screaming – I thought I had already been killed and gone to hell! Ah, the cruelty of the world!)

'Master Taplow,' Benjamin continued, 'you were involved with the monk Hopkins, acting as his courier?'

The tailor licked his lips. 'Aye, that's the truth. Will you tell that gaoler to give me some wine?'

'Of course.'

'Ah, well.' Taplow scratched his head. 'Yes, I was Hopkins's courier. I took messages to the Lord Buckingham, pretending I was delivering suits or looking for trade at his London house.'

'Did Buckingham ever reply?'

'No, he did not.'

'What else did you do?'

Taplow edged closer. God forgive me, he looked like a mud-coloured frog crouching there in the half-light. I had to cover my nose against the terrible stench and just wished my master would finish the business.

'What else did you do?' Benjamin asked again.

'Different errands for Hopkins. Leaving messages here and there, but nothing in particular.'

'Why did you do it?' Benjamin gazed at the man. 'Why should a tailor become involved with some mad, treasonable monk? Especially a man like you, Taplow, who accepts the reformed doctrines of Luther?'

Taplow's eyes fell away.

'Once I was a Catholic,' he stuttered, 'till my wife died. Hopkins was the only priest who cared.'

I stirred, forgetting the discomfort in the cell, as I caught my master's suspicions. Something was wrong here. Taplow was filthy, but looked well fed and, for a man facing a horrible death, too calm and serene.

'Did you take messages to anyone else?'

He shook his head. Benjamin stretched across and grasped the man's hand.

'Master Taplow,' he whispered, 'there is very little I can do for you except make sure the gaoler gives you your wine, pray for your speedy death and that in Purgatory Christ will have mercy on your soul.'

'Aye,' Taplow whispered. 'Let my Purgatory be short.' Then he went back to lie down in the corner of the cell.

We hammered on the door for the gaoler and returned to the main gates of the prison where Benjamin left a coin and instructed the sadistic bastard to do what he could for poor Taplow. Then we left, through the old city gates, skirting its wall as we hastened along alleyways and runnels down to the river quayside at East Watergate. Benjamin hardly spoke but kept muttering to himself. Only when I ordered the boatman to take us to Syon did my master break free of his reverie.

'Strange, Roger,' he remarked. 'Here we are. We have just witnessed an old lady's strangling and a silly tailor imprisoned in squalor who, in a few hours' time, will be burnt horribly to death. Death seems everywhere,' he continued, 'and red-handed murder is a constant visitor in our lives.'

I sat and let him brood. Indeed, looking back over the years, I have become surprised, not that people murder each other but that, given our love of bloodshed, they don't do it more often. Anyway, I just tapped my boot against the bottom of the boat and looked over the river, busy with huge dung barges emptying their putrid waste in midstream. Benjamin stayed lost in his own thoughts but I caught his unease. Old Wolsey loved to lead people by the nose, in particular his nephew and myself, and relished his little games of sending us unarmed into darkened chambers full of assassins. (Just wait until I've finished this story and you'll see what I mean!)

At last we reached the great Convent of Syon, its gleaming white stone crenellations peeping above a green fringe of trees. We disembarked and made our way up a gravel path, through the gatehouse and into the guest room. The white-garbed nuns fluttered around us excitedly, pleased to welcome visitors to their famous house. A beautiful place Syon, with its cool galleries and passageways, high-ceilinged chambers and pleasant gardens. Mind you, this was no ordinary convent. The nuns were some of the best doctors in Europe and saved many a person from death but old Henry put paid to them, flattening the convent and pillaging its treasures. The great bastard!

A lovely house Syon, whose occupants tended the sick and brought about many a cure. Mind you, they could do nothing for Johanna, the love light of Benjamin's life. I have mentioned her before: the daughter of a powerful merchant, seduced and abandoned by a great nobleman whom Benjamin later killed in a duel. Johanna, however, had become witless, her beautiful hair streaming down about a pallid face, her mouth slack, her eyes vacuous.

Whenever Benjamin was in London he always visited her. He would sit and hold her, rocking her gently to and fro as if she was a child whilst she, muttering gibberish, rubbed salt into his wound by believing he was the nobleman come back to claim her. The meetings were always heart-wrenching. I could never stand and watch so would walk away to wink and flirt with the young novices. At last Benjamin would drag himself away and Johanna, screaming for her lost love, would be taken away by the gentle sisters. This time was no different and my master left Syon with the tears streaming down his face. As usual he grasped my hand.

'Roger,' he urged, 'if anything should happen to me, swear you will protect Johanna!'

And, as usual, I would swear such an oath. Oh, don't worry, I kept it! Years later when The Great Bastard pulled down the monasteries and emptied the convents I took Johanna into my own home. Indeed, I have made her immortal: my old friend Will Shakespeare wrote a play about a Danish prince called Hamlet who moons about the stage wondering whether he should kill his murderous mother. I don't like it and I told Will that he should reduce it to one act with Hamlet throttling the silly bitch immediately! But, you know old Will Shakespeare. Shy and quiet, he hid his face behind his hands and laughed.

Nevertheless, I helped him out with one scene where this Danish prince sends his betrothed Ophelia mad. (May I say, having watched the play, I'm not surprised.) Anyway poor Ophelia emerges as a tragic woman who drowns herself in a river, flowers in her hand, hair spread out like a veil around her. Well, Ophelia was really Johanna and the river is the Thames. I always think it was a nice touch.

We walked back to the quayside, Benjamin still disconsolate.

'Can't anything be done?' I asked. I searched round for a crumb of comfort. 'Master,' I added rather hastily, 'some people spend their Purgatory after death but individuals like Taplow or poor Johanna go through Purgatory here on earth.'

(I was always like that, ever ready to give a tactful word of comfort.) Benjamin gripped my wrist and nodded but, just as we were about to step into the boat, he clapped his hands together.

'Purgatory,' he muttered.

'Yes, Master?'

He glanced at me strangely. 'When is Taplow about to die?'

I looked up at the sun. 'Two hours past noon. Why?'

Benjamin pulled me into the boat. 'Then come quickly. We must see him. We have to see him die.'

We arrived too late. Smithfield Common was packed. The horse fair had been abandoned, the stalls cleared and the shops deserted. All of London had poured on to the great open waste, heads craned towards the stake on the brow of a small hill just next to a three-armed gibbet. The crowd was thick as hairs on a dog and we were unable to force our way through. As I have said, all of London was there, bodies reeking of sweat beneath rags, serge and silk, minds and hearts intent on watching a man being burnt to death. We peered over their heads.

Taplow, standing on a high stool, was already tied to the stake, his arms and legs tightly pinioned, head and face partially covered by a white fool's hood. Already small heaps of green faggots were laid about the stool, with dry

weeds on top as high as the victim's groin. The masked
executioners walked round as if they were involved in some
artistic endeavour, positioning the faggots for the best
effect. The crowd, held back by serried ranks of soldiers,
was already growing restless and shouts of 'Get on with it!',
'Let the poor sod die!', rang out, followed by the usual
volleys of refuse.

'We must get closer,' Benjamin muttered.

'Why, Master?' I begged.

'A man is going to die.'

I stood on tiptoe. 'It's too late. The torch has already
been put to the kindling.'

I watched the executioner light the faggots but apparently
the kindling was too green and the fire didn't catch. Benjamin looked in desperation at the gatehouse of St Bartholomew's Priory: the balcony was already full of important,
well-dressed people who had brought their children for a
day out; they had also brought sugared apples, dishes of
marzipan and jugs of wine to make their enjoyment complete.

Benjamin pulled one of Wolsey's warrants from his
pouch, one of those old letters written by the Cardinal so
Benjamin could gain access to any place he wanted. My
master seized me by the arm and pulled me over. The
captain of the guard outside St Bartholomew's let us through
and we went under the darkened archway and up some
steps into the chamber which led out on to the balcony.
Once again Benjamin used his warrant, pushing his way
through the grumbling spectators until we had a good view
of both the execution scene and Smithfield Common. The
catcalls from the crowd had now intensified at the
executioners' bungling of their job.

(Believe me, it's a terrible way to die! Once, whilst in
Venice, the Inquisition caught me, tried and condemned me
to burn in the great piazza before St Mark's. I was actually

tied to the stake and the kindling lit but, once again, fortune intervened. However, that's another story!)

Anyway, looking back over the years I can imagine what that poor bastard at Smithfield felt. The Inquisition were effective, his executioners were fools. Torches were again put to the kindling but the fire only teased the victim's feet and ankles. The poor fellow screamed.

'Oh, Christ, son of David!'

As he did, the crowd fell silent. Benjamin just stared fascinated and I studied him rather than the condemned man for, as I have remarked before, Benjamin had a horror of public executions.

'Why are we here, Master?' I whispered.

'Shut up, Roger!' he hissed.

The flames were now strong enough to reach the two bags of gunpowder tied to the man's neck. There was a loud explosion and the flames roared fiercer. The victim's head was thrust back and the fool's cap fell off. The fire was now an intense sheet of flame. Taplow's lips continued to move though his throat was so scorched he could not make a sound. The fire now reached his face, blackening his mouth, swelling the tongue, pushing the lips back to the gums. His limbs began to disintegrate into a bubbling mass of fat, water and blood.

'Christ have mercy on him!' Benjamin muttered. 'I just wish I could have seen his face clearly for one last time.'

The execution stake was now hidden beneath its wall of flame. I stared out over the crowd. They looked like some great beast with gaping mouth and hungry eyes, then I caught a movement over near the great elms at the far side of the common. (The branches of these trees were often used as makeshift gibbets.) I saw a red-haired man jump down from one of the branches as if he, too, was sickening of the scene and was preparing to leave. I glimpsed the black robes and wondered why Southgate would be so interested in such a grisly execution. I asked the same of Benjamin as we walked out of a postern gate of St Bartholomew's back towards the river, but my master was only half-listening.

'I can't tell you the reason,' he murmured. 'Not yet, Roger. Not while we're trapped in this tangle of lies!'

Chapter 6

We took a barge back to Richmond to find the palace in turmoil. The King and his Cardinal were preparing to leave and the courtyards were full of sumpter ponies, officials and chamberlains. Porters thronged the stairs and galleries carrying packages and bags. Huge four-wheeled carts, each pulled by six horses, were lined up in front of the main doors as Fat Henry moved his furniture and belongings elsewhere for another round of pleasure. The royal standard of England no longer fluttered on its pole, a sign that Henry and Wolsey had already departed with a small advance party though Doctor Agrippa had remained, waiting for us in our chamber.

'You had a useful visit to the city?'

'Interesting,' my master replied.

Agrippa, like a little spider in his black garments, came up beside Benjamin and handed him a small sheaf of documents and two fat purses.

'Your uncle wishes you a safe journey. This silver will ease your passage and there are the usual letters of accreditation.'

I took down our saddle bags from the hook in the wall and flung them on the bed.

'And you, my good doctor?' I asked. 'You will stay safely in London?'

Agrippa crept near me, pushing his face close to mine. I caught his strange perfume and gazed into those clear, glass-like eyes.

'I wish I could go, Roger,' he murmured. 'I wish I could die, but my time has not come.'

Benjamin watched us both strangely.

'Then what is all this?' I asked, refusing to be cowed. 'Why do you talk of death? Agrippa, have you no flicker of friendship for us? What does my Lord Cardinal think will happen at Templecombe? And what does the tortured brain of that royal madman really want?'

Agrippa's face softened. He blinked, and when I looked again, his eyes were light blue, childlike in their innocence.

'Roger, Roger,' he whispered, 'I am the Cardinal's man in peace and war, at least for the next ten years. But when the prophecy is fulfilled and the cow rides the bull and the priest's skull is smashed, I shall be free.'

(At the time I had not a clue what he was talking about but, in hindsight, he was, of course, referring to Boleyn's ascendancy over Fat Henry and Wolsey falling like a star from the sky of royal preferment.)

'Before you leave,' Agrippa continued, 'for friendship's sake, I will give you this advice: *Age Circumspecte.* Act wisely!' Then he spun on his heel and left the chamber.

Oh, well, we forgot Agrippa's strange advice as the next few days passed. Benjamin remained locked in the sombre mood which had dogged him since he had witnessed Buckingham's execution. Where possible he would seize scraps of parchment and draw lines, muttering to himself and scratching his head.

I was left to my own devices. I wandered back into the city and even thought of revisiting my old haunts but, near Whitefriars, a counterfeit man recognised me. Instead of the usual friendly salutations, he scuttled away down the alleyway to sell his information to men like Waller and others to whom I owed debts. A petite, pleasant-faced doxy, however, caught my eye and for a few hours I became old Shallot again, whiling away the time, telling the most outrageous stories and making her laugh both in the tap-room and on her feather-filled mattress in the chamber above.

Lovely, lovely girl! She had eyes as bright as buttons, a sharp wit and the most beautiful pair of shoulders I have ever clapped eyes on. Ah, well, she's gone, for golden girls and golden boys must, in their turn, go to dust. A nice little phrase. I coined it but my good friend Will Shakespeare seized it for himself. That's the way with scribblers, they are for ever borrowing other people's quotations.

Refreshed and a little more composed after my love tryst, I went back to Richmond where Benjamin asked me to accompany Southgate to collect stores from the Tower. I reluctantly agreed and we went in silence down the mist-shrouded Thames to that narrow, evil fortress. We had to wait awhile; the troops there were drilling in preparation for being shipped to some Godforsaken town in the Low Countries to wage one of Fat Henry's futile, forgotten wars.

Now you will hear the old buggers tell you how their hearts are kindled and the blood bubbles in their veins at the prospect of war: banners snapping angrily in the breeze; war horses caparisoned for battle pawing the ground; brave young men in shining armour, their faces flushed with the prospect of war; swords sharpened, helmets plumed. It's a load of bollocks! That's how it begins but it ends in maimed bodies, chopped limbs, blood spurting like fountains. Green grass turning rusty brown, rivers choked with corpses.

Always remember old Shallot's military theories. First, where possible, run! Secondly, if that's not possible, surrender. Thirdly, volunteers never live till pay day. And I know! I have fought in too many battles and lost my boy in one, the only child of my third wife. I called him Benjamin because he wasn't like me, rotten and twisted, but tall and noble. A brave heart, oh sweet Jesus, he went to Ireland with Essex's armies and died in the bogs of Antrim. Oh,

Lord, I miss him still! It's true what the Greeks say: 'Those whom the Gods love always die young'. In which case I'll live for bloody ever!

At the Tower, on that distant autumn day, the young men were preparing for war. The smithies were busy beating the rivets of armour into place, fashioning sallets, lances, swords and all the necessary equipment for killing. The young men practised in the dusty yards, swinging swords against each other or dodging the deadly quintain, the stuffed dummy with a club on either end so, if you didn't move quickly enough, you got a nasty bruise on your head. Old Shallot, as always, kept well away from this but Southgate seemed fascinated by it. After we had collected what we came for, he returned for one more look and broke his disdainful silence.

'I wish I was going to war.' His chilling blue eyes stared at me. 'Don't you, Shallot?'

'Oh, yes,' I lied. 'I dream of it every day.'

Southgate smirked. 'When we get to Templecombe, you'll wish you had.' He flicked a hand at the sweating soldiers. 'At least they'll know their enemy.'

We left Richmond two days later, early in the morning, just after first mass. Our small cortège milled about in the courtyard near the large double-barred gate of the palace.

Mandeville and Southgate slouched on their horses, both dressed in leather quilted jackets, their feet encased in long riding boots. They were armed with dirks, swords and daggers and wore large travelling cloaks. Behind them, as if carved in stone, were their two secretaries, Cosmas and Damien, who sat pulling their horses' reins, eyes fixed intently on Mandeville. A short distance away were the Santerres: Sir John shouting orders and beside him his wife, riding side-saddle, her desire to leave apparent in the agitated remarks she made to her husband. Rachel looked as pretty as a picture, her lovely body warmly covered by a grey riding cloak lined with miniver fur. The rest were servants and grooms with our baggage piled on a sturdy, four-wheeled cart.

'Mistress Santerre looks beautiful,' I whispered to Benjamin. 'She puts us all to shame. I tell you this, Master, if we met a pretty maid I suspect she'd fall in love with one of the horses before she took to any of us!'

Benjamin laughed. 'I just hope we will be safe, Roger,' he murmured.

'Oh, Lord save us, of course, Master! As bullocks on thin ice.'

(Looking back, I wish I hadn't said that. Words uttered in haste often have a prophetic ring to them; within a month Benjamin and I would be fighting for our lives on icy waters in Somerset.)

Soon we were ready. Mandeville, who saw himself as the King's own commissioner and therefore self-appointed leader, shouted orders; the great gates swung open, and he led us out. As we rode towards London, one of Mandeville's secretaries unfurled the pennant on a pole he carried bearing the royal arms of England, showing all and sundry that we carried the King's own warrant. As we passed people stood back on either side, loud-mouthed apprentices and washerwomen in leather clogs stopping their noisy clatter and waiting for us to pass. We reached the muddy cobbles of the city, going through Bowyers Row and up towards Cripplegate. On the corner of Carter Lane, with the mass of St Paul's cathedral towering above us, we had to pause whilst labourers using ward hooks pulled down the still smouldering, blackening timbers of a burnt-out tenement to ensure no spark ignited neighbouring houses.

At last a city official, wearing the blue and mustard livery of the Corporation, decided the burnt-out tenement had been sufficiently destroyed and we were allowed to pass on.

Now, as I have said, Mandeville led us, the Santerres

behind with their small retinue whilst we were at the back just before the cart. I looked hungrily around, drinking in the sights of London: the beaver hats, lined with green velvet, of the wealthy merchants, the shabby caps of the artisans and, above all, the ornate head-dresses covered in clouds of gauze of the court ladies stepping out for a morning's shopping. We reached St Paul's, the great copper eagle on its weather vane dazzling in the weak sunlight. (I remember it well for the sun shortly afterwards disappeared and we did not see it for weeks.) We had to halt as cartloads of bones dug up from the cemetery were taken down Paternoster Row to the charnel house.

As we did so, a ragged urchin slipped from the crowd and passed a piece of parchment to Sir John Santerre. I was about to tell my master when we heard the sounds of music coming from beyond the wall of St Paul's. Benjamin waved me over and we looked through the open gate. A group of musicians stood in the angle of one of the buttresses of the cathedral playing tambour and fife whilst the Dean and Chapter, garlands of roses on their heads, danced in solemn procession around the severed head of a buck which had been placed on a pole, its brown eyes staring glassily over those who now rejoiced at its death. At the foot of the pole the succulent body of the deer lay sprawled, blood still seeping from the severed arteries of its neck. I stared in astonishment at Benjamin.

'It's a custom,' my master muttered out of the corner of his mouth. 'Every month the city verderers have to deliver a fat buck for the Dean's kitchen; in thanksgiving the Dean and Chapter perform this dance.' He cleared his throat. 'God knows why, when they call themselves churchmen.'

I looked at the sleek, well-fed clerics performing their silly jigs.

'It's hard to decide, Master, which are fatter, they or the buck.'

'Never mind that,' he murmured. 'Did you see that message being slipped to our bluff Sir John?'

I nodded.

'I wonder what it said, Roger?'

'God knows, Master. Your uncle weaves such tangled webs!'

We heard Mandeville calling us and continued our journey up towards Cripplegate, forcing our way through the lawyers and serjeants of the coif who were assembling outside the door of the Priory of St Elsing-Spital for their last mass of the Michaelmas term.

We reached the old city walls and passed through the gates. Above us the decapitated heads of traitors, crowned with laurels or ivy, gazed down at us, their eyes and mouths turned black by the pecking of ravens. We had to pause awhile as the body of a suicide, dragged by the feet, was taken by city bailiffs to be dumped in the city ditch. This was followed by a cart full of putrid offal, heading for one of the brooks near the Barbican. A beggar ran alongside the cart and came whining towards us, hands extended. Mandeville drove him away so he passed further down the group and tugged at Benjamin's leg.

'Master, Master, a penny, a penny!'

Benjamin's hand went to his wallet and he gasped as he stared down at the beggar. Despite the ragged head-dress and mud-stained face, I recognised our good Doctor Agrippa.

'*Age Circumspecte!*' he hissed and disappeared into the crowd.

'What does he mean?' I asked. 'He told us that before.'

'A pun, Roger. The old Latin tag, "Act wisely", perhaps a warning about the *Agentes.*'

'Magnificent!' I murmured. As if I hadn't realised that already.

We reached Red Cross where the city dwellings gave way

to fields and small copses and, an hour later, we were in the open countryside.

I won't bore you with the details of our journey across southern England. The roads were still hard so travel was fast and easy as Mandeville used the royal messenger service to obtain good food and warm beds at priories, monasteries, taverns or royal manors. We travelled in three distinct groups: the *Agentes*, the Santerres and ourselves.

No one was really at ease. Lady Beatrice ignored my wandering eye, young Rachel dared only smile shyly at us, whilst the *Agentes* were a law unto themselves. Southgate and Mandeville, their two mutes behind them, travelled at the head of the procession, whispering to each other. My master, preoccupied with Hopkins's riddle drew me into discussion about its meaning, only to reach the conclusion it would tell us nothing until we had reached Glastonbury or Templecombe.

For the rest, when the opportunity presented itself, we questioned Sir John about the legends of Arthur, the Grail and the wonders of Glastonbury Abbey, but never once were the Templars mentioned, as if they were a forbidden subject, a treasonable offence even to refer to them.

Twenty years ago I took the same journey to look at the ruins of Glastonbury, destroyed by Fat Henry and his evil spirit, Thomas Cromwell. Sad, nostalgic, the countryside had hardly changed and, if I closed my eyes at certain parts, I was back with Master Benjamin and all those people, now long dead, travelling to a place where conspiracy, treason and sudden death became part of the very fabric of our lives.

The only difference then was the weather for it turned cold and hard, the clouds massing thick above us as if the sky intended to fall and crush out all life on the face of the earth. A cold, biting wind chilled our fingers and stiffened the muscles of our body and, just as we crossed into Somerset, the long-awaited snow began to fall. At first in soft flurries but, by the time the gables, spires and turrets of Glastonbury came into view, a veritable blizzard raged.

Now I am an old cynic. I have seen men and women betray and kill each other without batting an eyelid. (So much so that, although I believe in God, my great difficulty is accepting that he believes in us!) Glastonbury, however, would challenge the most hardened hearts, a place of mystery and mysticism which catches you by the throat and provokes the mind to strange dreams.

The land itself is relatively free from trees, low, flat and well beneath sea level. The abbey was great and sprawling, a veritable palace behind its high walls and, from the brow of a small hill, Sir John Santerre pointed out the chapel, the abbey church, the cloisters, the hall, the abbot's kitchen, guest houses and gardens, all quite distinct in spite of the falling snow.

However, what caught my imagination was the great Tor or hill overlooking the abbey which jutted like a giant's finger up towards the heavens, making the small church on its summit a most suitable meeting-place between God and man. If the abbey was a marvel of man's work, the Tor was God's answer for in that flat land it looked like one of the high places mentioned in the bible where the ancient patriarchs went to talk to Yahweh. Even Mandeville and Southgate murmured in admiration. Benjamin and I just stared speechlessly down at the abbey, then up at the great Tor.

'Oh, yes,' Santerre declared proudly. 'This, gentlemen, is Avalon. The island of glass, the island of apples, Arthur's last resting place. Once,' he continued, 'everything beneath the great Tor was covered in marsh, meres and pools, but the monks have drained these dry and turned the land into one of God's great wonders.'

I forgot the falling snow and biting wind.

'What is that?' I pointed to the great Tor.

'What you see, Master Shallot. A high place,' Santerre replied. 'Sacred even before Christ was born. The ancient tribes used to come here by boat, led by their leader the Fisher King, to worship on the Tor. Some people say,' he lowered his voice, 'that inside the hill are secret passageways, halls and chambers used by the ancient ones. People have entered its secret paths and entrances and have either never returned or, if they were fortunate enough to do so, came out with their minds mazed, their wits scattered.'

'And why should Arthur come here?' Benjamin asked.

'To be healed,' Santerre replied. 'There has always been a monastery here but, in ancient times, when the meadows were flooded you had to use secret routes and pathways to reach it. Arthur's great fortress lies further north at Cadbury, a huge hill which still bears the remnants of a formidable fortress. Legend says Arthur's Sword was thrown into one of the pools here after the Grail, kept in the monastery, was brought to him too late. If he had drunk from it, the wounds received in his last dreadful battle against his nephew Mordred would have healed. So, Arthur now lies buried beneath the Abbey.' Santerre wiped the snowflakes from his face as he stared round at us.

'Chilling legends,' Mandeville interrupted, his dark face damp with snow. 'But, remember, we are here on the King's own business and the legends of this place sent Buckingham to his death.'

With that he kicked his horse forward and we made our way down the trackway to the ornately carved gateway of Glastonbury Abbey. A porter let us in and we were taken into a great yard. Lay brothers hurried about, unpacking the carts, and we were escorted into the spacious, white stone guest house: a large solar on the ground floor with above it chambers for each of the abbot's guests. Servitors took our wet clothing and served us cups of mulled wine, followed by earthenware bowls full of a meaty soup which warmed our hands and removed the chill from our stomachs.

We sat in chairs before a great log fire. Only when we were rested and our bags unpacked did the abbot, Richard Bere, together with a young sub-prior and other monks of the abbey, enter the guest house to greet us. Bere was a frail, white-haired man, one vein-streaked hand clutching an ash cane, the other resting on the arm of the sub-prior. (A great man, Bere. He carried out many building works at Glastonbury. After him came poor old Richard Whitting, who was abbot when Cromwell sent his agents in. Whitting died a horrible death. The abbey was plundered and pillaged, its treasures looted, its roofs pulled off, and what was once man's homage to God became a nesting place for foxes, ravens and kites. Ah, well, enough of that.)

On that cold, snow-laden winter day Bere and his brethren were most welcoming, but the abbot's anxious lined face and short-sighted eyes betrayed his fear at having the powerful *Agentes* within the sacred walls of the abbey. He had a pathetic wish to please and I hated Mandeville for his arrogance as he rapped out his orders. We would stay the night, transfer our baggage to sumpter ponies and make our way to Templecombe, he instructed.

'But,' Mandeville boomed, standing over the abbot, 'we shall return, Reverend Father, to ask questions about the traitor Hopkins. You will produce any memoranda or books held by him and, above all, the manuscript he was so fond of studying with its doggerel verses which drew him and others into the blackest treason.'

'We are the King's loyal servants,' murmured Bere defiantly. 'Brother Hopkins, God rest him, was a man lost in the past but the manuscript he studied will be handed over.'

He smiled at all of us, nodding courteously to Lady Beatrice, then with his silent monks around him, walked wearily out of the guest house.

We rose early the next morning awoken by the clanging

of the abbey bells. I opened the shuttered window to look out on a countryside blanketed in snow. The blizzard had passed but the sky threatened more. We gingerly broke the ice in the washing bowl, washed, changed and joined the others in the small refectory below.

A lay brother came over and took us into the abbey church to hear morning mass and, believe me, for the glory is now gone, the abbey church of Glastonbury was the nearest thing to heaven on earth. Soaring pillars, cupolas and cornices leafed with gold; huge walls covered in brilliant, multi-hued pictures depicting scenes from the bible. The Lady Chapel in blue, red and gold marble; the choir and rood screen of carved, gleaming oak which shimmered in the light of hundreds of candles. The air was sweet with incense which wafted round the marble high altar like the spirits of the blessed.

So much space, so much beauty. The choir stalls were each carefully sculptured and the wood polished till it shone like burnished gold. Banners of different colours, scarlet, red, green and blue, hung from the hammer-timbered roof whilst around the church were carved statuettes of the most breathtaking beauty depicting the Virgin Mary, St Joseph, St Patrick, and the whole heavenly host. I knelt and gazed around in astonishment.

Yet now it is all gone, nothing left. Henry's agents saw to that. I know many of you are of the reformed faith and in your minds perhaps rightly so, but if you had seen what I saw then, you'd still mourn. You'd weep at the destruction of such sheer glory.

After mass a lay brother offered to take us on a tour of the church and other interesting sights of the abbey. The Santerres demurred, Rachel claiming she felt unwell, but Mandeville and Southgate eagerly joined us. We were shown the great marble slab covering Arthur's coffin and the chalice well which provided water for the brothers. My master peered down this as if expecting to see a vision at the bottom.

'Is it true,' he asked, 'that the Grail might lie beneath the waters of this well?'

The seamed, yellow face of the old lay brother broke into a grin.

'So legend says,' he wheezed. 'Many have searched yet nothing has been found.'

We also visited the holy thorn, a wild rose bush supposedly sprung from Joseph of Arimathea's staff. I tell you this – the legend is true. Even in that bitter weather the plant was beginning to blossom and, when it bloomed at Christmas, the abbot as was customary would send a cutting to the King. After this, at Mandeville's insistence, the old brother took us into the library, a long room, its walls covered with heaped shelves of books. Benjamin's hands positively itched to take down the leather, jewel-embossed tomes (so did mine for other reasons), but Mandeville shook his head.

'We have seen enough for today,' he murmured. 'Such matters are to be examined at our leisure. Templecombe's our destination. We must be there by noon.'

We returned to the guest house and found our companions ready to leave. Outside in the courtyard lay brothers were moving baggage from the carts to sumpter ponies whose iron-shod hooves scraped the cobbles, their hot breath hanging like clouds as they whinnied in protest at being taken from their warm stables. I searched out Rachel. She still looked pale so I plucked up courage to speak.

'Mistress, is there anything wrong?'

She smiled thinly. 'Nothing, Roger.'

(How I thrilled at her use of my first name!)

'The journey has been exhausting and I will be glad to be home.'

I would have dallied longer but the venerable Bere came

down to wish us farewell. Mandeville was as curt as ever. He leaned over, patting his horse's withers.

'Father Abbot,' he declared for all to hear, 'we thank you for your hospitality but we shall return. Certain questions need to be asked to which truthful answers must be given.'

He then gave the order to move off and led us out of the abbey gate.

Our journey was cold and uncomfortable, a brutal reminder of the comforts we had left behind. The sky, grey and lowering, threatened more snow whilst the previous day's fall carpeted the hedgerows and fields, choking the ditches and making the trackways slippery and dangerous. Never once did we stop even in Templecombe village but made our way through the sleepy hamlet, the houses on either side all boarded up, the only sign of life being columns of smoke and the occasional villager foraging on the outskirts for fire-wood. These seemed happy enough – burly, red-faced peasants who doffed their caps and shouted salutations to their Lord of the Manor, genuinely pleased to greet his return.

We were making our way up a trackway towards the main gate of the manor when suddenly an old hag slipped out of the trees on one side of the path and stood squarely in front of Mandeville. She was a veritable night bird in a dirty cloak with a hood half-covering her greying wisps of hair. Her face was lined and raddled, the toothless mouth slack, displaying reddened gums, yet her eyes were full of life. She wiped her dripping, hooked nose, clasped her hands together and cackled. Believe me, if I had seen her in any other place, I would have dismissed her as a witch from a mummer's play. One of those old beldames who like to proclaim themselves keepers of secret mysteries. But this old bird was more sinister, a veritable crow, a harbinger of bad news. Mandeville gestured at her to get out of his way. She just laughed and stepped back, her eyes bright with malice.

'Welcome to Templecombe!' Her voice was surprisingly strong and powerful. She made a mock bow. 'Sir John Santerre, your lovely wife and the beautiful Rachel.' The old crone licked at the saliva frothing on her lips.

'Get out of my way, woman!' Mandeville ordered.

'Yes, I will. I will.' The old crone cringed back. 'When I have told you my news.'

Mandeville leaned forward. 'And what news is that?'

'There will be deaths!' the old woman proclaimed, one bony finger streaking up to the grey clouds. 'Death by fire! Death by iron! Death by rope! Death by water! And you, Sir Edmund Mandeville, emissary of a king who is not a king, the hand of death lies over you! The Midnight Destroyer sits at your right elbow whilst the Lord Satan squats at your left. You all,' she screamed, her eyes blazing, 'you all have entered the Valley of Death!'

'What do you mean?' Southgate shouted. No languid lisping now, I noted.

The old woman sagged, her chin falling to her breast. She looked up from under grey, bushy eyebrows.

'You have had your news, now I'll be gone!'

And, before any of us could do anything, she flitted like a ghost back into the trees.

Mandeville glared furiously at Sir John Santerre.

'Who the devil was that?'

'One of your tenants, sir?' Southgate accused.

Santerre shrugged. 'She's a crazed old woman who says she has visions. She's lived in a hut in a clearing just beyond the trees for God knows how long.' His eyes were lowered. 'Some people call her mad. Others say she is Hecate, Queen of the Night.'

'She's just an old woman.' Rachel spoke up, her voice muffled behind her cloak. 'Pay no attention to her, sirs. She's a veritable Cassandra who sees doom and death in the flight of a sparrow.'

Mandeville coughed and spat. 'If she accosts me again,' he grumbled, 'I'll burn the bitch!'

And on that uncomfortable note we continued our way along the track. A porter opened the double-barred gate, shouting a welcome to the Santerres as he led us along the old causeway which wound past birch, oak and yew trees up to the front of the house.

Chapter 7

Let me tell you about Templecombe. The Templars had first built it as a fortified manor but later generations had embellished it to make it more comfortable. A massive stone edifice built in a square about a spacious inner court-yard, three stories in all, its roof was of grey slate. Although we could see the old arrow-slit windows, more sophisticated owners had added rounded oriels, jutting bays and ornate chimney stacks. The stone gleamed as if freshly washed whilst every window was glazed, some with pure glass, others, despite the poor light, even displaying brave heraldic emblems in a variety of hues.

On our arrival, the great door was flung open. Servants gathered on the steps and for a while all was confusion as stewards, bailiffs, cooks, huntsmen and pages hurried down to greet the Santerres. Despite Sir John's brusque ways, I saw he was a well-respected, even loved, lord of the soil. Servants took our baggage, grooms led our horses away, as the Santerres proudly escorted us in.

Despite its bleak exterior, Templecombe proved to be a jewel. The entrance hall was gleamingly panelled, the wood carved and sculpted. The floorboards, the great sweeping staircase, its balustrade and newels, were fashioned out of the most expensive materials. We were taken to the main hall, a long lofty chamber dominated by a hammer-beamed roof with an oriel window at one end depicting the Lamb of God carrying a standard. Other large windows, with cushioned seats beneath, were on either side of the cleverly carved fireplace above which hung a canvas painting of Adam and Eve being tempted by the serpent. A great log fire crackled in the hearth, the room was lit by squat wax candles fixed on metal spigots around the walls and, at the far end, under the oriel window, was the dais and high table. The floor was paved with marble flagstones, black and white so it looked like a chessboard, and on this had been laid the thickest rugs from Persia, India and Turkey. There were chests of cypress and cedar, small tables bearing trays, silver cups, pewter tankards and flagons. Cloth of gold and exquisite tapestries hung on the walls, their fringes reaching down to the wooden panelling. Everything seemed to boast the power and wealth of the Santerres.

'He owns rich fields,' Benjamin whispered, 'and the wool from his flocks is famous even in Flanders. Sir John has a finger in every pie and is well known to the harbour masters all along the south coast.'

This rich Lord of the Manor now stood in the middle of the hall revelling in his ostentatious show of wealth whilst servants placed high-backed chairs in front of the fire. At Santerre's insistence we sat and warmed ourselves with possets of hot wine and slices of sugared pastry. Even Mandeville, tired after his ride, relaxed and murmured his appreciation.

The greatest change, however, was in Rachel. She'd cast aside her cloak and even her veil so her jet-black hair fell down on either side of a face now glowing with happiness. I had eyes only for her but Benjamin was all agog with interest in the room and kept looking around, murmuring his admiration.

'Come.' Rachel stood, smiling at both of us. 'Whilst our elders and betters take their rest, let me show you round our home.'

She then took us on a tour, chattering excitedly like a

child. The house, as I have said, had three stories, each a perfect square bounded by four polished galleries, three rooms leading off each. Even on the top one where Rachel showed us our chambers, the air was warmed by sweetened braziers and the atmosphere was comforting with gleaming wainscoting, coloured cloths, woollen carpets, carved chests and chairs. Everything was clean and bright in the candle-light. Even the corbels and cornices of the ceiling had been freshly painted.

Rachel explained that her step-father had not stinted in his refurnishing of his new home. Now and again, however, we caught glimpses of its Templar past: black Beauce crosses printed on the walls which the passage of time had not faded; old arrow slits through which you could glimpse the snowy fields beyond; small gargoyles, some depicting wyverns or dragons, others the faces of long-dead knights.

Gradually we realised that despite the wealth, warmth and comfort, Templecombe held an eerie, sinister air. Even as Rachel flitted before us down passageways and galleries, I could feel other presences, as if ghosts hiding in the shadows watched her pass then trailed behind us, looking for some weakness they could exploit. Benjamin's shoulders twitched and on one occasion I saw him shiver.

'A strange place,' he murmured as Rachel walked ahead of us. 'The dead do not lie at rest here.'

At last Rachel had shown us everything but, still full of enthusiasm, said there was more to see outside. Benjamin and I hid our exasperation, took our cloaks and followed her into the snow-covered grounds. We visited the outhouses, stables, smithies, brewing rooms, barns – slipping and slith-ering, though Rachel was as sure-footed as a cat. We went through a clump of yew trees into a clearing where a small church stood, a simple primitive affair with steep tiled roof and a small entrance tower. Rachel pushed the door open and beckoned us in.

If the manor was opulent, the old church was positively

bleak. A baptismal font stood near the doorway, a row of squat white pillars on either side of dark transepts, then through a rood screen into a plain, stone sanctuary. On either side were stalls, their seats up, each displaying a scene from the bible. Benjamin looked at these and exclaimed in delight.

'Look, Roger!' He pointed to one of the raised seats where centuries earlier a carpenter had carved a bear climbing a tree. The scene was so vivid and lifelike you almost expected the bear to move or the tree to bend. Rachel sat on the sanctuary steps and watched us.

'I love this place,' she murmured, gazing up at the black roof beams. 'It's so simple, so pure. My step-father wanted to tear it down but my mother and I refused to allow it.' She smiled at us, then her face grew solemn and her eyes widened. 'The Templars used to meet here,' she continued. 'This was their chapel.' She shivered and pulled her cloak close. 'Very evil men,' she whispered, 'with such dark practices, their ghosts still linger here. Mother's always saying the house should be exorcised.'

'Do you think they were guilty of such terrible crimes?' Benjamin asked.

Rachel stood up. 'Perhaps, but not committed here. Let me show you something.'

She led us out of the church, round the back and through a wood. The line of trees suddenly ended where the ground fell away and, beneath us, was a large lake, the water turning to ice and, in the middle, a mist-shrouded island. On this, amongst the few trees growing there, stood a low dark building which, in the fading light, had a desolate, sinister air.

'The Templar house,' Rachel explained. 'Just a long stone room but legend has it that the Templars used it for their mysteries. I have never been across.' She gestured to the barge nestling amongst the frozen weeds. 'Others go over

114

but I wouldn't set foot there even in the height of summer! That island frightens me.' Her face brightened. 'Come,' she added, 'you must be exhausted and I prattle on. Supper will be served soon.'

She took us back to the house where a servant showed us up to our rooms. We each had a small chamber. Mine was between those of Cosmas and Benjamin. Mandeville, Southgate and Damien were on the other gallery. The rooms were probably once Templar cells but now they were luxuriously furnished. Each had a large fourposter bed, an oaken wardrobe, a table, stool and chair, whilst the arrow-slit windows had been widened and filled with tinted glass. A log fire crackled in the hearth and two capped braziers had been moved in just inside the door. My room was as warm and smelt as fragrant as a summer's day. For a while I sat on the edge of the bed until Benjamin joined me. He seemed tired and perplexed and, without invitation, began to summarise what had happened so far, ticking the points off on his fingers.

'First, Hopkins was a monk, a Benedictine from Glastonbury but he also served as a chaplain for the Santerres here at Templecombe as well as for the outlying farms.

'Secondly, he had a passion for Arthurian legend and lore and searched for the Grail and Excalibur. He discovered an ancient manuscript in Glastonbury's library with a doggerel verse which no one understands.

'Thirdly, Hopkins told Buckingham that he could lay hands on these precious relics. My Lord of Buckingham come to Templecombe thinking the relics might be hidden here, or maybe just to verify with Hopkins that what he had been told was the truth. Sir John Santerre was approached but panicked. He believed Buckingham's search for the relics masked some subtle treason, and so the *Agentes* were alerted. Buckingham then wrote to Taplow in London but this correspondence was seized by our good friends Mandeville and Southgate. Buckingham was arrested: he went to the block whilst poor Taplow was burnt at Smithfield. The Santerres were investigated but cleared of any suspicion.' Benjamin paused. 'What else?'

'The murdered agents?'

'Ah, yes. Fourthly, two of Mandeville's agents who had been placed in the Buckingham household and first alerted their masters to Buckingham's so-called treason, were murdered with a garrotte string as was Hopkins's sister but we have no clue as to who the murderer was. Fifthly, there is a secret coven or conspiracy linked to the ancient order of the Templars who are also searching for the Grail and Arthur's Sword. God knows who these could be. The abbot and his brothers at Glastonbury? John Santerre? Or even worse, Mandeville or Southgate. After all, there is suspicion that the order has an accomplice close to the crown.

'Sixthly, we have been sent here to find the Grail and Excalibur – though there's fat chance of that – as well as to assist our two dark shadows to root out the activities of these Templars.

'And, finally, we have the warnings of that crone. Why did she deliver the message then? Who told her to? Was it the monks of Glastonbury?'

'Master, she is a witch.'

Benjamin shook his head. 'Nonsense, Roger. I don't believe in such powers.' He got up and started pacing up and down the room.

My master was like that: once his mind probed a mystery or problem, he became physically agitated, gnawing away at it until he had satisfaction. A true Renaissance man, Benjamin Daunbey. He didn't believe in witches, sorcerers and warlocks. I did. When you meet the likes of Mabel Brigge, you quickly recognise someone who has made a pact with Satan and acquired occult powers! A beautiful demon, Mabel! To kill someone, all she did was fast for

116

three days and concentrate her mind on destroying the life of her enemy. I watched her do this and bring about the destruction of one of England's greatest noblemen but that's another story.

Benjamin stopped pacing up and down.

'Do you agree with what I have said, Roger?'

'Well, of course, Master. It's all happened, hasn't it?'

'Of course not.'

'If you say so, Master.'

Benjamin came and sat down beside me. 'Less of your sarcasm, Roger. We know only what we have been told or made to see. How do we know Buckingham committed treason? How do we know he wrote those letters to Taplow?'

'Because the mad bugger confessed!' I interrupted. 'We met Taplow in prison and saw the poor bastard die!'

Benjamin pulled a face. 'No, the man we met in prison was not Taplow but someone else.' He smiled at my snort of disdain. 'Don't you remember, Roger? Think of that prisoner, with his fat arms and legs. Oh, he was covered in dirt and spoke like an actor reciting his lines but he made one mistake. Taplow was supposed to be a Lutheran but the prisoner said he believed in Purgatory. No Lutheran would have said that.

'Now, when we went to Smithfield I caught a glimpse of the dying Taplow. Oh, he had the same colour hair as the man we met in prison but he was much more emaciated.'

I closed my eyes and thought back. Taplow, in his prison cell: the fat on his arms and legs, the chubby, well-fed face beneath the dirt, the reference to his soul going to Purgatory, the fire at Smithfield, the thin, broken body I had glimpsed. My master was right.

'Why?' I asked.

'Let's remove Buckingham from our investigations,' Benjamin replied. 'He was a great nobleman with Yorkist blood in his veins and Henry wanted his head. The good Duke was foolish enough to make enquiries about certain precious relics and the King's agents closed in. I suspect his letters to Taplow produced during his trial were forgeries, whilst Taplow himself with his tenuous links with Buckingham was used as a catspaw. You know our gracious King. Taplow, the poor sod as you would put it, was tortured, bullied, to say what he did in court but then Mandeville had to make sure he did not tell the truth afterwards. He was removed to some far cell and a minion brought in to act his part. Mandeville thought we would be satisfied with that. He never dreamt that we would go to witness the execution or, even if we did, would get close enough to realise the man being burnt at the stake was not the same person we'd questioned at Newgate. I would have suspected nothing if the counterfeit Taplow had not made reference to Purgatory. So . . .'

'So,' I finished for him, 'we can ignore everything the little bastard in Newgate told us!'

'Yes, a pack of lies.' Benjamin drew in his breath. 'But if one part of the pie is rotten,' he concluded, 'how do you know the rest is true? What if there is no Grail or Excalibur or secret Templars? And why were those agents murdered?'

'Mandeville might have killed them,' I suggested. 'Perhaps they objected to the destruction of Buckingham and the web of deceit to which they'd been party?'

'Possible,' Benjamin murmured. 'Possible.' He rose and absentmindedly patted me on the shoulder. 'But come, Roger, we have to wash and change. Our hosts await us.'

My master wandered out and I unpacked my belongings, washed, changed and went down to the sumptuous banquet Santerre's cooks had prepared for us.

The high table was covered in pure silk cloths, bathed in light by countless wax candles which winked and dazzled on the silver trenchers, flagons, glass goblets and knives with precious pewter handles. The meal was delicious: beef and venison pastries and different wines, blood-red claret as well as light, sweet Rhenish.

Conversation was desultory for we were all exhausted though Mandeville declared that tomorrow he would spread his net. Certain questions had to be answered by Sir John and then we would return to Glastonbury Abbey. I ignored the sinister bastard and drank fast and deep with eyes only for Rachel. Dressed in a sea-blue gown with matching head-dress, each studded with small mother-of-pearls, she looked so beautiful!

(I see my little chaplain snigger because he knows I have talked about her before. All right, the little sod's reminding me of the truth, so I'll tell it.)

Yes, I was jealous, that's why I drank deep. I could not but notice how tenderly Rachel looked at Benjamin and jealousy, a flame so quickly started, is the most difficult fire to extinguish. After a while I became so deep in my cups I grew surly, said I felt unwell and trotted off to bed where I could nurse my hurt as well as conceal my bad manners. I lay on my fourposter ready to bemoan what had happened but the next minute I rolled over and sank into the deepest sleep. God knows when the banquet ended. I remember half-waking and seeing my master bend over me.

'Are you well, Roger? Is it something you ate?'

'Yes, yes,' I murmured bitterly, half-asleep. 'Something I ate.'

My next awakening was more harsh. I was in the middle of my favourite dream, standing in the dungeons, sipping a cup of claret whilst masked torturers had Fat Henry spread-eagled on the cruellest rack. I could smell smoke and hear the most terrible screams. Suddenly I shook myself awake, realising it was no dream; smoke was drifting under my door and, in spite of the thickness of the walls, I could hear the most awful groaning and crashing.

'For pity's sake, fire!' I shouted.

I opened the door and went out. The gallery was filled with smoke, the guttural screams and crackling sounds coming from the chamber occupied by the secretary, Cosmas. Quick-witted as usual, I shouted: 'Fire!' and dived back into my room with only one thought in my mind. The cornerstone of Shallot's philosophy: when danger threatens, collect your possessions and flee like the wind. I ran to find my master who was still fully dressed.

'For God's sake, Roger,' he said, 'what's happening?'

'For God's sake, Master!' I snarled back. 'Isn't it obvious? The silly bastard next door started a fire and I have no desire to join him!'

Benjamin stared at my cloak full of the little trinkets and valuable possessions I had collected.

'Roger, Roger, don't be so modest, you can't break the door down with those!'

He snatched the cloak out of my hand and threw it on the bed. Outside, I could hear doors opening on the gallery and running footsteps. At Benjamin's urging I helped pick up a wooden chest. We staggered out and began to use it as a battering ram against the locked door.

Mandeville and Southgate appeared, followed by the other secretary, Damien, his pallid face even more ghastly as he stared in terror at the fire enveloping his brother's room. He beat the air with his hands and made the most heart-rending cries. God be my witness, Mandeville was as tender with him as a mother with a baby. He grabbed the poor creature by the neck and drew him close, then gazed savagely across at us.

'Come on, you poltroons! Break the bloody door down!'

Assisted by Southgate and two sleepy-eyed, half-dressed servants we hammered again at the door until it buckled, creaking and groaning, before snapping back, breaking the lock. The smoke billowed out, forcing us to drop the chest. Benjamin scurried back to his room and brought napkins soaked in water, flung these at us and told us to cover our mouths and eyes. Other servants appeared led by Santerre. A chamber was opened and I realised that, like many wise householders, Santerre used one room to store huge vats of water against the very fire we were now fighting.

Benjamin and I, however, were first into the room. My master staggered over and opened the nearest window and, as the smoke cleared, we saw that the huge fourposter bed was now a sheet of flame.

It was one of the most curious things I had ever seen. You must remember Templecombe was made of stone and the chambers on the top gallery had no wooden wainscoting so the fire hadn't spread. Oh, two rugs on the stone floor were smouldering but the fire was contained. It looked as if the entire bed had simply erupted into a ball of flame.

Even then, as servants pushed by us with buckets of water and began to douse the flames, I knew there was something wrong. Both the braziers near the door had not been disturbed. The fire in the hearth was now a heap of white ash. So where had the flames sprung from? I concluded that I had done enough and was getting ready to sidle away when a servant pushed a large bucket of water into my hands and I realised that, under Santerre's direction, a human chain had been formed. At first the water made no difference but eventually the flames began to die until what was left of the bed was nothing but black smouldering ash.

Mandeville was the first to approach it and, amongst the remains of the bed, we found the charred body of Cosmas. His corpse was nothing but burnt flesh, his features indistinguishable. I glimpsed white teeth and a gaping jaw but the sight of the eyeballs turning to water and the blackened flesh of the man's hands proved too much. I fled back to the privacy of my own room to retch and vomit. Further down the hall, Santerre shouted for the windows to be opened, canvas sheets to be brought, and issued curt requests that Rachel and his wife go back to their rooms.

Mandeville's curses rang out interspersed by the awful, mournful sounds of the dead man's brother. At last I stopped retching and washed my hands and face with a cloth. When I turned Benjamin was standing there.

'What caused that?' I gasped.

'Death by fire!' my master repeated. 'And it was no accident, Roger. Cosmas was murdered. Burnt alive!'

Benjamin would say no more. I finished cleaning my mouth and hands and went back to the dead man's chamber. The flames were now extinguished, windows had been opened in the top gallery and the smoke was beginning to dissipate. Two servants, their mouths and noses covered by rags, removed Cosmas's remains in a canvas sheet. The burnt bed was broken up and pieces tossed through the window into the courtyard below. Benjamin seemed most interested in the charcoal braziers and sifted with his boot amongst the white ashes of the fire but, muttering to himself, claimed he could discover nothing untoward.

By the time we returned to bed, dawn was breaking. A few hours later Benjamin shook me awake.

'Come on, Roger, we have to break our fast. Mandeville's waiting for us in the hall below, talking about God's vengeance come to judgement.'

I rubbed my eyes. 'You still say it was murder?' I asked. 'Why?'

'The door was locked from the inside,' Benjamin replied. 'Cosmas remained wrapped in the bedding and was burnt alive. He had only one candle which was not powerful enough to start such a blaze so quickly whilst the fire was whitened ash.'

'What about gunpowder?'

'What do you mean?'

'Well, a trail of gunpowder from the bed under the door-way, then someone could have struck a tinder?

Benjamin shook his head doubtfully. 'We didn't see any such marks on the floor.'

(Now I see my little clerk shaking his noddle and giggling to himself. Oh, this master of the secret arts thinks my idea stupid. Well, let me tell you a short story. Many years later I was sent as emissary to Mary, Queen of Scots, when she was playing the two-backed beast with Bothwell. Mind you, I can't blame Mary: her husband Darnley was so pitted with the pox he had to drape a white veil over his face. Anyway, I told Mary about Cosmas's death then forgot all about it. That is, until a few months later when Darnley and his page boy, whilst staying at Kirk o' Fields Palace, were killed in an explosion. I often wondered whether Mary got the idea from me. Ah, well, that's another tale.)

Benjamin was truly perplexed by Cosmas's death: he did admit there were rare cases of human beings bursting into flames. (At the time I thought the idea was ridiculous until many years later when I attended a church in Holborn where the vicar, giving a fearsome sermon, abruptly burst into flames. I have never seen a church empty so quickly.) Anyway, on that snow-laden morning as Benjamin and I went deeper into the Valley of Death, Cosmas's murder remained a mystery. Only one thing stood out: Benjamin said there was a scorch mark on the outside of Cosmas's door but claimed it could be old. No other evidence of anything untoward could be detected. He waved his hands despondently.

'Who knows?' he sighed. 'Perhaps it was an act of God.'

I got up, washed, dressed, and Benjamin and I went down the great sweeping wooden staircase. We heard raised voices from the main hall but Benjamin insisted that we first walk out on to the porchway and take the morning air. We stood on the top step, an icy wind driving any sleep from our eyes and faces, staring out over the snow-carpeted grounds. Rooks cawed in the dark trees which ringed the house and I imagined demons nestling in the branches, mocking us. Southgate came through the door behind us.

'Sir Edmund Mandeville awaits you.'

'Oh dear,' I mocked. 'God can wait, but Sir Edmund . . . !'

And, with a mocking haste, I rushed back into the house, Benjamin following more slowly. Southgate caught up with me as I entered the main hall and saw Santerre and others sitting round the high table.

'One day,' Southgate hissed in my ear, 'your wit, Master Shallot, will take you to the scaffold. Or on to the point of someone's sword!'

'One day, one day!' I jibed back. 'Isn't it strange, Master Southgate, you are not the first to say that. And, even stranger, those who do say it meet violent deaths themselves.' I turned and looked him full in the face. 'Don't threaten me,' I whispered in false bravado, 'I am a fighting man!'

(Lord, the lies I told!)

'Your looks are as crooked as your eyes,' Southgate sneered.

(Oh, yes, I was a handsome rogue, tall with jet-black hair, olive-skinned but with a cast in one eye, I always thought it gave me a devil-may-care look.)

I noticed Southgate's hand had fallen to the hilt of his rapier. I gulped and peered over my shoulder to make sure Benjamin was behind me.

'When this business is over,' I scoffed, 'draw your hangar. But as you keep saying, our Lord God, Sir Edmund Mandeville, awaits us!'

Chapter 8

The group at the high table – Sir John, Lady Beatrice, Rachel, Mandeville and the white-faced Damien – had already broken their fast. Sir John clicked his fingers and servants placed a trencher before me with strips of dry bacon, small white loaves and a pot of thick creamy butter; blackjacks of ale were also served.

I gazed around and noticed how white and drawn everyone was. I smiled cheerfully, wished everyone a good morning and began to stuff the food into my mouth. Benjamin, of course, was more courteous. (A proper courtier, my master. He would have shamed an angel with his table manners.) He sipped from a tankard and stared at Mandeville.

'Sir, my condolences on the death of your secretary.'

Mandeville nodded slightly. 'Death, Master Daunbey. Death?'

Benjamin coughed. 'No, sir, you are correct. The word is murder.'

'But how?' Sir John stuttered. 'How in God's name, in my house? The man's chamber was locked. There are no secret entrances or passageways.' He looked away. 'At least not in that room.'

Benjamin smiled. 'So some exist?'

'Well, of course,' Santerre stammered. He shifted his feet nervously. 'Here, beneath us, are cellars and passageways.

The Templars often used them.' He smiled faintly. 'Now, I store my wines, wood for the fire and coals there, nothing singular.'

'What makes you think it's murder?' Mandeville asked sharply.

'Because, sir, beds do not explode into flames,' Benjamin replied. 'If my observations are correct, the mattress and blankets were turned into a roaring inferno within seconds. The braziers had not been moved, the fire was dead, the candle had spluttered out. And yet a powerful fire must have started so quickly it gave poor Cosmas no time even to get out of bed.' Benjamin sipped from his tankard. 'But who or why or how,' he continued, 'is as much a mystery to you as it is to me, Sir Edmund.

'As you say, the door was locked, no one else was in the room and the fire was meant to kill swiftly, expertly, and with little damage to anyone else. Go and check the chamber. The ceiling is of plaster and would take hours to ignite. The walls and floor are of stone. In many another house, the flames would have spread along the top story, but not here. Our murderer knew that!'

'But the bed and blankets,' I intervened (Old Shallot being intent on delivering his pennysworth!), 'would be as dry as tinder.'

'And why didn't Cosmas get out of the bed?' Santerre asked.

'Because,' Benjamin answered, 'he was seriously maimed. But how?' He shook his head.

'You think he was murdered?' Santerre asked.

'Yes, I have said so but . . .'

Mandeville tapped the top of the table with his empty tankard and glanced accusingly at Santerre. 'The question really is, who was behind this attack?'

Sir John pushed back his chair, his red face bristling with rage. 'Are you accusing me, Sir Edmund, or my family or servants? If so, say it!' He breathed in deeply through his nostrils. 'Remember where we are, Sir Edmund. This is not London but the South-West of England. Memories die hard here. Edward Stafford, my late Lord of Buckingham, was much loved and respected, so remember that. I can no more vouch for the loyalty of every one of my tenants than His Grace the King or my Lord Cardinal can guarantee the loyalty of every Englishman.

'Secondly . . .' Santerre paused to consider what he was about to say.

'Do go on,' Southgate put in silkily. The bastard was really enjoying himself.

'Secondly,' Santerre continued hastily, ignoring his wife's warning glance, 'memories of the Templars still survive here. In their time they were regarded as great magicians who brought prosperity to these parts. They had a reputation as healers, good lords who possessed the secrets of both heaven and earth. Do you think,' he looked straight at Mandeville and I admired the fellow's courage, 'do you really think, Sir Edmund Mandeville, that the people of these parts don't know the true reason for your presence here? That they do not know what you seek as well as your intention of rooting out any trace of an ancient order? Above all, they must know of your part in the destruction of my Lord of Buckingham as, God be my witness, I know mine!'

'Are you saying,' Southgate accused, 'that you sympathise with the dead Duke?'

'No, sir, I do not!' Santerre bellowed. 'And pray do not put words in my mouth. My Lord of Buckingham came here. He sat at this very table and, when he was gone, your two creatures came and asked me what he said. I told the truth. The rest was in your hands.'

Santerre pulled his chair back to the table. 'God knows,' he concluded softly, 'some of the Duke's blood may be on my hands.' He stared round the hall. 'I am not of these parts,' he continued, 'I was Hampshire born.' Santerre clutched his wife's hand firmly in his. 'But when I married Lady Beatrice, she took my name and I took her house. I came here to be a good lord as well as the King's most loyal servant! Think of that, Sir Edmund, before you sit at my table and hint about who was responsible for the death of your secretary! God knows, it wasn't me or mine!'

Southgate sneered. Mandeville simply stroked his dark face as if weighing up carefully what he was to do next.

'Sirs,' Benjamin intervened tactfully, 'before any judgement is passed, we must recognise the truth of what Sir John says. My Lord of Buckingham was of these parts. We have come here to disturb legends which are a part of the very soil of these lands. Sir Edmund Mandeville, think about what has been said. Your two agents, Calcraft and Warnham, may have been followed to London and killed by one of the Duke's retainers or by these secret Templars. Sir John cannot be held responsible for the loyalty of every one of his servants, and Cosmas's death, God rest him, is a mystery.'

'What intrigues me,' I asserted, 'is that the witch we met yesterday prophesied such a death. Don't you remember, Sir Edmund? Death by fire, by rope, by steel and by water? And may I remind you that none of us were exempt from that curse.'

My words created an eerie silence.

'I should have had that witch brought in!' Mandeville cursed.

'The witch can't be blamed,' Rachel declared softly. 'She only spoke the truth: this house is haunted. The spirits of the Templars wander its passageways and galleries. Cosmas's death is not the first tragedy to have occurred here.' Her face hardened. 'Oh, yes, there have been other deaths here, haven't there, Mother?' She did not wait for a reply. 'My own father was killed in a riding accident. Servants have slipped downstairs. An old nurse hanged herself in one of the barns. A gardener was found drowned in the lake. Suicides, or so the coroner declared.'

Rachel's sombre words chilled all our souls.

'Is this true?' Benjamin asked her parents.

Santerre nodded. Lady Beatrice rubbed her face in her hands, distraught, losing her air of frosty self-possession.

'Yes,' she answered reluctantly. 'Many say this house is haunted. The common people do not blame me or my husband for Buckingham's downfall but say his fate was starcrossed by this house. Sometimes, just sometimes, I wish I could burn the entire building to the ground!'

'We could always make a start,' Southgate quipped.

'Nonsense!' Benjamin replied. 'True, I accept the legions of hell are all around us. We fight, as St Paul says, against an invisible foe. Ghosts may walk but so do murderers. Cosmas's death had more to do with flesh and blood than curses, witches or ghosts.' He smiled bleakly at Rachel. 'Though I agree that the old witch has a most singular gift for prophecy. Sir Edmund Mandeville is correct – perhaps she should be brought in for questioning. However, before we consider that, let's establish if anyone went into Cosmas's room.'

Damien the mute had been watching my master's lips intently. He tugged me by the sleeve and pointed to Santerre's wife.

'Lady Beatrice, did you go into Cosmas's chamber?' Mandeville asked.

'Yes, earlier in the day I did. I am mistress of this house and I have to see that all is well.'

'As did I,' Sir John added. 'For the same reason.'

'I saw a maid going in,' Southgate declared. 'A brownhaired lass with a white coif on her head. She was carrying blankets and linen.'

'That would be Mathilda,' Sir John replied. 'But she's a simple country girl with hardly a thought in her head. Nevertheless, I'll question her.'

'I don't think a maid,' Benjamin asserted, 'would plot murder. Sir John, how long did yesterday's evening meal last?'

'About two hours.'

Benjamin stared down at the table top. 'Roger was the first to leave, then you, Master Southgate, followed by Lady Beatrice and Sir John. Finally you, sir,' he pointed at Mandeville, 'with your two clerks.'

'And what time did you leave?' Southgate asked.

Benjamin blushed. 'I didn't. Lady Rachel and I remained here. She collected a book from her father's library containing all the Arthurian legends, a copy of Malory's *Arthur of Britain* and the *Knights of the Round Table*.'

My heart chilled and I gnawed at my lip to hide my disappointment. Rachel had caught my eye but it seemed her interest was in my master rather than me.

'What are you implying?' Mandeville asked.

'I am implying nothing. I'm just curious if anyone visited poor Cosmas's chamber.'

A chorus of denials greeted his question. Mandeville stood and picked up his cloak, thrown over the back of a chair.

'We were to travel to Glastonbury today but first I must deal with this dreadful business. Sir John, I will need some sort of box to serve as a coffin for poor Cosmas. This can be placed in your manor chapel and perhaps tomorrow, on our way to Glastonbury, we can leave it at the village church. I also have letters to write. His Grace the King will not be pleased by what I have to say. Master Southgate?'

Both the *Agentes* took their leave, followed by a silent, doleful Damien.

Lady Beatrice and Rachel murmured their excuses whilst

Sir John stretched, grumbling that it was all a dreadful business but the affairs of the estate demanded his attention.

Benjamin watched him leave. 'I wonder where Sir John is really going?' he muttered.

'If he had any sense he'd stay here and keep an eye on his daughter,' I quipped back. 'You did not tell me, Master, that you spent the night down here in the hall playing cat's-cradle with Mistress Rachel?'

Benjamin smiled. 'She's beautiful, isn't she, Roger? But she's not for you and she's certainly not for me. This is no game. We are surrounded by death, murder, plot and counter-plot. There is no time for dalliance. Trust no one except me until this matter is finished.'

He stared round. 'Roger, despite the quilted cushions, the golden clocks, the silver spoons and Venetian goblets, this house has the stink of death about it. I did not wish openly to agree with her but Mistress Rachel was correct. There is something about this place which reeks of ancient sin and, the sooner our task is completed, the better.'

'Do you think the secret Templars exist?' I asked.

'Possibly. Such societies or covens batten on their own secrecy. They create an exclusive world and, despite its green fields and pleasant villages, the King is right – England seethes with discontent. Great lords with Yorkist blood in their veins hold high office. There's a growing dislike of the Church. The Scots still threaten in the north whilst in Europe great alliances are formed which leave England isolated. In such an atmosphere secret societies like the Templars flourish. You'll always find the strongest weeds on a dung hill.'

'And the Grail and Excalibur?'

Benjamin shrugged. 'The King wants them or, more importantly, if he can't have them, he wants to make sure no one else does. I cannot make sense of that rhyme. What are the waters of Jordan?' He pulled a face at me. 'That's why I was talking to our young beauty last night. Is there, in this God forsaken place, some stream, river, house or church bearing the name Jordan? And where could Moses' Ark possibly be?'

'And could she help?'

'No, nor could her father – or so Mandeville told me last night after you had retired. So Master Hopkins's riddle is still shrouded in mystery.'

'Did he leave any papers?'

'None whatsoever. According to Mandeville, before he left for his fateful journey to London, Hopkins cleared out his entire chamber, the very one you are now using.' Benjamin pointed to the fire flickering in the great hearth. 'He stripped his chamber of everything, and what he couldn't burn, he destroyed.'

'A strange act.'

Benjamin shrugged. 'Perhaps he had a premonition about what might happen in London. Or maybe someone gave him a warning. Or perhaps he knew that Warnham and Calcraft in Buckingham's retinue were really the King's agents.' Benjamin sighed. 'Whatever, Master Hopkins took his secret to the grave.' He leaned closer. 'Roger,' he whispered, 'I wish to stay here, but you go back to your chamber, collect your boots, cloak and that broad-brimmed hat you wear. Sir John will leave within the hour. When he does, I want you to follow him from afar off. I know it will be hard in a snow-covered countryside but see where he goes to.'

The prospect didn't appeal to me but, there again, neither did the thought of lounging around Templecombe. So I slipped back upstairs, taking more careful note of my surroundings, particularly the small gargoyle's heads in the cornices of the ceilings and, above all, the great blackened Beauce crosses. Why hadn't they faded with time? Were they being constantly re-painted and gilded as some sort of memorial to that ancient secretive order? I reached the chamber, found the door half-open and cursed my own stupidity. I don't trust myself and, apart from Benjamin, I certainly didn't trust anyone else yet I had forgotten to take the key down with me.

I pushed the door open quietly. A young woman sat with her back to me on the far side of the great fourposter bed. Her head was covered in a white coif with a white shawl shaped in the form of a triangle going down her back like a liripipe. I heard the clink of coins, smiled and tiptoed round the bed.

'Good morrow, Mistress,' I said, leaning against a bed-post. I glanced at my purse in her lap and the coins scattered on the bed beside her. 'Do I owe you something?'

The young woman just stared back like a frightened rabbit. I caught a glimpse of auburn hair and large blue eyes in a suntanned face. She seemed to be about seventeen or eighteen years old.

'I asked you a question, Mistress. Do I owe you some money? If not,' I continued sarcastically, 'can you tell me why my purse is in your hand?'

I stepped closer and the young woman rose and made to flee but I seized her by the wrist. She struggled.

'I am sorry,' she pleaded, her voice betraying a thick country burr. 'Oh, sir, I am sorry but I saw it lying there and the temptation was too much for me.'

I pulled the girl closer, caught the faint perfume of lavender and roses and noted appreciatively how, under the brown smock, her plump breasts rose and fell in agitation.

'You're Mathilda, aren't you?'

'Yes, sir, I'm the chambermaid and I am also responsible for the linen cupboard.'

'And you prepared the beds for Sir John's guests?'

The girl nodded, still wide-eyed.

'Including the bed of the man who died?'

Now the girl's face paled. 'Yes, sir, but as I have told Sir John and Master Devil . . .'

I laughed at the girl's pun on Mandeville's name. With

his black garb, Italianate features and fearsome reputation, Sir Edmund must appear as Master Lucifer himself to the peasants of Templecombe Manor.

'I saw nothing untoward,' she repeated. 'You are hurting me, sir, let go of my wrist!'

'Why should I? You are a thief. You could be hanged for what you have done.' I looked at her in mock sternness. She caught the mischief in my eyes and pressed against me.

'Oh, come, sir,' she said. 'Perhaps you could give me one of these coins and send me away with a beating? I have been wicked.'

She pressed her body closer against me. I could feel her soft breasts and noted how slender and long her neck was. I released her hand and grasped her firmly by the buttocks, small but ripe. The girl touched the leather belt round my waist.

'You could use that,' she said thickly.

Well, you know Old Shallot. Like a jousting knight, my lance was ready! The girl's body was curved and slender and my hands were straying to the ribbons on her bodice. Then I thought again. Old Shallot's rule: never force yourself on a woman. And, like the romantic fool I was, I thought Mathilda was only offering herself in an act of desperation. I tapped her gently, picked up a silver coin and thrust it into her soft, warm hand.

'Don't do it again,' I growled. 'Now, begone!'

I heard her trip across the floor and the door closed behind her. I stood, eyes closed, congratulating myself on my newly found sanctity – then cursed at the sharp knock on the door. I went across and threw it open, exasperated that my holy moment had been so brutally shattered. Mathilda stood there, her bodice unlaced, breasts as ripe as any fruit, half-spilling out of her dress.

'I really do think,' she murmured mischievously, 'that I deserve correction.'

Well, what could I say? Old Shallot has another rule: never resist temptation twice. And within five minutes, we were both as naked as when we were born, bouncing merrily across the great fourposter bed. She was young and vigorous, a warm and comely maid, and what she lacked in skill, Mathilda certainly made up for in enthusiasm. She laughed and screamed until I had to smother her mouth with kisses. Even now, years later, I still remember poor Mathilda. A small, warm flash of sunlight in that grim, murderous place.

Sometime after, pleasantly exhausted, I collected my horse from the stable, saddled it and led it down the causeway out of the manor gate. A fresh sheet of snow had fallen in the night which now lay two or three inches thick, the cold wind freezing it hard. The countryside looked like some vision of hell; white, silent fields and black trees against a grey sky. Rooks cawed as they foraged hungrily for food but, apart from that, nothing except the eerie, deathly silence of a countryside in the grip of winter. Lord save us, I would have given a bag of silver for the sounds and smells of old Cheapside! I had already gathered from the groom that Sir John had not left so, when I came to a small copse of trees, I took my horse deep inside, hobbled it and sat on a boulder. I sipped from a wineskin, remembering Mathilda's warm charms and waiting for Sir John to come. My buttocks began to freeze and I was wondering whether to return when I heard the clop of the horse's hooves and glimpsed Sir John riding vigorously by.

Despite the icy ground underneath, he was urging his large roan horse on with all his might. A few minutes later I followed, using dips and bends in the track to keep myself hidden. He reached the crossroads, deserted except for a lonely scaffold post and the rotting cadaver of a hanged man still in its gibbet jacket. I watched Sir John take the path to Glastonbury and knew there was little point in tracking him any further. The Lord of the Manor had apparently lied to us. He must have some urgent business with the monks to make this cold, lonely journey.

I turned my horse back, looking forward to the warmth of Templecombe Manor and feeling rather sleepy after my exertions with young Mathilda. The turrets and gables of Templecombe were almost in sight beyond the trees when my horse whinnied and shook me awake. A group of masked men had slipped like ghostly shadows from the trees on either side of the track. They were all dressed in black, though I glimpsed the white three-pointed cross of the Templars daubed crudely on the shoulders of their cloaks.

'What is it you want?' I shouted, desperately trying to turn my horse's head so I could flee like the wind.

One of the figures moved. I heard the click of a crossbow and a bolt whirled warningly above my head. The man holding the crossbow approached; his voice, muffled by the mask he wore, ordered me to dismount.

'Piss off!' I shouted. I desperately tried to draw my sword but my belly was churning with such fear that I was unable to grasp the hilt.

'Get down!'

The group drew closer. I glimpsed naked steel and, as you know, that has only one effect on Old Shallot. I get this indescribable desire to flee. One of the masked men tried to seize the bridle of my horse.

'Damn you all!' I screamed and, pushing my horse forward, sent him sprawling with my foot.

Hands clutched at my legs whilst the horse, thoroughly alarmed, reared, flailing his iron-shod hooves. I had now regained some of my little courage, drew my sword and whirled it round my head like Sir Lancelot of the Lake. My only desire was to keep these hideous creatures at bay whilst I desperately looked for a gap in the ring of steel surrounding me. I felt my sword bite flesh, a scream, then I struck again. I don't know what really happened for I had my eyes closed, lashing out with my sword, whilst my horse, who had more courage than brains, took care of itself.

I heard hoof beats and opened one eye to see my attackers run back into the trees, two of them not moving as quickly as they would want. I admit, I was quaking with fright and this had its usual effect on Old Shallot: weak legs, wobbly belly, heaving chest and total panic. When my master found me I had dismounted and was squatting on a patch of snow, busily emptying the contents of my stomach. Benjamin heard the faint crackling in the undergrowth but took one look at me and gave up any idea of pursuit. Instead he took the wineskin from the horn of my saddle and forced me to drink. He looked around and saw the patches of red on the snow.

'A terrible fight, Roger?'

(God bless him, he was so innocent.)

'I did my best, Master,' I said humbly. 'There must have been at least a dozen of them,' I lied in mock modesty, 'and I doubt if four of them will live to greet tomorrow's dawn.'

'Who were they?'

'God knows!' I snarled. 'They were hooded, capped and masked, though they had crude Templar crosses painted on their cloaks. I think they were more than just a maurading band of outlaws.'

Benjamin walked into the line of trees and stared through the snow-dripping darkness.

'A dozen you say, Roger?'

'At least, Master.'

'Then why didn't they kill you immediately?'

'I don't know!' I snapped. 'But when they come back, I'll ask them!'

'No, no, you have been brave enough, Roger. I think they either wanted to question you or give you a warning. What it does prove,' Benjamin continued, 'is that they have the manor watched. They must have seen you follow

Santerre.' He looked over his shoulder at me. 'And why aren't you pursuing him?'

'There's no need. For some reason the pompous bastard has decided to return to Glastonbury. He must have pressing business there. Perhaps,' I added, 'Santerre's a Templar and has gone to warn his masters that one of Mandeville's men has already been killed.'

I got up and drained the rest of the wineskin.

'I'd give a bag of gold,' Benjamin murmured, 'to know what has taken Santerre to Glastonbury. Perhaps you should have followed him.'

'And do what?' I shouted, my legs still shaking with fright. 'Wandered into the monastery and said, "Oh, what a coincidence! What are you doing here, Sir John?" Anyway,' I nodded into the trees, 'perhaps those bastards would have struck before I reached Glastonbury. There are enough woods, marshes and fog-shrouded moors to hide a bloody army in this Godforsaken land!' I patted my horse, whispering my thanks to him, then mounted. 'I'm going back to Templecombe,' I moaned. 'I'm tired, wet, pissed off, really pissed off, Master, and I have had enough!' I looked evilly at him. 'Anyway, what were you doing here?'

Benjamin remounted and grinned at me. 'I am still intrigued by that witch. I was trying to find the place we met her yesterday morning when I heard you shouting and the sounds of ambush so I rode to investigate.' He pushed his horse nearer and grasped me by the arm, his long dark face, usually solemn, wreathed in smiles.

'Come on, my warrior prince,' he murmured. 'What's a few footpads to a man like Shallot, eh?'

(I felt like telling him those bastards had aged me by years, but I suppose we have to keep up a brave face.)

'Come on.' Benjamin kicked his horse forward. 'Let's see if we can find where the old witch lives.'

Moaning and groaning, I rode alongside. We were almost

near Templecombe gates when Benjamin and I both decided that we had found the gap in the trees through which she had fled and, despite my warnings, he insisted on going in.

If the old witch was a prophet, then so was I, for we had hardly ridden a bow's length into the trees when Benjamin declared himself lost. The wood was thick, the undergrowth covered in snow; even in summer it would have been difficult to follow the trackway. It was already getting dark and so, to my relief, Benjamin decided to turn back.

Chapter 9

At Templecombe we found everyone going about their own business. After stabling our horses, my master muttered that he had business to attend to and wandered off to his chamber. I went looking for Mathilda and found her working in the buttery with the other maids. She threw me a warning glance, telling me with her eyes to stay well away. I begged a tankard of ale from a surly cook and went to warm myself before the hall fire until my master roused me.

'Come on, Roger, we have work to do. I have been thinking about that riddle. Perhaps the old Templar chapel can provide an answer.'

I was warm and sleepy but my master kept haranguing me: compliance seemed the easiest way out so I put on my boots, grabbed my cloak and accompanied him down to the Templar chapel. The door was open. Inside, Mandeville and Southgate were standing near the baptismal font.

'So the wanderer has returned?' Southgate sneered. 'What brings you here?'

'The riddle,' Benjamin replied.

'We've already thought of that,' Mandeville muttered. 'But there's no Jordan water here, or Moses' Ark.' He pointed down the church. 'Damien's in the sanctuary. We found a pinewood arrow box.' Mandeville bit his lip. 'What's left of poor Cosmas has been sheeted, coffined, and lies before the altar. It's the least we could do.' He forced a

141

smile. 'I would appreciate it, Master Daunbey, if you would go there, say a prayer and offer Damien your condolences.'

Benjamin agreed. We walked down the dark, dingy nave under the simple rood screen into the sanctuary. The makeshift coffin lay on trestles before the altar. Six purple candles, three on either side, flickered in heavy iron holders. Someone had nailed a simple crucifix to the top of the lid with the name 'Cosmas' scrawled in black beneath it. On a prie-dieu, at the foot of the coffin, knelt the dead man's brother, his shaven head bowed, his shoulders shaking with silent sobs. Mandeville came up behind us.

'The coffin will lie here tonight,' he whispered. 'Tomorrow we will take it down to the village church.' He then strode off as Damien turned, his eyes red with weeping, his white face now puffy. Before, he had always been rather frightening but now he looked pathetic with his tear-stained cheeks, grieving eyes and red gaping mouth which could only make gurgling sounds as Benjamin took him by the hand and tried to convey his condolences. The poor mute nodded, his hideous face twisted into a smile, but when he looked at me, his eyes narrowed. Oh no, I thought, here we go. Old Shallot's a suspect again! I tried to look sympathetic but that only made matters worse and the fellow waved his fingers in the air as a sign for us to go and, turning his back, resumed his prayers. We left and he followed us to the church door. We heard it slam behind us and the key turn in the lock.

'The poor fellow wants to be alone,' Benjamin murmured.

'I understand that,' I replied. 'But must he look at me as if I am the murderer?'

Benjamin linked his arm through mine and we walked back to the manor house.

'I know the truth, Roger. But they think differently. After all, you were the first to leave the dinner table. You could have prepared that fire and retired to bed.'

'How could I?' I cried. 'Moreover, Master,' I dragged my arm away, 'you know Cosmas was a professional spy, an agent. Didn't he lock his chamber door?'

'Unfortunately not,' Benjamin replied. He looked at me, his face innocent. 'Don't forget, Roger, the key was on the inside of his chamber. Cosmas thought he was safe. After all, he was protected by the King's chief agent. Remember the old proverb: "It's easy for the hunter to forget how quickly it is to become the hunted." Anyway,' he seized my arm again, 'do you always lock your chamber?'

I wondered if my master knew something about my tryst with Mathilda but he had that distant, innocent expression. Benjamin at his most inscrutable.

'Did you really think,' I asked, quickly changing the subject, 'the chapel could pose a solution to Hopkins's riddle?'

'Not really, but the riddle must refer to a place. Either here at Templecombe or, more likely, Glastonbury.'

'There's one other place, Master.'

'Such as?'

'The house on the island.'

Benjamin's face beamed in surprise. 'Of course,' he breathed and, turning round, went back past the chapel and down to the lakeside.

We stood staring across the icy water at the mist-shrouded island. God knows, it was a most desolate place. The water was covered with a film of ice whilst above it a grey mist boiled. It almost disguised the island and its strange Templar house for we could only glimpse the tiles of its roof.

'I wonder what used to happen there?' Benjamin whispered.

I shivered and stamped my feet. You didn't have to have the soul of a poet to conjure up what could have been; in my mind's eye I had a vision of Templars in their faceless conical helmets, red and white crosses on their black cloaks, moving across the island at the dead of night, the barges being soundlessly poled whilst, at prow and stern, huge cresset torches spluttered and flared in the darkness. Why would they go there? I wondered. Some macabre rite? A Satanic mass? The conjuring of evil spirits? Or to indulge in illicit sexual pleasures?

'We should go across,' Benjamin commented.

'Not now, Master,' I said, trying to hide my panic. 'It's growing dark. Heaven knows how thick that ice is. And, if we have to go, I would like to be armed.'

Thankfully, Benjamin agreed and we returned to the manor house. I was cold and stiff, so went back to my chamber to warm myself. I lay on the bed for a while wondering if Mathilda might return, before drifting into a troubled sleep where ghastly figures, masked and hooded, danced on a lonely island before a terrible demon god.

Benjamin shook me awake.

'Santerre has returned,' he whispered. 'Let's go down and see where he really went.'

We found Sir John and his family in the great hall, sitting on the coffer-box chairs before the fire. Santerre seemed cheerful enough, shuffling his feet, warming his hands, and loudly declaring how good it was to be back in his own home and with his own people. He smiled and waved us over.

'A good day's business,' he bellowed. 'Despite the snow, all seems well.' He picked up a brimming wine goblet from the small table beside him. 'And you, sirs, you feel at home now?'

Benjamin made the usual tactful responses. I just stared at Santerre's cheery face. The man's a consummate liar, I thought. This bastard, with his bluff ways, merry eyes and welcoming invitations, nearly had me murdered this morning. Santerre patted his stomach.

'God knows, I have an appetite!' he bellowed, smacking his lips. He grinned at his wife. 'Good food, eh, wife?'

Lady Beatrice caught his mood and laughed back.

'Only the best for the Lord and Master!'

'Pork roasted in a lemon sauce, with slices of mutton, heavily garnished.' Santerre rubbed his stomach. 'This cold weather puts the wolf in your belly, eh, Master Shallot? A bowl of claret and afterwards a game of dice?'

Mandeville and Southgate walked stiff-legged into the hall. Both men were not amused by Sir John's high spirits during a time of mourning.

'Have you seen Damien?' Mandeville snapped.

'Yes,' Benjamin replied. 'About two or three hours ago.'

'But that was in the chapel.'

Benjamin shrugged. 'You asked, we answered!'

Mandeville stared into the fire. God knows, perhaps I have a sixth sense, but the hair on the nape of my neck prickled with fear.

'He can't still be praying,' Southgate insisted.

The good humour drained from Santerre's face. Rachel and her mother looked agitated. Benjamin got briskly to his feet.

'Talk is futile. Let us go to the chapel. If he's not there, perhaps he went for a walk in the grounds?'

We all left, going through the kitchen, out across the courtyard and down the trackway to the church. The door was still locked and, when I peered through the shuttered windows, I could see no sign of candlelight.

'Damien!' Mandeville roared. He tried the handle but the door was locked. 'Damien!' Mandeville shouted again and, losing his poise, hammered with his fists against the metal-studded door.

'Mother!' Rachel cried. 'Come with me.'

The two women went down the side of the church, shouting Damien's name through the shutters. Mandeville continued his knocking. Santerre sent for servants and, at his direction, they dragged out a huge log drying in the stables for Yuletide.

Mandeville supervised them as if he was besieging a

castle. Ropes were wrapped around the log and the servants swung it backwards and forward, hammering at the door until it groaned, cracked, then snapped back on its hinges.

'Everyone is to stay where they are.' Mandeville wiped the sweat from his face. 'No one is to enter this church until I say.' He went in. 'The key is still in the lock,' he exclaimed. 'And even the bolts were drawn shut!' He walked up the church shouting for Southgate to join him.

We all clustered silently by the door until a chilling moan from Mandeville and a despairing shout of 'Oh, no!' sent us hurrying into the church. In the nave nothing had been disturbed. Santerre ordered the torches to be lit. In the sanctuary we found Damien sprawled over the prie-dieu. A small crossbow bolt had been sent smashing into the back of his skull. He had been thrown violently forwards, the blood which had spurted from nose and mouth splattering the base of his brother's coffin. Mandeville pulled the corpse back, turning him gently in his arms like a mother would a child. In the flickering cresset torch Damien's face looked horrible: the eyes half-open, the mouth silent for ever now, blood caking his face from brow to chin. Mandeville laid the corpse gently on the floor.

'Some bastard will pay for this!' he hissed, the glint of madness in his eyes.

Santerre stepped back, spreading his hands. 'Sir, do not threaten me. You saw the door was locked from the inside.'

'Where's the other key?'

'On a ring on my belt. And where I go, it goes.'

Southgate leaned over and patted Benjamin on the chest. 'You saw Damien last?'

'What are you implying?' my master retorted. 'Do you accuse me or Shallot of this murder? And if so, how?' Benjamin pointed to the dead man. 'He saw us out of the church and locked the door behind us.'

Benjamin spun on his heel, grabbed a torch from Sir John

Santerre and walked down the nave, beckoning me to follow him. We stopped at the far end just under the small choir loft where there was a recess leading up to the tower. Benjamin gestured with his hand. 'Sir Edmund,' he shouted. 'Put the corpse back as you found it and come here!'

The two *Agentes* were about to object but had the sense to see what Benjamin was doing. They joined us at the far end of the church, Benjamin shouting at the Santerres to stand back.

'Don't you see, Sir Edmund?' he exclaimed. 'Someone could have been hiding here when we came into the church earlier today. We talked and you left, then Damien ushered us out and went back to the prie-dieu. Now, let's pretend we are the assassin, standing here with a crossbow looking up towards the sanctuary.'

He lifted the torch and Mandeville followed his gaze.

'Yes, yes,' he muttered. 'I see, Master Daunbey. Poor Damien was kneeling at the entrance to the sanctuary screen, an easy target for someone lurking here with a crossbow.'

Benjamin lowered the torch close to the paved stone floor, scrabbling round with his fingers.

'Look, in the torchlight you can see a dark stain. I agree it's hard to distinguish between our footprints but this stain, this wetness, shows someone stood here for some time, their cloak and boots heavy with snow. They must have come here even before Damien. When we all left, and he locked the door behind us, the murderer committed his crime.'

Southgate clapped his hands slowly. 'Most ingenious, my dear Daunbey. But how did the murderer leave?'

Benjamin shouted at Santerre now walking down the nave towards us.

'Sir John are there any secret entrances to this church?'

'None,' Rachel replied.'For God's sake, Master Daunbey, see for yourself.'

147

Benjamin asked for more torches and we went round the walls studying the floor. Nothing but hard stone. The only other entrance was a small door to the left of the sanctuary but that was closed with a padlock, rusting with age, and obviously had not been opened for years.

'There's no sacristy here?' I asked.

'None whatsoever,' Sir John replied. 'When the Templars used this church, the priests would vest for mass either in the manor or here in the sanctuary.'

Benjamin took his torch and walked along the walls examining the shutters of each window. All were closed, their clasps firmly in place.

'A veritable mystery,' he murmured. 'The murderer was locked in but how did he get out? Sir John, these shutters, they are locked from the inside?'

'And from the outside,' Santerre shouted.

'Oh, sweet heaven!' Benjamin breathed.

He led the group out of the church and, in a ring of torchlight, examined each window and the snow beneath. However, this only deepened the mystery for the outside latch on each shutter was also down and, apart from the fresh footprints of Lady Beatrice and Rachel, there was no sign that anyone had used the window to get in or out.

'Well,' Southgate declared, as we gathered outside the door of the church again. 'Damien's dead, murdered!'

'Death by steel,' I replied. 'Don't forget the witch's curse.'

'If it's witchcraft,' Mandeville grated, 'I'll see the old bitch burn within a week!' He glared at Rachel. 'You are right, Mistress, this house is cursed. Two of the King's most loyal servants have died here, foully murdered. The place should be burnt down.'

'Nonsense!' Benjamin interrupted. 'Damien was killed with a crossbow bolt and ghosts don't leave stains on the floor. We know how the murderer got in and where he lurked, the only problem is how he got out.' Benjamin drew himself up so his shoulders were no longer stooped. 'Can't you see what is happening?' he exclaimed. 'The assassin has marked us down for death, but first he is playing with us like a cat does with a mouse. The fear of death is often worse than death itself. Cosmas and Damien's murders are meant to torture and punish us as well as unnerve and divert us from our true mission. Two men are dead. Yet, Sir Edmund, I am confident the assassin will eventually make a mistake.'

Mandeville viciously kicked at the snow with the toe of his boot. 'But when, Master Daunbey, when?' He looked at his lieutenant. 'Southgate, have Damien's corpse removed. Sir John, I will need a chest. Tomorrow you will move both bodies down to the village church.'

Mandeville strode off, then stopped and turned. 'Southgate, before you do that, I would remove everything from Damien's room, all papers and documents. Sir John, dismiss the servants. I need to see you all in the hall.'

We obeyed and went in to sit in a sombre half-circle round the fire. No thought of food or drink now as Mandeville strode up and down in front of us, so angry he seemed impervious to the roaring flames of the fire.

'Tomorrow,' he began, 'we must go to Glastonbury. The snow lies thick but not deep enough to hinder justice.' He wiped his mouth on the back of his hand. 'I could ask where each of you were today but what's the use?'

I glanced quickly at Sir John. Apart from Benjamin and I, he was the only one who had left the manor so his cloak and boots would have been covered in snow. Had he gone to Glastonbury or come back by a secret route to Templecombe to hide himself in the church? Or was the assassin already here? Could it have been one of the footpads who tried to ambush me earlier that day? I glanced up. Mandeville was staring at me as if trying to read my thoughts.

'We must be careful,' he murmured, drawing in deep

breaths to calm himself. 'We must not start accusing each other of murder. Any one of your tenants, Sir John, and I mean no offence, could be the assassin. Perhaps Master Shallot is right, we must not forget that damned witch.'

'She may know something, Sir Edmund,' Benjamin tactfully intervened. 'But the murderer of Cosmas and Damien must be in this household.'

Mandeville agreed. 'Sir John, tomorrow morning at first light, I want all your servants gathered here in the main hall. And pray, sir, do not object. This is the King's business.'

He pushed by the chairs and strode out of the hall. Benjamin nodded apologetically to Sir John, beckoned to me and hastily followed. Mandeville was already half-way up the stairs.

'Sir Edmund,' my master called, 'a word!'

Mandeville looked down, his eyes glowing with a murderous rage.

'Piss off, Daunbey! In there I have to be courteous but I'll never forget that you and that bloody rogue of a servant were the last to see my clerk alive!' He came back down the stairs. 'You think it's a game, don't you?' he snarled. 'I have lost two good men. Four, if you include Warnham and Calcraft.' Mandeville pushed his face only inches away from that of Benjamin. 'You may not like what we are, the King's agents, his tools, his spies. You may not even like the King, but he wears the Crown of the Confessor. A strong prince is infinitely better than ten strong princes fighting for the crown.'

'I accept what you say,' Benjamin quietly replied. 'But that is not the matter at issue.'

Mandeville looked away. 'You are right,' he breathed. 'It is not. I have lost many agents but Cosmas and Damien were like flesh and blood. I mourn their deaths.'

'Then, sir,' I exclaimed, 'it is a time for honesty!'

I approached, shrugging off Benjamin's warning touch.

150

'We are the only ones you can trust. Warnham and Calcraft died before we ever entered this play. So let me ask you honestly, the man we met in Newgate wasn't Taplow, was he?'

The anger drained from Mandeville's face. He beckoned us further down the gallery and into a window embrasure where no one could eavesdrop. He stared through the paned glass and smiled apologetically.

'You are correct, Taplow died at Smithfield but the man you met was not him.'

'Why?' I asked.

'The King's orders.'

'And those letters Buckingham wrote?'

Now Mandeville's face paled. He still had a flicker of morality in him.

'Our King always wanted Buckingham dead, as did the Lord Cardinal. It was simply a matter of fitting a noose round his neck.'

'And Hopkins?' I insisted.

'A stupid priest who may have been a secret Templar and had access to hidden knowledge.'

'And the rest . . . the Grail, Excalibur, the Templars themselves?'

'Oh, that's all true.'

'Come, Sir Edmund,' Benjamin mocked. 'Just tell us what is really true!'

Mandeville leaned against the wall and ticked the points off on his fingers. 'First,' he whispered, 'the King wanted Buckingham dead. He was powerful, over mighty, had Yorkist blood in his veins. He also hated the King because of Henry's seduction of his sister. Secondly, Buckingham wanted those relics, the Grail and Excalibur. God knows why. Perhaps as curios, perhaps as a talisman he could use in some conspiracy against the King. Thirdly, Buckingham may not have been a traitor but he undoubtedly entertained treasonable thoughts, perhaps was a secret Templar. Fourthly, Hopkins was a conniving priest, a possible Templar, with an open distaste for our King. Fifthly, Taplow the tailor was a Lutheran, also involved in treasonable practices.'

'Such as?' I brusquely interrupted.

'He had tenuous links with Buckingham and also with Master Hopkins. I admit the letters Buckingham supposedly wrote to him were forgeries, as was Taplow's evidence at Buckingham's trial. The poor bastard was tortured so much he would have confessed to anything.'

'So why,' Benjamin asked, 'didn't you allow us to interrogate the real Taplow?'

Mandeville stared through the frosted glass.

'I asked a question, Sir Edmund?'

'Taplow was promised his life if he supported our destruction of Buckingham but in Newgate he began to recant.' This most sinister of spies shrugged. 'For a short time one of my agents took his place.' Mandeville smiled mirthlessly. 'I wondered if it would work. What made you suspect he wasn't the person he claimed to be?'

'Lutherans don't believe in Purgatory, the Taplow we met did.'

Mandeville sniffed disparagingly.

'Did you know Mistress Hopkins was murdered?' Benjamin asked.

Mandeville shook his head. 'We thought she wasn't worth the bother of watching.'

'Well, someone thought she was important and garrotted her. By the way, do you know who killed Warnham and Calcraft?'

'If I did,' Mandeville snapped, 'the murderer would be hanging on the gibbet at Smithfield!'

'So how much of the rest do you think is true?' I asked.

'Oh, the Grail and Excalibur exist. The King is most insistent on that.'

'And the Templars?'

'Oh, yes, we have been hunting them for years. They are a secret organisation existing in cells of six or seven. No single coven knows much about the others but they are powerful, spread like a net through France, Spain, Scotland and England. They are particularly strong here in the South-West.'

'Who is their leader?'

'A Grand Master, but we don't know his name or which country he lives in.'

Mandeville suddenly put his finger to his lips and stepped out of the window embrasure. He looked down to the gallery where the Santerres now stood outside the hall door.

'Sir John,' Mandeville called, 'I should be grateful if you could stay in the hall. Certain questions must be asked.'

'Look,' Benjamin continued, 'why are the King and his agents so interested in this secret society?'

Mandeville waited for the Santerres to withdraw before he answered. 'The Templars are particularly hostile to the King and have supported most of the Yorkist rebellions. They circulate stories about the Princes in the Tower still being alive and, during the present King's father's reign, they supported the two imposters, Lambert Simnel and Perkin Warbeck. If you remember your history, Master Daunbey, you may recall the fiercest rebellions were here in the South-West. When the King was a boy, rebels from the West Country made him flee from the city whilst the pretender, Perkin Warbeck, actually laid siege to Exeter.'

'Is Santerre under suspicion?'

'Yes and no. Santerre has proved to be a most loyal subject of the King but Hopkins served him as a chaplain and Buckingham came here looking for those relics.' Mandeville snorted with laughter. 'Matters are not helped by the two recent murders.'

'And Lady Beatrice? Her maiden name is Belamonte.

Her first husband, Lord of Templecombe, was Sir Roger Mortimer.'

Mandeville shook his head. 'Her loyalty is really beyond question. After all, it was Lady Beatrice who urged Santerre to confess everything about Buckingham to my two agents.'

'And the monks at Glastonbury?'

Mandeville smiled bleakly. 'A pretty mess. Strong links probably existed between the Templars and the abbey. Hopkins was a member of that house and the monks do guard the remains of Arthur whilst this mysterious riddle was found in a manuscript of their library. Mandeville gnawed at his lip. 'I have been honest with you. Now, sir, be truthful with me. What do you know?'

My master described what had happened on the trackway earlier that day.

'Probably members of the Templar coven,' Mandeville commented.

'They could have been responsible for the deaths of Cosmas and Damien,' I added.

'Thus we must resolve the matter,' Benjamin declared. 'The servants of this house could, one or all, be either the assassins or in their pay.'

'We shall deal with them in the morning,' Mandeville snapped.

'There's something else,' Benjamin continued. 'Sir Edmund, we must solve the riddle. Yet, as far as I can see, this house or the chapel have nothing even vaguely resembling the waters of Jordan or Moses' Ark.' He shrugged apologetically. 'I have wandered round the galleries but there's no painting or carving to arouse my curiosity. Only two other places remain: Glastonbury Abbey and the desolate building on that lonely island in the middle of the lake.'

'When we were at Glastonbury,' Mandeville answered, stroking the side of his face, 'I told the abbot to send one of his lay brothers to Taunton with a message for the sheriff to bring armed men to Templecombe. I expect them tomorrow morning. Once they have arrived we will interrogate the servants, cross to the island as well as hunt down that bloody witch.'

'And the two murders?' I asked. 'Do we have any further evidence?'

'Nothing,' Benjamin replied quickly. 'One man dies in his bed which mysteriously catches fire. Another is killed by a crossbow bolt but the only door is bolted and the windows shuttered. We have established the assassin had been tramping round in the snow, yet Lady Beatrice and Rachel are wearing the same clothes as they were this morning and, as far as I know, never left the house.'

'Both of you did,' Mandeville tartly replied.

'But why should we kill Damien? Others were in the house.'

Mandeville caught Benjamin's steady glance. 'Well, before you ask me, Master Daunbey, I stayed here, though Southgate did leave to ride the estate.'

He tilted his head and stared down the gallery. 'And, of course,' he whispered, 'there is always Sir John Santerre.'

I looked sharply at my master. He tugged his ear lobe, our agreed sign for the other to remain silent. Benjamin did not fully trust Mandeville and was unwilling to admit that Sir John Santerre might have gone to Glastonbury.

Our meeting then broke up, Mandeville stalking back into the hall whilst we returned to our chambers. Benjamin became lost in his own thoughts so I left him alone and lay on my own bed thinking about Mathilda until the bell sounded for supper.

Despite the rich food, the meal was a sombre affair. Benjamin tried his best to make light conversation but Mandeville and Southgate were withdrawn, Sir John Santerre lost in his own thoughts, Lady Beatrice looked anxious whilst the pale-faced Rachel merely toyed with her food. Once the table had been cleared and everyone was preparing to leave, my master suddenly stood up.

'This house must be searched,' he declared. 'Every room, every closet.'

'What for?' Mandeville asked.

'I don't really know though I will when I see it.'

Santerre bristled with rage.

'You may accompany us,' Benjamin added softly.

'Must it be now?' Lady Beatrice asked.

'I agree,' Mandeville insisted. 'Either now or tomorrow when Sir Henry Bowyer will arrive with armed men from Taunton.'

Sir John flinched. 'Is that necessary?'

'Yes, I sent the message when I was at Glastonbury. The sheriff's men will be able to assist us. Now, after the death of two of my colleagues, I need them for my own protection. Anyway, I am sure you prefer myself and Master Daunbey to search the house rather than clod-hopping shire levies?'

Sir John did not demur but insisted that he join us. Servants were called, torches and lamps brought and we began our search. Believe me, Templecombe proved to be an even larger house than I thought. The cellars were huge and cavernous but contained nothing remarkable; beer barrels, wine tuns, cut logs, sea coal and other stores. At the far end of the cellar, we found one chamber where the door was padlocked and barred. Santerre hastened to open it but told us not to bring any torches in.

'Gunpowder and oil are stored here,' he explained. 'We use it for taking rock from the local quarries.'

The door was opened and I went in. The room was nothing more than a dry, musty cell. Benjamin followed, studying the coiled slow fuses, jars of oil and small barrels of gunpowder piled there. He cocked his head to one side and I could see that something had caught his attention.

'What is it, Master?'

'Nothing, nothing at all.'

We continued our search and, I tell you this, if any place was haunted, it was Templecombe, particularly those cellars. We then returned upstairs, going from room to room, only to discover nothing untoward.

At last Mandeville himself called off the search, rubbing his eyes and yawning.

'We have done what we can,' he commented. 'Tomorrow we search the church and cross to the island.'

Benjamin objected. 'There are still the servants' quarters.'

Mandeville made a face. 'Let the sheriff's men deal with them. Sufficient unto the day is the evil thereof.'

We returned to our chambers, Benjamin joining me in mine. He sat on the edge of the bed and began to recite all he knew as if memorising some poem: 'Buckingham dies, the agents die, garrotted to death.' He looked up. 'Did you know you can garrotte someone in a few seconds?'

'Is that relevant?' I asked. I felt so tired I just wanted to go to sleep.

'No. No,' Benjamin murmured absentmindedly. 'Then we come here and a witch warns us, prophesying death by various means. Cosmas is burnt to death in his bed; Damien killed by a mysterious archer who apparently can pass through thick walls, but there's no clue to the riddle, no sign of the Templars and not a shred of evidence to indicate where the Grail or Excalibur lie.' He rubbed his chin. 'But there must be a solution. Perhaps the sheriff's men will help.'

Chapter 10

We were awakened the next morning by Sir Henry Bowyer's rough arrival accompanied by at least a dozen likely-looking rogues. These were not shire levies but professional soldiers who acted as the sheriff's posse in the pursuit of criminals. Bowyer was a short, squat man with very little hair and a cheery red face. He was always smiling and greeted us most amicably as we broke our fast in the great hall.

Nevertheless, he was a man you wouldn't trust. He had piss-holes as eyes, foul breath, decaying teeth and an attitude towards Mandeville which can only be described as servile. The sort of man whose head has been turned by success and left him staring in the wrong direction.

Bowyer's troopers, as professional soldiers are wont, soon made themselves at home in the courtyard and outhouses: within an hour, Sir John was receiving complaints of food being stolen from the kitchen; jugs of wine mysteriously emptying; and chickens, full of life the night before, suddenly being killed, plucked and spitted over makeshift fires. Santerre, however, had problems of his own as Mandeville, assisted by Southgate and a servile Bowyer, had the great hall cleared and turned into a shire court. He and Bowyer sat at the high table, the Santerres and ourselves were treated as onlookers. Mandeville then gathered all the servants, cooks, scullions, chambermaids, Mathilda included, even the men from the stables. He addressed them in short, pithy sentences and promptly began his interrogation of each of them.

'How long have you served here?' 'Does the word "Templar" mean anything to you?' 'Did anyone approach the chapel yesterday afternoon?'

The servants were good but simple people, local peasants who simply shook their heads and stared wide-eyed at this powerful lord from London. Nevertheless, I admired Mandeville's skill for, as he questioned, I caught the unease of some of them. Nothing really significant: a flicker of the eyes, a slight paleness of the face. Answers given too quickly and too readily. Mathilda herself was very ill-at-ease, shifting from foot to foot. Mandeville sensed this and closed like a hawk for the kill.

'You are the linen maid?'

Mathilda nodded.

'Aren't you curious about these strangers staying in your master's house?'

She shook her head.

'So you have not abused your position by searching our belongings?'

Mathilda's eyes flickered quickly towards me.

'No, Master,' she murmured.

'I can vouch for that,' I exclaimed. 'The girl didn't know I was in my room when she was changing the linen. She's the complete opposite to me, Sir Edmund, honest as the day is long.'

Benjamin looked strangely at me but a ripple of laughter lessened the tension and Mathilda was dismissed. The others came up. Mandeville asked the questions, or sometimes Southgate. Occasionally, to show his power, the sheriff would try to hector, though Mandeville kept him firmly under control. At last it was finished but before the servants were dismissed, Mandeville ordered their quarters to be searched. Sir John and Lady Beatrice vehemently objected to this, so Benjamin offered to supervise the soldiers and ensure it was not used as a pretext for theft or pillage.

This search, like the questioning, proved fruitless so Mandeville brusquely dismissed the servants. I watched them leave, paying particular attention to Mathilda and how she held the arm of a grizzle-haired, thickset man who appeared to be her father. I noticed he had a slight limp; I recalled the attack on me the previous day and the wounds I had unwittingly inflicted, but decided to keep the matter to myself. After that we made a thorough search of the chapel, its walls, flagstones and altar, but there was nothing. We even looked under the ancient stalls the Templars once sat in, and I confess (as is the wont of old Shallot) I did little work but spent most of the time admiring the brilliant carvings on the misericord of each stall. The first three enthralled me: a man, miserably clutching a winding frame, being birched on the buttocks by his wife; a tapster drinking; and two peasants disembowelling a slaughtered pig. Each carving was a breath-taking picture in itself. Benjamin came over to join me.

'The Templars,' he declared, 'would come into the stalls and raise the seats. The carvings were placed on the reverse, not only for ornamentation's sake but to make the seats heavier.' He grinned and pointed to the woman birching her husband. 'The local craftsmen always enjoyed themselves, depicting scenes far from sacred.'

Mandeville, however, had finished his search which proved just as fruitless as the previous day's and told us to leave. We all moved out of the church down to the lake which glistened brightly, though the island itself was still mist-shrouded. A number of barges were hidden in the trees along the lakeside and Mandeville and Santerre ordered these to be brought together. They were cleaned of frozen mud, made ready, and we all clambered aboard, Bowyer's soldiers poling us across.

God be my witness, that island was the most mysterious I had ever visited. It was damp, cold, eerie and uncanny. The trees were too close together and the snow-covered gorse seemed to have a life of its own, blocking our passage with its thick stems. We struggled through, soaking ourselves to the skin.

'Have you noticed anything?' Benjamin breathlessly whispered. He stopped and looked up at the tangle of gaunt branches above him. 'No birds here! No rooks, no crows, nothing at all!'

I stopped and listened, straining my ears for any sound above the crashing of the soldiers or the muttered curses as men slipped on the icy ground underfoot. This raucous noise only seemed to emphasize the ominous silence of the island and reminded me of a story I had heard from a traveller who claimed to have sailed the Western Ocean and come across islands inhabited by ghosts of dead sailors. I shivered and muttered a curse. Mandeville and the others had now drawn their swords and were cutting their way through. The *Agentes*, in particular, seemed to be affected by the oppressive mood of the island and were taking out their fears in the hacking blows of their swords.

At last we reached a clearing and the desolate building we had glimpsed from the shore. It was of yellowing sandstone with a dark, red-tiled roof, no windows but thin, trefoil arrow slits in the walls. The iron-studded door was padlocked. Santerre apologised, he had no key, so Southgate hacked the padlock off and kicked the door open. We walked in and torches were lit. Believe me, the sombre atmosphere of that place seemed a living thing which clutched the heart and dulled the spirit. Nothing in particular, just a yawning emptiness, a cold chilling air which had little to do with the ice and snow outside.

'A home of death,' I muttered.

'Or a very sacred place,' Benjamin replied.

Mandeville ordered the soldiers to stand round the walls, taking their torches which spluttered bravely against the darkness. I had the almost childish impression that if we kept within the pools of light everything would be fine but, beyond the flames, shadows lurked and powers even darker waited to catch you by the throat. The floor was hard paving stone, the walls lime-washed, the room devoid of even a stick of furniture.

The soldiers grew uneasy and grumbled amongst themselves so Mandeville shouted at them to begin the search. Those men were professional foragers and, if there was a loose paving stone or secret passageway, they would have found it, but there was nothing. Benjamin, however, just squatted, moving like a spider from one paving stone to another. He stopped, exclaiming in surprise, so we gathered round as he scraped the floor with his finger.

'Candle grease,' he observed. 'Someone has been here and fairly recently.'

Other drops were found but nothing else so Mandeville ordered us to resume our search. I kept a wary eye on Santerre for this bluff manor lord, usually afraid of nothing, stayed near the door like a child frightened of a dark, strange room.

'Is anything wrong?' I asked.

Santerre shook his head but his face was pallid and I saw the beads of sweat on his cheeks.

'What is it?' I muttered.

The soldiers pushed by us, eager to get out. Santerre just shook his head.

'Nothing,' he muttered.

'Are you sure?' Benjamin asked, coming up beside him.

Again Santerre nodded. Benjamin looked up at the white-washed wall above the door. He waited until the rest had left.

'Sir John, I think something is very wrong and

Mandeville, in his haste, has overlooked it.'

Santerre just stared at him.

'It's the walls,' Benjamin continued. 'They have been recently white-washed. Now why was that done, eh?'

'I don't know,' Santerre mumbled and trudged off to join the others.

We crossed back to the other bank, Mandeville striding away from the barge, shouting orders at Southgate. A cart pulled out from the courtyard, driven by a soldier taking the two coffins down to the village church where the priest would sing a requiem and those two pathetic brothers be buried and, in time, forgotten. Mandeville made ready to follow. The pompous Bowyer was ordered to stay at the manor but Sir Edmund waved us over.

'You will come with us to Glastonbury, though first we have one further task to accomplish.'

He refused to say any more so we collected riding boots, hats and cloaks from our chambers. A white-faced Mathilda sped by me in the gallery but Benjamin was shouting for me so I decided not to accost her. We collected our horses, took leave of Santerre and galloped down the frozen, cobbled track as if Mandeville intended to waste no time in reaching Glastonbury before nightfall. We rode a good way along the track before Mandeville slowed, leaned over and talked quietly to Southgate. Eventually they reined in.

Southgate declared, 'Yes, this is the spot,' and I realised we were going witch-hunting. We dismounted. One soldier was ordered to guard the horses whilst another, a lean whippet of a man with leathery skin and sea-blue eyes, was beckoned over by Mandeville. Sir Edmund grasped the soldier by the shoulder and introduced him.

'Bowyer calls this man Pointer because he is a skilled hunter. If anyone can find his way through the tracks and forest paths to where that hag lives, Pointer will!'

The man grinned wolfishly, showing jagged teeth. He

was well named. I have seen better looking hunting dogs. Mandeville fished in his purse and brought out a silver coin, rolling it in his fingers. Pointer watched it greedily.

'Find this old bitch's hut and two of these are yours.'

Pointer needed no further encouragement and I was too intrigued to object to floundering through the frozen bracken. Pointer set off through the trees with a loping stride. God knows how he did, they were clumped together and the undergrowth beneath made more treacherous by a carpet of snow. On no occasion did Pointer seem bemused or in doubt but led us on, disregarding the ankle-deep snow and the sudden flurries and falls from over-hanging branches.

(On reflection, men like Pointer are not so rare. Once, in the wild dark woods of Muscovy, I was hunted by men and dogs in one of the most terrifying escapades of my life. I had been invited to a banquet by some mad Russian prince. What I didn't know was that I was the entertainment afterwards! Before the hunt began, the mad bastard told me that if the yellow-haired mastiffs did not tear me to pieces, I'd be pulled apart by horses. You can be assured I needed no further encouragement to run on that occasion, but that's another tale.)

Now I dislike the countryside at the height of summer, but that forest was bewitched. I protested loudly against the darkness, nature's traps and, above all, kept thinking of those assailants who'd attacked me yesterday.

'A natural place for an ambush,' I cried.

Mandeville grinned and wiped the sweat from his face.

'That's why I told no one back at the manor of our visit. I want to give this old bitch the surprise of her life.'

At last the trees gave way to a clearing. At the far end was a small rocky hillock as if huge boulders had been jammed together by the hand of some mythical giant. At the base of this cliff was a large cavern. Mandeville drew his sword and we followed suit, though God knows what we expected to find. We strode cautiously across as if the old hag might appear at the mouth of the cave, uttering curses and dire prophecies, yet everything remained silent.

Benjamin stopped and pointed to the entrance. There had been a light snowfall the previous night but it looked as if someone else had been here, visited the witch then gone back to the line of trees, covering their tracks by using a switch of old branches so no imprint could be seen. We entered the cave. The fire which should have flared at the entrance was a pile of wet ash and the oil-topped torches were extinguished. Mandeville lit one of these and we went deeper in.

A strange place – carvings on the wall which, Benjamin explained, must be centuries old. The cave itself was surprisingly warm and we realised we were walking through a gallery which led us into a lofty underground cavern. It was furnished like any room. The rushes on the floor were clean and sprinkled with herbs. A cooking pot hung on a tripod though the logs beneath were now blackened cinders. I glimpsed a chest and coffer, table and stool. In the far corner was a bed and, beside this, slumped like a disused doll, lay the witch. Benjamin hastened over and grasped the woman's shoulder.

She turned, arms flailing, head back, eyes open – but the gaping mouth would utter no more prophecies, her breath cut off by the red garrotte cord round her scrawny neck.

Mandeville just cursed and lashed out, sending a stool flying. Southgate crouched by my master and felt the nape of the old woman's neck, trying to ignore those staring, popping eyes.

'She's been dead for hours,' he commented. 'Her skin's cold as a dead snake's.'

He got up and wiped his hands. 'Sir Edmund, the old witch apparently played her part and now she, too, has been removed.'

'I agree,' Benjamin replied.

'But who killed her?' Mandeville snapped.

'I suspect the same people or person responsible for the murders of Cosmas and Damien, not to mention your agents in London.'

Benjamin pointed at the grotesque corpse. 'She was only a paid player, a silly old woman. The murderer knew we would make her talk. She may have been killed any time in the last two days.'

'You mean someone from Templecombe?' Southgate asked.

'Possibly,' Benjamin replied. 'One of the family, or a servant, or perhaps by the Templars themselves.' My master shrugged. 'We are strangers and how long did it take us – ten to fifteen minutes – to come here? Yet there must be secret routes and trackways into the forest. The murderer probably came by these, killed the old woman and went back, making sure he removed all trace of his movements.'

We could do nothing further. Mandeville said he would report the woman's death when we returned to Templecombe and so we continued our cold journey through the bleak Somerset countryside. We arrived at Glastonbury just after dark. The trackways were nigh impassable, the weather so icy we could hardly talk, and Mandeville shouted with relief when the walls of Glastonbury came into sight.

A lay brother let us in through a postern gate where others took care of our horses and baggage. Once again Abbot Bere came to greet us in the guest house, accompanied by a monk who had been absent at our earlier meeting. A vigorous young man, ruddy-faced and bright-eyed, he was scholarly and courteous. I liked him, whilst he and Benjamin struck up an immediate rapport.

'This is Brother Eadred, our archivist and librarian,' Abbot Bere declared. 'He will assist you in your enquiries. He knows our manuscript room like the palm of his own hand and is a *peritus*, an expert in Arthurian life.'

'Did you know Hopkins?' Southgate brusquely enquired, taking off his coat and shaking the damp from it.

'Yes,' replied Eadred. 'Brother Hopkins was a man not at peace with himself or his order. He was not a historian but a collector of legends. He found our monastic rule hard to bear so spent every second he could in the library.'

Eadred patted the old abbot gently on the shoulder. 'Reverend Father did all he could for Brother Hopkins. He arranged for him to be released from his vows and work as a chaplain in Templecombe and the surrounding villages and hamlets.' The librarian's face broke into a boyish smile. 'He wasn't even good at that: he claimed he had found the key to mysterious secrets and hastened off to tell My Lord of Buckingham.' He became solemn. 'In the end Hopkins destroyed himself and others, and brought the King's wrath down on this community and elsewhere.' He stared squarely at the *Agentes*. 'Though, I tell you this, sirs, John Santerre is a loyal subject of the King.'

I bit back my questions as Mandeville began to list what he wished to see the following morning: Arthur's tomb; the manuscript in which Hopkins had found the riddle; and any other matter the reverend Abbot and Brother Eadred thought might assist us in our search.

Eadred coolly agreed, informed us that food would be sent across and bade us all a courteous good night.

'I don't like him,' Southgate grated as soon as the monks left. 'I don't like this abbey and I think there's some sort of link between this place and Sir John Santerre.'

'Why?' I challenged. 'What proof do you have?'

'Well, after Sir Edmund finished his interrogation this morning, I had a word with a few of the servants, men from the outlying farms. Santerre apparently did not go round his estates yesterday as he claimed. So where was he, eh?'

We kept our mouths shut and Mandeville and Southgate stomped away. We made ourselves at home, ate the simple food sent across to us from the refectory and retired to bed.

Early the next morning Benjamin attended mass in the abbey church then roused me. We breakfasted in the small refectory of the abbot's guest house on light ale and spiced oatmeal heated with boiling milk. Mandeville and Southgate joined us, the soldiers who had accompanied us being billeted elsewhere. The two *Agentes* were full of themselves, eager to exert their power in this famous abbey so, when Brother Eadred joined us, Mandeville insisted that we go straight to the library.

We left the guest house, going through stone-vaulted passageways into the cloister garth. The study carrels were empty because of the cold weather: snow and ice covered the deserted garden though from the abbey church we could hear the faint chanting of Lauds.

We found the library wondrously warm, being ingeniously heated by hot pipes which also gushed water into the latrines. I remember this well for I have never seen the like since.

I did, however, discuss such a marvel with Sir John Harrington, the Queen's nephew, who has since devised an ingenious system to build a water closet so that privies and latrines can be cleaned by pulling a chain and releasing water. Very clumsy, though I've had one installed here at Burpham.

Of course, Benjamin was at home in the library, exclaiming with delight at the smell of parchment, pumice stone, ink and newly treated vellum. He took down volumes from the shelves, undid their clasps and, chattering like a child, pointed out the beauty of the calligraphy. Some letters were pictures in themselves, containing miniature dragons, wyverns, centaurs and other mythical beasts. Mandeville and Southgate just stood watching patronisingly until Sir Edmund clicked his fingers.

'I want to see the Hopkins manuscripts.'

169

Eadred stared at him in mock innocence. 'No such books exist, Sir Edmund.'

'Don't play games with me!' Mandeville snarled. 'I don't know the bloody title but I wish to see the ones Hopkins studied!'

'Oh, you mean the *Legends of Avalon*?'

Eadred went and opened a great, iron-bound coffer and brought out a thick folio, leather bound and fastened by two small clasps. He placed this gently down on the table and we all gathered round.

'It's not really a book,' Eadred explained. 'It's actually a collection of legends about Glastonbury and this area.'

'And what did Hopkins find?'

Mandeville undid the clasps and pulled back the leather cover. At first we couldn't see anything on the white backing but then Eadred brought across a candle, held it near the page, not quite close enough to scorch, and sea-green writing began to appear.

'A subtle device,' Eadred murmured. 'God knows how it is done.'

Time and again he wafted the candle flame and, for a while, the writing became quite distinct. Benjamin borrowed a quill and a piece of parchment and copied the verse down, word for word. It was no different from that Agrippa had quoted:

'Beneath Jordan's water Christ's cup does rest,
And above Moses' Ark the sword that's best.'

Mandeville chanted it like a child learning a rhyme.

'What the hell does it mean?' he added.

Eadred invited us to sit round the table.

'How did Hopkins discover this?' Benjamin asked.

The monk spread his hands. 'Perhaps an accident because, though the manuscript contains famous legends, there's nothing new in it. What I suspect is that he was inspecting the binding and moved the candle to study it more closely to see if there was a gap between the cover and its backing: underneath the candle flame the writing must have appeared.' Eadred pointed to the white page where the lettering was beginning to fade. 'I was here when Hopkins discovered it. He didn't tell me but became so agitated and excited, he left the book open with faint drops of candle grease on it. I repeated what I had seen him do. The rest you know.'

Mandeville leaned over and tapped the book. 'And there's nothing else in here?'

'Nothing at all.'

'Then,' Mandeville leaned towards Southgate, 'my colleague here who is an expert in secret writing, codes and ciphers, will take this to another table and study it carefully.'

I looked at Southgate in mock surprise. 'You can read!' I exclaimed. 'You can truly read?'

Well, that got the bastard really enraged.

'I studied at Oriel!' he snapped. 'Theology, Philosophy, Logic and Mathematics!'

'Then I beg your pardon, sir.' I slapped my own wrist. 'It just goes to show you shouldn't judge a book by its cover, eh?'

Southgate picked up the manuscript and stalked away. Mandeville glared at me whilst Eadred and Benjamin seemed preoccupied with their fingers.

'This is no laughing matter, Shallot,' Sir Edmund declared. 'Brother Eadred, on your allegiance to the King, do you know the meaning of Hopkins's riddle?'

'Before God, Sir Edmund, I do not!'

'Is there anything in this abbey that has even the vaguest reference to Jordan's water or the Ark of Moses?'

Eadred smoothed the table top with his fingers. 'The Jordan is a river in Palestine,' he replied. 'What in God's

171

name, Sir Edmund, would that have to do with an abbey in Somerset? And as for the Ark of Moses, this was the sacred chest fashioned at the foot of Mount Sinai to contain the sacred tablets of stone. Where on earth would that be?'

Sir Edmund was not easily put off.

'Yet you have a rose bush,' he retorted. 'Which, you claim, was planted by Joseph of Arimathea. Don't play games with me, dear monk. Your abbey proudly proclaims that this Joseph of Arimathea came here, bringing the Grail with him. According to the book of legends you have just shown us, Arthur came here to drink from the Grail, whilst one of his knights, Sir Bedivere, reputedly took Excalibur down to Narepool which is only three miles from Glastonbury. This is still owned by the abbey and, according to the annual accounts you submit to the exchequer, provides 5,000 eels a year for your kitchen.'

Sir Edmund half-raised himself from his seat and pointed a finger straight at the monk's face. 'Before God, sir,' he threatened hoarsely. 'If I find even the vaguest reference to an Ark or to Jordan's water in this abbey or any place in your possession, I shall see you stand trial at King's Bench in London on a charge of high treason!'

'Then, Sir Edmund,' Eadred replied coolly, 'discover such evidence.'

Mandeville shoved back his chair and walked to the door.

'I shall inspect this abbey myself!' he shouted over his shoulder. 'Southgate, when you have finished with that manuscript, look around carefully.' He left, slamming the door behind him.

Eadred seemed unmoved by Mandeville's threats.

'Perhaps we should go,' he whispered, glancing sidelong at Southgate who sat poring over the book. 'Sir Edmund does not believe me, yet he'll find nothing in this abbey or elsewhere.'

We left the library, went round the north part of the

church and into the abbey church through the Lady Chapel, now covered in sheets and dust.

'Abbot Bere,' Eadred explained, 'is now digging a crypt. This will run under the Lady Chapel and Galilee porch.'

He pulled the sheets aside and led us down some steps. The crypt was a high vaulted room, the roof being supported by thin ribs of stone which spread out from the centre, giving the impression of a bursting star. The crypt was not yet finished and, strangely enough, was the only place in that entire abbey where Eadred seemed rather nervous and unwilling to linger. We then returned to the Galilee porch, past another small chapel and into the great white-stoned nave. We examined the north and south transepts, went under the ornate rood screen and into the sanctuary beneath which lay Arthur's tomb.

'Is there any way,' Benjamin asked, 'that the tomb can be reached?'

Eadred shook his head. 'Of course not. The coffin is sealed in a great vault below. Only the Holy Father can give permission for such a tomb to be opened.' Eadred spread his hands. 'And why should it be opened? The Grail and Excalibur were seen centuries after Arthur's death and the monks who reinterred his body here would scarcely bury such sacred relics.'

We agreed and continued our tour out of the church, following the snow-covered, pebbled paths past the Chapter House, dormitory, rear dorter, monks' kitchen, into the abbot's garden; the latter was enclosed by a high brick wall and carpeted by snow but in the summer must have been beautiful. My eyes, however, were continuously drawn to the great Tor which loomed high above the abbey and the small church of St Michael on its summit.

'Could that contain anything?' I asked.

Eadred smiled and shook his head. 'Everyone who comes here thinks that, yet compared to the abbey, the church is

173

quite new. You are welcome to go there but your climb would be fruitless. I strongly recommend that we leave such arduous duties to your two companions, who will undoubtedly have asked themselves the same question.'

Chapter 11

We returned to the guest house, Eadred ordering mulled wine from the kitchen to warm us. He and Benjamin soon became immersed in a discussion on alchemy and the philosopher's stone: the librarian also offered to take my master to see Narepool at the bottom of which, according to legend, Arthur's Sword still lay. I became bored and wandered back to the library.

Thankfully, Southgate had gone. Some of the brothers were busy in the scriptorium but I was greeted courteously and no one objected when I began to leaf through the manuscript Southgate had left upon the table.

Brother Eadred was correct. The manuscript contained a collection of writings describing the legends of Glastonbury, Avalon, Arthur, the forging of Excalibur, and even the fanciful story of how, when Christ was a boy, Joseph of Arimathea brought him to Glastonbury to buy tin and precious oils from the natives. The book also contained writings on topographical and biblical matters of a general nature; one entry caught my eye. I remembered what Agrippa had told me and a faint suspicion stirred.

I closed the book hastily and sat thinking, trying to apply my discovery to the murderous maze I found myself lost in. I resolved to keep silent on it.

(Oh, excuse me a minute, my little chaplain is jumping up and down, splattering the parchment with ink. 'Tell me!

Tell me!' he whines. 'There are no clues, no indication, no resolution to the mystery.' I pick up my black ash cane and rap him smartly across the knuckles. Hasn't he read the Book of Ecclesiastes? 'There's a time and place under heaven for everything.' So let me tell my tale. The little turd would never dream of standing up during one of Will Shakespeare's plays and shouting, 'Tell us what happens! Tell us what happens!' He would be pelted with fruit. In fact, that's not a bad idea . . . If he's not careful, he'll get my empty wine goblet on the back of his little noddle. Ah well, good, that settled matters.)

Suffice to say we spent two fruitless days at Glastonbury and left as we came with only two scraps of information: first, Hopkins had been a monk at the abbey, and secondly had discovered his famous riddle there. Brother Eadred rode with us for a while, two or three miles from the abbey gates. At the crossroads he bade us adieu and warmly clasped Benjamin's hand. My master then turned to us.

'Please ride on,' he asked, 'all of you. I wish to raise a personal matter with Brother Eadred.'

I was a little hurt, Mandeville outraged.

'What is it?' he spluttered.

'Sir Edmund,' Benjamin quietly insisted, 'it is a matter of conscience, a confessional matter!'

Well, who could object? Sir Edmund made a sign and the soldiers, myself included, followed him further down the track. I looked round and saw my master in earnest conversation with the monk. Whatever he was saying clearly discomfited the librarian. Even from where I stood, I glimpsed Eadred's agitation. After a while Benjamin caught up with us.

'What was it, Master?'

'Not now, Roger,' he whispered.

We continued on our journey to Templecombe. No snow had fallen during our stay at Glastonbury but the sky was growing overcast and threatening. Once we were past the village on the road up to the major, Sir Edmund, recalling my story about the ambush, ordered the soldiers to fan out before us. We made our way slowly. A biting wind tore at our cheeks, turning our fingers to blocks of ice, whilst our horses scrabbled to maintain a secure foothold. Suddenly, just as we rounded the bend and were able to glimpse the gables and turrets of Templecombe above the trees, one of the soldiers came riding back so fast his horse, slithering and clattering on the path, almost crashed into Mandeville's mount.

'What is it, man?' Southgate snarled.

The soldier's face was like a ghost's. The fellow opened his mouth soundlessly and pointed back down the track. Mandeville pushed his horse forward and we rounded the corner. At first, in the fading light, we could see nothing but the icy path, the snow-covered trees on either side – but then the flicker of a candle flame caught our eyes. It seemed to be standing in the snow, a little metal cap protecting it against the biting breeze, but as we approached closer, my stomach turned. Our horses became skittish. Mandeville and Southgate loudly cursed for the dirty white candle was held in the snow by a greyish-green, severed hand.

'Witchcraft!' Mandeville breathed.

'I'm not passing that!' one of the soldiers exclaimed.

'Remove it!' Mandeville ordered Southgate.

'In this matter, Sir Edmund, I would prefer not to act.'

'Come on, Roger,' Benjamin ordered.

We both dismounted and went to examine the obscenity. The hand was decomposing, the bloody stump of its wrist had turned into a black, congealed mess. The nails were discoloured, the fingers beginning to flake. The breeze shifted and we caught the stench of putrefaction.

'What is it?' Benjamin asked.

(Oh, I knew what it was! Even though I was still an

177

innocent youth, Old Shallot had met the most fierce and sinister of warlocks, magicians and witches: men who used dark powers to unhinge the mind of their opponents. You take Shallot's advice on this: the power of witchcraft lies in what you can make other people think. I recently recounted such a theory when I met Will Shakespeare and Richard Burbage at the Globe. Old Will, God bless his kind eyes, was really taken with the idea: in a play he is now busily writing, he has a scene where witches, on a blasted heath in Scotland, put insidious ideas into the mind of a murderous nobleman called Macbeth.)

On that frozen trackway, however, I just stared at the grotesque thing lying in the snow; the hand seemed to be thrusting up through the earth as if some ghoul was struggling to rise from its grave.

'It's the Hand of Glory,' I explained.

Benjamin looked puzzled.

'A powerful talisman, Master,' I continued. 'The witch cuts the hand from a murdered man then fashions a candle out of human grease which is lighted and put into the hand. It's a way of calling up demons, a curse as well as a warning.'

Benjamin edged nearer. 'Do you think it works?'

I shrugged. 'Oh, I could call Satan up from hell, Master.'

Benjamin glared at me.

'But whether he'd come is another matter.'

(I once said the same thing to Will Shakespeare and, sure enough, it's in one of his plays. I think it's *Henry IV Part 1*, where Hotspur and Glendower are talking about magic.)

'Well,' Benjamin got to his feet, 'if it comes from hell, it can go back there!' And he kicked both the candle and the hand into the undergrowth. The flames sizzled out as Mandeville and Southgate dismounted and joined us. Both he and his companion looked pale and I could see all joy had gone out of their task. Mandeville stared into the darkness then up at the rooks cawing around us.

178

'This place is hell-touched!' he murmured, kicking the snow where the Hand of Glory had lain. 'Perhaps we should leave it, go back to London and return in the spring with soldiers?' He chewed his lip. 'I could deploy all my agents in the area, root out what is really going on.'

'And what will the King say?' Benjamin asked quietly. 'Above all, what will my dear uncle think if we now return, empty-handed, to report the deaths of Cosmas and Damien? I want justice, Sir Edmund, and you want vengeance. Murder is like a game of hazard. So far this silent assassin has won every throw, but sooner or later he will make a mistake.'

(It just shows you how times have changed. God rest them, Mandeville and Southgate could be wicked men, true minions of the King. Nevertheless, they had some kind of conscience. Not like Walsingham and the next generation of spies and 'agents provocateurs'. You take a man like Christopher Marlowe: I was with him when he was murdered in that private house. He and his killers, men like Frizier and Skeres, not to mention Poley, were devils incarnate who feared neither God nor man. Poor Kit! A bad man but a brilliant poet. He died far too young.)

We continued on our return to Templecombe. The Santerres were waiting for us with Bowyer who looked as if he had really settled in, shirt open at the collar, stubby feet enclosed in buskins whilst his fat face was flushed with drink and his breath smelt like a wine press. He and Sir John now appeared to be bosom friends and I secretly wondered if the Santerres had suborned this bumbling servant of the crown. Mandeville, however, was not at all pleased and gave the sheriff a scathing look.

'Was your visit to Glastonbury profitable?' Sir John asked as we warmed ourselves before the great fire whilst Lady Beatrice and Rachel served spiced wine.

Mandeville just muttered a curse and Southgate would

have launched a vitriolic attack upon the abbey if Sir Edmund had not told him to shut up and drink his wine. Sir John, full of himself, tried to humour them.

'Tomorrow,' he said, 'let us take a break from affairs of state. There have been no fresh falls of snow and I know where my dogs could rouse a fine hart.'

Bowyer and Southgate immediately brightened at the prospect of a good hunt. Even Mandeville agreed and, from the discussion which followed, I gathered both agents were keen huntsmen with an inordinate love of the chase. I also wondered if Sir John Santerre, despite his bluff bonhomie, was skilled and well-versed in seeking out a man's weakness and pandering to it. Had he sought mine out? I wondered. Had Mathilda been deliberately sent to my room?

I stared at Rachel, whose fawnlike eyes were now smiling at Benjamin. Did she, too, play a role? Were we all being bought off? I with Mathilda, Benjamin with Rachel, Bowyer with good food and drink, and the *Agentes* with the prospect of a good day's hunting. I remembered Mandeville's words as we approached the house. Was the sinister influence of the Temple beginning to work its effect?

Now, I tell you this, I am a rogue born and bred. I have great difficulty in distinguishing between my property and anyone else's, or at least I used to, but I do not like to be dismissed as stupid. True, we had discovered nothing at Glastonbury or of why Cosmas and Damien had been killed. I stared around. Bowyer was drunk, Benjamin lost in his own thoughts or seduced by Rachel's flattery, Mandeville and Southgate were revelling in the manor's hospitality whilst Santerre, whose conduct was suspicious to say the least, played the role of smiling host.

I slammed down my cup and stood up. Bowyer's and Southgate's conversation about the coming hunt faltered and died as I went to stand and warm my backside against the fire.

'Roger?' Benjamin looked at me, puzzled. 'What is the matter?'

I glared round. 'I'm tired,' I began. 'I'm cold and I'm exhausted.' I held my hand up, fingers splayed, and counted the points off like a teacher in front of a group of scholars. 'Cosmas is dead. Damien is dead.' I stared at Santerre. 'The old witch is dead. If you send men into the forest you will find her frozen corpse in that cave she called her home. Finally, on our return from Glastonbury, we were threatened with witchcraft.'

Santerre exclaimed in surprise. Bowyer looked at me drunkenly. I glared at Benjamin and the *Agentes*.

'Well, aren't you going to tell him?'

'Roger,' Benjamin intervened, 'it's best if you keep a still tongue in your head.'

'Bollocks!' I replied. 'As we came up the trackway of your house, Sir John, we found a Hand of Glory with a lighted candle in its fingers.'

The Santerres just stared, open-mouthed, back at me.

'I'm bloody frightened!' I bawled. 'In the stinking alleys and runnels of Southwark and Whitefriars, the Hand of Glory is a powerful talisman, a warning to us all. Someone here wishes our deaths. Someone at Templecombe or on the estates around. And I for one don't intend to play coney in the hay!'

I stalked out of the hall, quite pleased with myself, and went back to my own chamber. A few minutes later Benjamin joined me. He slipped through the door and pulled up a stool as I lay on the bed.

'Roger, why the outburst?'

I propped myself up on my elbow and looked at him.

'Outside, it's dark, cold and more snow has fallen. Bowyer's drunk as a lord, Mandeville and Southgate are scared, whilst you seem more absorbed in Rachel than anything else.'

Benjamin smiled and shuffled his feet. 'Is that the problem, Roger? Are you jealous?'

I threw myself back on the bed with a laugh. He grabbed my wrist.

'Tell me why you spoke Roger? You usually keep a still tongue in your head. The dutiful, sharp-witted servant who sees all and says nothing.'

I just stared up into the darkness. 'Perhaps you are right, Master, but I *am* frightened. We are threatened, attacked, two of our companions murdered. We go chasing around this frozen, benighted countryside and discover nothing. Yes, I wish Rachel would look at me as she does at you.' I gazed at him beseechingly. 'But here I'm like a duck out of water, Master. If these were the alleyways of Paris or the runnels of London I could hide or strike back. But what happens if we have been sent here to die, one by one?'

Benjamin shivered and folded his arms. 'We have found something,' he replied. 'I saw the look on your face as we left Glastonbury.'

'What did Eadred tell you?' I countered.

'I asked why Sir John Santerre had such close links with Glastonbury?'

'And?'

'At first Eadred tried to bluff, claiming Sir John was a local landowner, but then he confessed that Santerre was funding Abbot Bere's construction of the crypt but told me if I wished to know more, I should ask either Sir John or the abbot. So,' Benjamin smiled, 'what did you find, Roger?'

I told him of my discovery. Now, perhaps it was the poor light but Benjamin's face paled. (Excuse me for a minute, my little clerk is again insisting I furnish such clues immediately. No I will not! As Shakespeare says, 'Every tale has its own metre and beat.' He'll have to wait!) I'll be honest, at the time, I did not recognise the true value of my discovery but Benjamin did.

'Master,' I begged, 'does it mean anything to you?'

'Yes and no,' Benjamin slowly replied. 'When we searched Templecombe's rooms a vague suspicion of how Cosmas died occurred to me. I also thought of something in the church the afternoon Damien was killed.' He narrowed his eyes and shook his head. 'But they are only pieces, Roger. By themselves they mean nothing.'

He left me to sulk until a servant came to announce dinner was ready. I went down to the hall and found Santerre still intent on lavishing hospitality on his guests. The high table was covered in a silk sheet cloth, the best glass and silver had been laid out, whilst the savoury smells from the kitchen and scullery teased our nostrils and mouths with the sweet fragrance of roast duck, meat pies, quince tarts and the sugary odour of fresh marchpane.

Santerre had changed into a doublet and hose of grey-silver whilst his wife and daughter both looked resplendent in gowns of blue satin trimmed with gold. Santerre bubbled like a stream in spring. He assured the drunken Bowyer that he would always be welcome at Templecombe and I recalled the friendship formed between Pilate and Herod. Southgate was in his cups though Mandeville looked sub-dued and stared speculatively at me as if my outburst had revealed a side of my character he had not noticed before.

The meal was almost over and I had downed at least four deep-bowled cups of claret when the small red stain appeared on the table cloth. At first, I thought it was spilt wine but then it spread and I noticed little splashes coming down from the ceiling above. I gazed up into the darkness but the rafters were cloaked in blackness.

You've drunk too much, I thought, but then Benjamin noticed the spreading pool and splattered drops.

'Look!' he cried, pointing to the widening scarlet stain. The chatter and laughter died down. We all sat watching the drops fall and the scarlet blot widen. Benjamin was the first to recover his wits, standing up and pushing back his chair.

'What's above us, Sir John?'

'A small solar. A chamber with windows looking east. We only use it in summer.'

Benjamin ran out of the room and I followed. Behind us the shouts and exclamations grew as the scarlet stain spread. We ran upstairs, knocking aside startled servants. I glimpsed Mathilda's white face then ran into the gallery, pushing open the door to the solar.

The room was cold and dark, the windows shuttered. Benjamin cursed the darkness but, as in any good household, there were boxes right inside the door containing rushlights and candles. Benjamin lit one of these and we walked into the centre of the room. At first we could see nothing so crouched on our haunches, edging forward like crabs, feeling the soft woollen carpet. I touched something wet and sticky. Benjamin pushed the rushlight closer. God forgive me, I could have screamed in terror. Resting in the centre of the carpet, severed at the neck, eyeballs rolled up in their sockets, was the decapitated head of the witch.

Grotesque in death as it had been, now putrefaction tinged the face a greenish hue. The congealing blood from the severed arteries of the snow-soaked head drenching the carpet and seeping down between the floor boards. My stomach heaved. We heard the door behind us open but Benjamin shouted for everyone to stay out.

'Come on, Roger,' he whispered. 'There is nothing we can do here.'

Outside in the gallery Benjamin told the rest of the group what we had found. Lady Beatrice became hysterical, crouching against the wall, covering her face, whilst Rachel tried to comfort her. Santerre was shocked sober whilst Sir Edmund and Southgate were torn between a mixture of anger and fear.

'Clean the mess!' Benjamin snapped at Santerre. 'Just roll up the carpet, take it and its grisly contents downstairs and have it burnt. The floor can be scrubbed.' He looked at Sir Edmund. 'Roger is correct. The Angel of Death walks this accursed house!'

'Who could leave such a thing there?' Southgate murmured.

'One of the servants, someone we don't know,' Benjamin replied. 'But the head and the Hand of Glory come from that poor hag. Oh, by the way, where's our noble Sheriff Bowyer?'

'Drunk as a bishop,' Mandeville snarled. 'Now sleeping like a baby in his cot down in the hall.'

Benjamin made to walk away.

'Master Daunbey,' Mandeville caught him up at the corner of the gallery. 'For God's sake, man, what am I supposed to do? My job is to trap conspirators, plotters . . . not stumble around in the dark after some secret assassin.'

Benjamin muttered something to himself.

'What is it? What is it, Daunbey?'

My master looked up, his face as hard as stone, the skin drawn tight. 'I was just thinking of what you said, Sir Edmund. This is not poor Buckingham, is it? Or some pathetic tailor like Taplow being trapped in his little cage and taken off to the slaughter house. And Templecombe is not some abbey where you can tap your toe and play the great lord. So how does it feel, Sir Edmund, to be the hunted instead of the hunter?'

And spinning on his heel, my master stalked off to his chamber.

(My little clerk is muttering that Benjamin was acting out of character. That's not true! Benjamin was a kind, gentle man. He always hated bully-boys and was correct to do so. Mandeville and Santerre had arrived at Templecombe wanting to make everyone dance to their tune. Instead, they had stumbled into a veritable snake pit.)

I wandered round the galleries for a while for the dinner

was both spoilt and finished. Sure enough, after a while I
caught sight of my quarry, little Mathilda, her chubby arms
full of blankets, tiptoeing along without a care in the world.
I followed her up to one of the other floors and caught her
by the elbow.

'Mathilda, my sweet, a word.'

She whirled round but she was not frightened and I
glimpsed the sparkle of triumph in her eyes. I drew her into
a shadowy window embrasure.

'You weren't looking for gold, were you?'

She pouted prettily.

'The money was secondary, wasn't it?' I continued. 'What
were you looking for? Did you kill that clerk in the fire?
What secret device did you use?'

She sighed and sat down in the window seat.

'Master Shallot, you and your fellow clod-hoppers wander
into Templecombe.' She looked out into the icy darkness.
'You are in a place hundreds of miles from London with a
few paltry soldiers to guard your back. The Devil and his
assistant trapped my Lord of Buckingham, a man much
loved in these parts. He was hustled up to London to have
his head cut off with less mercy than we would treat a
chicken. His lands are seized and the monks at Glastonbury
bullied as if they are the inmates of some prison.'

She looked squarely at me. 'Oh, yes, we have heard of
that.' She flounced the sheets in her hand. 'And what do
you expect? To come tripping through without a by-your-
leave? These are ancient lands, Master Shallot. Arthur and
his knights rode here, or so Master Hopkins told us. The
Templars are much feared but also respected for their
knowledge.'

Now, I can take a sermon from any pretty woman and
Mathilda was no exception, but I also caught the threat in
her words. I clapped my hands mockingly. 'So what does
all this make you, Mathilda, my dear? A thief looking for
gold?'

Even in the darkness I saw the flush on her cheeks.

'I am no thief!' she snapped. She drew herself up. 'I am a poor widow. My husband died two years ago from the sweating sickness. Aye, Roger, we marry young in Somerset. I have a child.'

'You also have a father,' I retorted.

She caught her lip between her teeth.

'You do have a father,' I continued smoothly. 'A tall, grizzle-haired fellow who now walks with a pronounced limp. Where did he receive his wound?'

'It was an accident.'

'Nonsense!' I snapped. 'Do you want me to call Mandeville and Southgate and have him dragged into the hall? I'll wager a piece of gold that his wound resembles a sword cut. Your father was one of those who attacked me.'

She mumbled something.

'What was that?'

'If they wanted to kill you,' she whispered, 'they would have done. We have no quarrel with you or your master. They simply wanted to frighten you.' She grasped me by the hand. 'Please, Roger, leave my father be.' She stared through the window. 'This place is full of ghosts,' she murmured.

'And the Templars?'

She lowered her head. I pulled out my short stabbing dagger and held it between my fingers.

'Nothing in life is free,' I whispered. 'You and your father are no threat to me but those you work for . . .'

Mathilda shook her head. I sheathed my dagger and got to my feet.

'Wait!' she seized my wrist. 'Roger, we are small fleas on a very big dog. We take our orders, issued here and there in a whisper.'

'And where does the dog live?' I asked.

Mathilda peered fearfully down into the garden and got to her feet. 'If you wish to meet the dog,' she whispered, 'you'll find him on the island.' And she slipped like a ghost into the shadows and ran down the gallery.

I stood staring out of the window into the shifting, cloying mist and wondered about Mathilda's ghosts trooping back to their worm-eaten beds. I had learnt enough so returned to my own chamber, secured the lock and, fully clothed, lay down for a fitful sleep.

Chapter 12

The next morning we rose early and broke our fast hastily in the hall for, despite the grisly warning issued the night before, Southgate was determined on a morning's hunting though Bowyer was still suffering the effects of being too deep in his cups. Mandeville, imperious as ever, ignored us as he issued instructions to a bleary-eyed sheriff to send for more men. His attitude towards Santerre was distinctly cool.

As we went out towards the stables I heard Sir Edmund whisper to Santerre that the matters at Templecombe were beyond his brief: he would plan his return to London where he would advise the King to send Justices into the area. If he expected this to frighten Sir John he succeeded. When the King's Justices came south they would arrive with troops and issue writs raising levies from the surrounding country-side, empanel juries, collect evidence, and not move away until the matter was settled. Santerre was about to protest but Mandeville dismissed him with a curt move of his gloved hand.

'These matters will wait!' he snapped. 'Today we hunt, tomorrow we go.'

The rest of the party were waiting for us in a courtyard full of yapping dogs; long, lean greyhounds, black, white and brindled. They stood straining at their leashes whilst, on the other side of the yard, a pack of mastiffs whimpered in protest at the muzzles on their grizzled snouts and the

189

lash of their whippers-in. Maids hurried round with cups of hot posset, stable boys and ostlers shouted as horses were brought out, saddled and made ready to mount. Southgate's and Bowyer's were fiery, hot-tempered, rearing and kicking the air with sharpened hooves. It took some time for their masters to curb them.

At last we all mounted, downing one final cup of posset whilst the huntsmen were sent on before us, the barking of the dogs shattering the silence of the cold country air.

No more snow had fallen, the sky was still overcast but the air was crisp and a little warmer. We left by the back gate of the manor following a trackway through a wood. At first, we rode together but the freshness of the horses, particularly Bowyer's and Southgate's, meant we had to break up. We cleared the trees and stopped on the brow of a small hill which fell down to snow-covered fields, broken here and there by small copses and woods. The trackers and beaters were already there and in a flurry of snow, shouts, cries and yelping barks, the hunters moved down to meet them.

Roger and I hung back on the hill, watching the rest of the party go into a wood. There was a short silence then the dogs' barking grew into a raucous row; shouts and the shrill of hunting horns carried clear to us as a fat buck, together with two hinds, galloped from the trees and across the meadow in a flurry of snow. Santerre sounded the horn and led the excited hunters down the hill. The buck had already cleared one field. Behind him the dogs raced like dark shapes against the snow. The hunt was on.

It is difficult to describe exactly what happened. We were a party of horsemen charging down the hill. Santerre, the chief huntsman, Bowyer, Southgate, Mandeville, Benjamin and myself, Lady Beatrice and Rachel having declined to come. Bowyer and Southgate were the first to break away from the rest, their horses fiery, eager for the exercise after close confinement.

We all spurred and whipped as we reached the bottom of the hill to keep up pace for the snow underfoot made the going heavy, when both Bowyer's horse and that of Southgate suddenly took on a life of their own. They bucked, reared and shot forward like arrows from a bow. Benjamin and I followed quickly afterwards for it was apparent both riders were losing control. Now I realised something was wrong for, as you young men know, if a horse becomes uncontrollable the best thing to do is to dismount as quickly as possible. Bowyer and Southgate tried this but seemed incapable of getting their boots out of the stirrups whilst both were losing control of the reins.

Southgate managed to move his left foot and swung his leg over but his right boot was still caught. The horse reared, Southgate pitched out of his saddle and was dragged along, one boot still caught in the stirrup. Bowyer's horse was galloping even faster, heading towards the trees. Benjamin shouted at Santerre and Mandeville to follow the sheriff, whilst he and I raced after Southgate, now being dragged along like a rag doll. Benjamin drew level and, in a feat of horsemanship, leaned down and slashed his dagger towards the horse's belly, cutting Southgate's stirrup loose.

We dismounted and crouched beside him. God knows, he was a grisly mess: the back of his head and legs were a mass of wounds. He groaned, opened his eyes and lapsed into a swoon.

Bowyer was not so fortunate. His horse reached the trees where he was hit by a thick, low-hanging branch, knocked out of the saddle and, as his horse careered deeper into the wood, dragged through the brambles and undergrowth, his poor body smashing against each tree.

The hunt was called off: the whippers-in and the huntsmen despatched, Benjamin ordering them back to the manor and telling them to bring down two stretchers, wine and bandages.

Mandeville and Santerre soon returned from the trees;

the latter had a crossbow in his hand, Bowyer's corpse sprawled across the saddle bow. There was no need to ask: Bowyer's body was an open wound from head to toe, his face disfigured by a mass of bruises, and the slackness of his head showed his neck had been broken. Mandeville had had to shoot his bolting horse to cut him free.

'Southgate?' he asked wearily.

'He will live,' Benjamin replied. 'Or, at least, I think he will.' He pointed to Southgate's left leg. 'Broken cleanly, as is one of his arms. God knows what other injuries he suffered.'

Mandeville crouched in the snow beside his lieutenant. He looked pathetic.

'Everything is finished,' he groaned. 'The King will not accept this.'

Benjamin forced a wineskin between his lips, urging him to drink.

Bowyer's body was immediately sheeted, placed in a pinewood box packed with snow, put in a cart and sent off to Taunton.

Back at Templecombe, now over his shock, Mandeville paced around like an angry cat, hurling abuse at Santerre, telling Lady Beatrice to stop screaming and order servants to go down to the village and bring wise women to attend to Southgate. The injured man was taken up to his chamber.

Later in the day, two old women arrived. Mandeville, pale as a ghost, promised them anything provided his companion recovered. He then packed his belongings saying he would no longer stay in Templecombe and requisitioned carts and horses for a move to Glastonbury Abbey.

Any last vestige of merriment at Templecombe completely disappeared. The Santerres stayed well away from Mandeville who stalked the galleries and corridors shouting orders at both servants and the dead sheriff's soldiers. On one occasion he met Santerre inside the main hall. Mandeville pointed an accusatory finger at him.

'I'm leaving, Sir John, but I'll be back in the spring with His Majesty's Justices and a thousand pikemen!'

'Sir Edmund?' Benjamin approached him.

'What is it, Daunbey?' Mandeville snapped, not even bothering to turn his head.

'You are leaving Templecombe for Glastonbury?'

'Yes, I am quitting this hell-hole and recommend you do the same.'

'Southgate cannot be moved.'

'He'll die if he stays here,' Mandeville hissed.

'Then perhaps only to the village. Perhaps to the priest's house where he can be guarded by soldiers. Sir Edmund, I beg you, wait a while.

'We can't leave here,' Benjamin insisted. 'Although no snow has fallen, the trackways are frozen hard. Southgate will die before he even reaches the village. Moreover, what will the King say?'

Mandeville stared into the flames of the fire.

'I shouldn't have brought Bowyer here,' he moaned. 'I had forgotten about Buckingham.' He chewed his lip and looked at Benjamin. 'Bowyer was involved in the Duke's destruction. He was a marked man. But how?' he asked bleakly. 'How were those horses made to bolt? If you discover that, Master Daunbey, I promise I'll stay until this business is done.'

'Sirs!'

We spun round. Rachel, beautiful in a dark purple gown, stood in the doorway of the hall.

'Sirs,' she greeted us and stepped forward, a determined expression on her face. 'Sirs – especially you, Sir Edmund. My father is distraught, my mother hysterical. I object to you pacing round this house shouting at our servants like some freebooter. We, too, mourn Bowyer's death, and Master Southgate's wounds are being tended.' She looked appealingly at Benjamin. 'We are doing all we can,' she continued gently. 'Southgate will mend, God knows he was fortunate. A broken leg, a fractured arm. The rest are bruises which will quickly heal.'

Benjamin spread his hands helplessly. 'But the deaths and injuries occurred here, Mistress.' He tapped Mandeville gently on the shoulder. 'However take courage, Sir Edmund, Master Hopkins's riddle may be about to unravel.'

Mandeville looked up, startled. Rachel looked puzzled but Benjamin shook his head.

'Not now, there are other matters to deal with.' He gestured at me and we left the hall.

'What do you mean by that, Master?'

'Everything in its own season, Shallot. Now I want to look at Southgate's horse.'

We found the poor animal securely tethered and hobbled in a small, dank stable. It had been unsaddled but its coat was still covered with a thick, sweaty foam though it was now quiet and placid. Benjamin ignored my warnings: he went into the box, talking gently to the horse, smoothing its flanks whilst he examined its underbelly. Then, still talking quietly, he inspected its side.

'As I thought,' Benjamin murmured, coming out. 'Southgate spurred the horse.'

'I did the same but mine didn't bolt like a shot from a sling!'

Benjamin looked round the busy yard where servants were pulling out carts and hitching up horses under the watchful eye of Bowyer's soldiers. Benjamin pulled me into the shadows as Mandeville came out to issue curt instructions for the dead sheriff's body to be removed and informed the soldiers that he would stay at Templecombe for a while. Once he had gone, Benjamin led me back to the stable.

He plucked an apple from his pocket, God knows where

he got it from, and gave it to the horse who munched it greedily. Benjamin then dug his hand into the empty manger and plucked out the remains of the horse's feed. He examined this curiously, ignoring my questions, and went into the adjoining stable where his own horse was stabled and did the same. Benjamin muttered to himself, wiped his hands and shook his head.

'Ingenious,' he murmured. 'Come on, Roger.' He grabbed me by the arm. 'One final call.'

He led me back into the house and up to Southgate's chamber. The poor man now lay in a great fourposter bed while the two old beldames clacked and muttered to themselves as they fastened splints to his leg and carefully washed his naked, bruised body. Benjamin ignored them as he looked round the chamber.

'Southgate's boots,' he whispered.

I saw one lying under the dresser and pulled it out gingerly lest the spur catch my finger. Benjamin hid it under his cloak and hurried back to his own chamber like a schoolboy who has stolen a sweetmeat. He bolted the door behind us, sat on the bed and carefully examined the spur in the light of a candle flame.

'Perhaps it's washed off,' he murmured. 'But, as Pythagoras said, "Truth can only be found through experimentation".' He lightly scored his finger on the edge of the spur, gasped and quickly dipped it in the bowl of water on the lavarium before bathing it in a little wine.

'That hurt!' he grimaced.

'Master, you will tell me?' I asked.

Benjamin, his wounded finger clasped in a wet rag, grinned from ear to ear.

'Roger, Roger, isn't the human mind ingenious when it comes to plotting the destruction of another being? When I examined Southgate's horse I saw the spur marks. When I examined the manger where the feed had been put, I found oats and bran. When I examined my own horse's stable I found only traces of hay. And finally, when I scrutinised Master Southgate's spur, I found its sharpness tinged with mercury.'

'So?' I began slowly, trying to assemble all the facts.

'So,' Benjamin continued. 'I suspect Bowyer's and Southgate's horses were fed a rich diet of oats and bran both last night and this morning. Now you know, Roger, how that would affect an excitable horse who has had little strenuous exercise? It would become fiery and restless, something I noticed when Bowyer and Southgate left for the hunt. However, can you imagine what would happen if such a horse was not only spurred but goaded by a spur tinged with mercury?'

'It would bolt.'

'Which is what happened.'

'But, Master, Bowyer and Southgate, for all their faults, were expert horsemen. Why didn't they just dismount?'

'Ah! But what if the stirrups of their saddle had been changed, each being given a narrower set? Now, when you mount a horse, you simply push your boot in to the stirrup. That's the easy part. It's like anything else: you can get a small ring on your finger, the problem is getting it off. Remember, Bowyer's and Southgate's boots were wet and so leather would swell a little. Now, as they left Templecombe, the boots fitted snugly. They would not object to such a tight fit, in fact it would help them keep their restless horses under control, but once they had set spurs and the horses bolted, murder occurred.' He shook his head. 'There's no proof. Bowyer's and Southgate's saddles have now been returned to the stable and the original stirrups probably replaced. Nevertheless, that is how I believe the trap was set.'

'But the spurs would be kept in their own chambers?'

Benjamin shrugged. 'I don't think that need bother us.

There are probably keys to fit every chamber in this house. It would take only a few minutes to open a door, search out the riding boots and pour a little mercury over each spur.'

'And the murderer?'

'A vague suspicion as yet but I tell you this: if the murderer strikes again, it will be against us, Roger, so be on your guard!'

'What about Mandeville?'

Benjamin peered at me.

'He could be the murderer, Master. He knew where those agents were in London and about Mistress Hopkins. He could have killed his own men, Cosmas and Damien. Above all, he survived the hunt.'

'An allegation's one thing,' Benjamin snapped. 'Proving it is another.'

'And the riddle? Have you really resolved it?'

'Perhaps. I have remembered my schooling: baptism is often called "Jordan's water" after the river where Christ himself was baptised.' Benjamin grinned at my puzzlement. 'But let's leave that for the moment. More importantly, I can prove how Cosmas and Damien died. No ghostly intervention but a most subtle assassin.' He grasped me by the shoulder. 'Listen, Roger, go for a walk in the grounds or try and pour more balm on Mandeville's troubled spirit. Visit poor Southgate, flirt with young Mathilda, but come back here,' Benjamin peered out of the window, 'in about two hours.'

I did what my master asked, trailing around the house like a ghost though no one really wished to speak to me. Rachel had gone to her own chamber. Santerre and his wife were in close council with each other. Mandeville still sulked in the hall whilst the old beldames in Southgate's chamber cackled with laughter and asked if I wanted them to wash me? Of Mathilda there was no sight whatsoever and I realised that Bowyer's death had panicked many of the servants into leaving Templecombe.

I went down to the lakeside and stared across at that mysterious island. I wondered if I should climb into a barge and pole myself across but the mists still hung over the water, I was cold, frightened, and so, following Benjamin's instructions, returned to my own chamber.

I found the door unlocked as I had given my master the key before I left; the light was poor but I could see nothing had been disturbed so lay down on the bed, pulling the curtains around me. I was half-dozing when suddenly I smelt something burning, followed by a small bang under my bed which shook me awake. I pulled back the curtains and dashed out of the room to find Benjamin standing there, laughing at my shock.

'For God's sake, Master, what are you doing?' I bellowed.

Benjamin patted me on the shoulder. 'Stay calm, Roger, I could have blown you up but I didn't. Here.' He walked back into the room. 'Help me push your bed away.'

We did so, heaving and pushing until the bed moved a few inches and I saw the slight scorch mark on the stone floor beneath. Benjamin pointed to it.

'I think that's how Cosmas was killed: his door was locked but, before he retired, I suspect someone spread a coat of oil between the mattress and the bed support and then inserted a small bag of gunpowder.'

'How did they light that?'

'Oh, with a slow fuse.'

'*Oh*, I see,' I replied. 'They just knocked on the door and asked Cosmas could they light a slow fuse under the bed?'

'No, no, what they did was attach a slow fuse to the gunpowder and left it coiled under the bed.'

'And?'

'When the poor man was asleep, someone came upstairs and began to pull the thread attached to the slow fuse which was left lying out on the gallery. The slow fuse uncoiled like a snake, the assassin pulling it slowly across the floor until the end appeared under the door. A tinder was struck, the fuse lit and Cosmas died.'

'But they couldn't do that! Cosmas would notice.'

'No, he wouldn't. No more than you did. You came into the chamber, you were not looking for an almost invisible line of thread running from your bed underneath the door. Even if, in the poor light, you did see it, you would dismiss it. All the assassin had to do was take the piece of thread as I did, pull it very slowly, which hardly makes a sound, and murder is only a few seconds away. Like you, Cosmas would not hear the fuse. It's meant to burn slowly but very quietly. The only difference with you is that I used two grains of gunpowder and no oil. In Cosmas's case it was different.'

'But we saw nothing. Surely, as the slow fuse burns, it would burn the floor beneath?'

'No, it splutters not burns. And remember, Roger, the thread had been removed, the fuse destroys itself, and people coming in and out of the room, once the bed was on fire, would scarcely think it suspicious even if they saw the odd burn mark on the floor.'

'So how did you discover this?'

'What really intrigued me was the scorch mark on the outside of the door facing the gallery, as well as the damage done to the heavy bedstead. A brilliant piece of murder, Roger. The assassin did not have to enter the room and, in killing Cosmas, destroyed all the evidence except for that small scorch mark on the other side of the door.'

'The murderer could have destroyed the whole house.'

'No, as you noticed before, the floors in all our chambers are stone and there was no combustible material anywhere near. The bed would burn, its occupant die, but the fire would be discovered in time and the flames doused.'

199

'Why didn't Cosmas just get out of the bed?'

'Ah, now, that did intrigue me until I remembered the gunpowder. There was probably sufficient to injure him badly. Do you remember the corpse? The bottom half of his legs had disappeared completely. The gunpowder either killed the poor man or caused such grievous wounds as to send him into a swoon from which he would never recover. Meanwhile, the oil was ignited. The bed is old wood and would burn as quickly as stubble in the driest summer.'

I stared down at my own bed and accepted Benjamin's conclusions. The fuse would destroy itself, the gunpowder explode, poor Cosmas's legs would be shattered, and even if he wanted to, the fire spread so quickly as to prevent his escape.

'Well,' Benjamin looked round the room, 'all is safe here, eh? No fire, no flames. Now let us go to the church, and I shall show you how Damien died.'

We left the manor and went down to that silent tomb of a church. Benjamin pushed me in, locking the door behind us, and lit two sconce torches. The pitch spluttered and flared into life, making the place more eerie with dancing shadows.

'Now,' Benjamin murmured, 'let's assume I am the assassin. I have come into this chapel to commit murder. Cosmas's body is laid out and his poor brother will come in for the death vigil. Unfortunately, others arrive: Mandeville, Southgate and finally us. Eventually we leave and the murderer, hiding on those steps leading to the tower, is granted an additional advantage by Damien locking the door.' Benjamin walked over, past the baptismal font and stood looking down into the sanctuary.

'Now I have prepared everything well. The crossbow bolts and the arbalest have been hidden away. I have also lifted the catch, both on the outside and inside of one of the windows.' Benjamin, imitating the stance of an archer, pretended to fire a crossbow. 'Damien is killed. I make sure, then prepare to leave, but I want to make it appear that I entered and left the church like a ghost. This is how I do it.'

Benjamin walked into one of the small transepts and stopped beneath the window. He opened this and, from the darkness, picked up a long, narrow ladder, the type soldiers climb when scaling a castle wall, or a tiler might use when working on the roof of a house. Benjamin pushed this ladder through, then hoisted himself up and, with a great deal of huffing and puffing, disappeared down the ladder. I heard it scrape as it was lifted away and his voice sang out.

'So you see, Roger, this is how the murderer left.'

'Very good,' I called out. 'But how do you close the shutters, both from the inside and the outside?'

'Oh, very easily,' my master replied. 'Stand back!'

I did so. The shutters slammed shut and I even heard the catch fall. I ran out. Benjamin was standing a few yards away from the church, the ladder still in his hand. It was apparent that he had used it both to slam the shutters and so knock the simple latch back into place. I walked over to him. He stood, as pleased as a school boy, grinning and clapping his hands.

'You see, Roger, I used the ladder to get out of the church. I leave no footprints under the window and use the same ladder to shut the window and force the catch back.' He blew on his cold fingers. 'I could have opened the outside latch in the same way.'

'But what about the one inside?'

Benjamin shrugged. 'That is neither here nor there. Do you remember when we went into the church with Mandeville and the rest? It was dark, anyone could have slipped along the transept and put the catch down. And don't forget, Roger,' Benjamin added, 'with the window slamming shut, the inside latch might just have fallen into place.' He took

201

the ladder and slung it into the snow-covered bushes.

'What now, Master?'

He put his arm round my shoulders. 'To be perfectly honest, my dear Roger, I don't really know. But go back to your room and wait for me there.'

Mathilda was waiting for me in my chamber. I grinned and seized her, but she was not in a playful mood. She looked fearfully around and I wondered if there were eyelets or spy-holes in the wall.

'Listen!' she hissed. 'You have not hurt my father, so listen to this. Tonight, the Templars will meet on the island.'

I shook my head disbelievingly.

'Yes,' she persisted. 'I tell the truth. It's all I can or will tell you. Go down to the lakeside. There will be a barge waiting for you but don't cross unless you see the lights. Study the island carefully and you will see.' She pushed me away. 'I'll do no more,' she repeated, and left.

My master came back, slightly bemused, lost in his own thoughts and I had to repeat two or three times what Mathilda had told me. He chewed his lip and looked at me.

'How do we know it's not a trap?'

'I don't think it is. It stands to reason, Master. That island, its awesome long house . . . We both know it lies at the heart of this mystery.'

'Does it?' Benjamin asked. 'Does it really?' and wandered away.

Chapter 13

The mood in the Santerre household was not conducive to any more festive banquets or grand meals. Mandeville kept to himself, fretting about Southgate and when the additional soldiers would arrive. So we snatched mouthfuls of cold food and went back to our own chamber to wait until midnight. It seemed an eternity in coming. We carefully watched the flame of the hour candle eating away the wax from ring to ring.

When it reached the twelfth, Benjamin and I dressed in boots and cloaks, put on our sword belts and quietly left. The house seemed asleep yet, as I have said, it had a life of its own. Time and again we stopped, hearts beating, the hair on our necks prickling with fear at the eerie, creaking sounds which seemed to match our every move. We crept down into the hall, through the kitchen and out by a small postern door.

The night was as black as the Devil would wish. No moon, no stars, just a cold biting wind moaning, shifting the gaunt branches of the trees and throwing icy flurries of snow on to our heads. I would have preferred to have lit torches but Benjamin was against this.

'We hunt creatures of the night, Roger. Let us become like them.'

We slipped and slithered out of the stable courtyard where horses moved and snickered, past the Templar church and down to the gleaming lakeside. We sat on our haunches, two black shapes against the snow, and peered through the mist at the faint outline of the island. At first we could see nothing, our eyes hurting and smarting at the strain as well as the biting night air. Then Benjamin stirred and seized my arm.

'Am I seeing things?' he hissed.

I stared through the bleak darkness. Still I could see nothing but then I glimpsed the light of a torch. One, perhaps two. The flames seemed to flicker as if someone was moving about on the island.

'Come on, Roger!'

Benjamin and I slithered down the bank. We saw the barge, pole resting in its stern, as if some ghostly boatman was waiting to take us across. We clambered in. Benjamin sat in the prow whilst I grabbed the pole, brushing the ice away, trying to close my mind and senses to the chill wind and the lapping of the cold black lake. At first I was clumsy but then my old skill returned. (Don't forget, I was raised in Norfolk where the skill of punting barges is as natural as walking.) Nevertheless, I make a confession: Benjamin and I were stupid. Now and again we made such mistakes. An excess of impetuosity, the rashness of youth. Time and again it nearly cost us our life and that night, on the frozen lake, was no different. I had made two, maybe three sweeps of the pole, when I felt a wet slipperiness beneath me. Benjamin spun round, his face a white mask in the darkness. He, too, had felt the dampness seep in and yet, due to the broad sweeps of my pole and perhaps the motion of the lake, we had already travelled yards from the shore.

'Roger, it's been holed!'

I let the pole slip and crouched, plunging my hand into the bottom of the barge. My heart jumped in fear as I felt an inch of icy water. I put the pole down and clambered on hands and knees round the barge, looking for the hole.

Now this is where my skill as a bargeman saved our lives. You see, on the Broads of Norfolk and Suffolk such accidents are common and the unwary make one of two mistakes, or even both. They try to reach the place they are heading for or else turn back to the shore. Sometimes, due to panic and fear, they try both. But take Old Shallot's advice: if you are in a boat or barge which has been holed, particularly one where the damage is malicious, stop rowing and block that hole for any further movement of the barge simply helps the water rush in.

At last I found it in the stern of the barge, a hole the size of a man's fist as if someone had taken a hammer and smashed through the bottom. I took off my cloak and immediately began to thread the fabric through the hole. My master, who had found a similar one on the port side, first tried his cloak but then cursed as it went into the lake and he had to stop the hole with the heel of his boot. For a few seconds, and it seemed like hours, we just crouched, looking at each other, as the barge danced on the glassy surface. I glanced quickly towards the island where the siren light still beckoned us on.

'I am sorry, Master,' I wailed.

'Oh, shut up, Roger!' he hissed.

I kept my hand pressed to the bottom of the boat, my fingers freezing in the icy water swilling round us, but I noticed it grew no deeper.

'Master?'

'Yes,' Benjamin hissed. 'Now, Roger, my friend, turn this barge round and pull us to the shore, swiftly, with all your skill. If there's another hole and the water swamps us, we will not survive for long in these icy waters.'

Now you know Old Shallot. My heart was pounding, my stomach spinning like a child's top. I wanted to cry, weep and beg the Almighty for mercy. I seized that bloody pole, swinging the barge round even as I felt the water beneath me slop and gurgle as if maliciously laughing at me, waiting to embrace us in its frozen grasp. The barge turned. I closed my eyes and began to pole.

'Roger!' my master screamed. 'You are going the wrong way!'

I opened my eyes and realised the barge had only half-turned and we were now running parallel to both the island and the shore. I began to pole and pray with a vigour which would have astonished any monk. In between snatches of prayer I cursed, using every filthy word I knew, until that bloody barge was heading straight back to the bank. The water lapped round my ankles. We had failed to discover a third or even fourth hole and still the water was rising.

My master manoeuvred himself round, using his hand to scoop out the icy water, shouting at me to pole faster. We skimmed across the surface of that sodding lake whilst all around us gathered the dark hosts of hell. The water rose higher but then, just as Old Shallot's courage began to crumble into blind panic, the barge shuddered to a stop; both my master and I ran ashore, grateful to fall sobbing on to the snow-soaked bank.

My master crouched, breathing in deeply to calm himself, whilst Old Shallot dealt with the threat in his usual formidable way.

'Bastards!' I screamed, jumping up and down on the bank, shaking my fist at the island. 'You murdering, sodding bastards! Come on, Master!' I seized Benjamin by the arm.

He trotted breathlessly beside me as I strode like a madman through the snow, back to that accursed manor.

'Roger, what are you going to do?'

'I am going to slit that bitch's throat for a start!'

'Roger, don't!'

'All right, I'll cut her head off! Master, I don't mind being shot at, hunted, trapped, attacked – but to die on a frozen lake at the dead of night!'

'Roger.' Benjamin grabbed me by my doublet. 'Listen! Mathilda will be well away now. Do you think she's going to wait for you to come back? There was always the possibility you might escape. No, listen, I know who the murderer is. I know where the Grail and Arthur's Sword could be.'

I stopped. 'Why didn't you tell me this before?'

'I had to wait. I suspected the murderer would strike at us, and what happened on that lake proved it. Now, Roger, I beg you, let us go back to our chamber, warm ourselves, snatch a few hours of sleep and tomorrow, as we break fast in the hall, I shall confront the murderer.'

Of course my master had his way. Anyway, by the time we reached our chambers my anger had been replaced by sheer terror at the danger we had just escaped. All the old signs appeared: I wanted to be sick, my knees kept quivering, and it took three deep-bowled cups of claret before I could even remember what day of the week it was. Naturally, I taxed my master on what he had learnt. He merely sat on the only chair in my room, shook his head and told me to sleep, and that it would be best if we shared the same chamber that night.

The next morning we woke none the worse for our terrible experience. Benjamin insisted that we shave, wash and change our linen and doublets before going down to the hall. On our way I looked for Mathilda but Benjamin was right, there was no sign of the little minx.

The Santerres were already at high table, Mandeville also. My master waited until a kitchen boy served us, then suddenly rose, locking the great doors of the hall as well as those to the kitchen and buttery. Mandeville broke free of his reverie. Sir John Santerre stared, a ghost of his former self. Lady Beatrice watched fearfully whilst Rachel sat like an innocent child waiting for a play to begin.

'Daunbey, what's all this?' Mandeville grated.

Now Benjamin had unmasked many a killer and brought numerous murderers to boot. Sometimes he played games, drawing the assassins into verbal battles in which they would confess. But this time it was different. He walked once, twice round the table on the dais, pausing for a few seconds behind each chair. Then he went round again and stopped between John Santerre and Rachel, putting his hand gently on the man's shoulder.

'Sir John, are you the killer?'

Santerre shot back in his chair. If a man's face could age in a few seconds, his did.

'What do you mean?' he stuttered.

'On our first day here you claimed you left Templecombe to ride your estates. You did not. Instead you went to Glastonbury.'

'There's no crime in that.'

'And, just before we left London, why did the beggar give you that note?'

'I . . .'

'If you lie,' Benjamin snapped, 'these matters will be laid before the King's Council in London.'

Sir John stretched over and, despite the hour, filled his wine goblet completely to the brim. He gobbled its contents like a thirsty man would the purest water. Mandeville was now alert as a hunting dog.

'Answer the questions, Santerre!'

Sir John put the wine cup down. 'When I was in London I paid people to ascertain if the Templar church near Fleet Street contained anything resembling the River Jordan or the Ark of Moses.'

'And did it?'

'No.'

'And Glastonbury Abbey?'

Sir John licked his lips. 'Both Abbot Bere and I wanted an end to all this nonsense.' He glanced at Mandeville. 'No offence, Sir Edmund, but no lord in the kingdom wants you or your sort prying round his estates. I used my wealth to fund the building of a crypt at Glastonbury. I thought that something might be found.'

'And has it been?' I asked.

'Nothing whatsoever.'

Benjamin stepped beside Lady Beatrice, who sat rigid in her chair.

'Lady Beatrice, what do you know of these matters?'

The woman's mouth opened and closed. She shook her head.

'Oh, yes, you know something. Your first husband's name was Mortimer?'

Lady Beatrice nodded.

'He came of a crusading line which has held the manor of Templecombe since time immemorial?'

Again the nod.

'And the Mortimer family motto is "*Age Circumspecte*" is it not?' Benjamin glanced at me. 'Shallot discovered that in the Book of Legends at Glastonbury Abbey.'

'Yes,' she whispered.

'What's that got to do with us?' Mandeville interrupted.

'Was your husband a member of the Templars?'

Lady Beatrice's eyes, glassy with fright, stared down the hall.

'I think he was,' Benjamin continued, whispering in her ear. 'When the Templars were dissolved some two hundred years ago, some escaped, assumed other identities, married and settled down. Your husband's ancestor was one of these. Nevertheless, the Templars continued meeting in secret, each coven acting like a small community, the mysteries of the Order being passed from one generation to another.' He moved slightly and rested a hand lightly on Rachel's shoulder. 'You were given these mysteries, weren't you, Rachel?'

209

Do you know, the girl just smiled and played with the ring on her finger.

'You are a Templar, aren't you?' Benjamin whispered. 'Your father passed the secrets on to you. In time you would have married and passed the mystery on to your first born. For generations,' Benjamin's voice rose, 'the lords of Templecombe have been members of the secret Templar organisation.' He paused. 'Oh no, not you, Sir John, nor Lady Beatrice, but I think you both had your suspicions.'

'Impossible!' Mandeville shouted. 'She is a mere chit of a girl.'

'She's eighteen summers old,' Benjamin retorted. 'And if you remain quiet, Sir Edmund, I will tell you what happened.'

He went round the table, stepped off the dais and stood looking at all of us. Santerre and his wife were like waxen effigies but Rachel, her face slightly flushed, leaned forward as if without a care in the world.

'The Lords of Templecombe,' Benjamin began, 'were always Templars. They kept the Order's secrets and in dark covens met their helpers, probably in the sombre house on that Godforsaken island. Now in the main these Templars lay sleeping like seeds planted in the soil, though sometimes they would burgeon, quickening into life, particularly in any uprising or rebellion against our Tudor masters. Nevertheless, they were content to sit, watch and wait. Hopkins was one of these, though deranged in his wits.'

Benjamin paused to collect his thoughts. 'The Templars always coveted the great relics, the Grail and Arthur's Sword, Excalibur, but these remained hidden. They were content with that, provided no one else discovered them.' Benjamin stared at Mandeville. 'Hopkins began the drama. He had a passion for the relics and believed their discovery would strengthen the Order. My Lord of Buckingham, also a Templar, was drawn into the mystery. He received a message from Hopkins and came to Templecombe but then blundered into the trap My Lord Cardinal had laid for him. Hopkins and Buckingham were killed.' Benjamin glanced at Rachel. 'But I suspect the Templars have a code. No one strikes at their interests and walks away unharmed. Moreover, there was a greater danger: His Grace the King was now interested in these relics and was insisting on a thorough search for them. So the Templars struck.'

Mandeville tapped the top of the table with his knuckles.

'You say Buckingham was a Templar?'

Benjamin smiled thinly. 'Oh, come, Sir Edmund, he could have been a Cardinal of Rome and his fate would have been the same. Don't play games. Buckingham was baited, trapped and killed because my uncle hated him and because he had royal blood in his veins.' Benjamin glared at him. 'Hopkins was a traitor, perhaps deserved his death, but Buckingham was innocent. His death was murder made legal.'

'I will tell My Lord Cardinal your words!'

Benjamin shrugged. 'Do so and dear Uncle will simply laugh and put it down to my youthful impetuosity. I only say what thousands think.'

Mandeville glared down the table at Rachel who sat, hands joined, like some novice at prayer. She seemed fascinated by Benjamin as if he was telling some mysterious tale on a cold winter's night and she was a spectator, not a party to it.

'I cannot believe,' Mandeville jibed, 'that this girl garrotted two experienced agents, Calcraft and Warnham.'

'Oh come, Sir Edmund,' Benjamin replied. 'I have heard how in Spain there are beggar children so skilled with the garrotte they can kill a fully grown man in a matter of seconds. It would have been simple for Rachel.' Benjamin spread his hands. 'Calcraft, and on another occasion Warnham, were invited down to a meeting in some tavern

211

by the riverside where Mistress Rachel was waiting to talk to them. After her coy glances and generous cups of wine, they were lured out into the dark so Rachel might speak where no spy could overhear. Perhaps they sat down. Mistress Rachel would find it so easy; a desolate spot, the garrotte cord in her hands, men in their cups. Just a few seconds, Sir Edmund, and the cord slips round their throat; fuddled in their wits they would struggle but only briefly before lapsing into unconsciousness. If the garrotte cord did not kill, the cold water of the Thames would. Then Rachel would flit back along the alleyways to Richmond Palace.'

'You have proof of that?' Sir John blustered, though his eyes betrayed him.

'Yes and no.' Benjamin replied. 'Except I was intrigued why a scarlet cord should be used. So, before I left London, I took it to one of the maids at Richmond Palace, and do you know what she said?'

Santerre shook his head.

'That it is a sort of material women might buy to serve as piping on their dresses, gowns or cloaks. At the time I dismissed this but later it was a piece which fitted the puzzle.'

Rachel, her lower lip caught between her teeth, shook her head disbelievingly. I felt a chill of fear at her complete imperviousness to what my master was saying.

'Hopkins's sister,' I intervened, 'was also a victim of the garrotte. Rachel, you see, overheard us as we left the hall in Richmond Palace. She subtly covered this up by appearing to be concerned about what dangers might face us here at Templecombe.'

'Why should she kill Hopkins's sister?' Mandeville asked.

'Because,' I replied, 'there was always a danger that Hopkins, who confided in so few people, may have said something to his sister which could have threatened her. And it was so easy.' I spread my hands. 'Rachel slipped out of

212

Richmond Palace and went hot foot to the house of Hopkins's sister who would, of course, admit her as a friend, the daughter of the lord whom her dead brother had served. Rachel would reassure her, they even shared a goblet of wine, before Rachel slipped the garrotte round her throat. The old woman died, Rachel searched the house for anything which might incriminate her, and then disappeared.'

'That poor old woman was murdered,' Benjamin declared, 'not because she had said or done anything wrong but simply because of what she might know. We tell the truth, I believe, Rachel?'

The girl stared back silently.

'Once we left London,' Benjamin continued, 'the real dance began, didn't it, Roger?'

'Oh, yes,' I replied. 'When we stopped at Glastonbury, Mistress Rachel sent a message, God knows how, to that old witch who was waiting for us with her prophecies. Look, it stands to reason,' I continued. 'No man, or woman could read the future so clearly. Even before we reached Templecombe our deaths were planned. The old hag was really a mummer mouthing lines taught to her and, once her part was played, she too had to die. An easy feat. There must be secret passageways and entrances out of Templecombe. Mistress Rachel used these, first to silence the witch; secondly, to cut off her hands and head in order to frighten us on our return to Glastonbury.'

'And the deaths of Cosmas and Damien?' Mandeville asked.

Benjamin gave a pithy description of how both men had died.

'Cosmas was the easiest,' he concluded. 'On our first evening here, after you had all retired, Rachel allegedly left the hall to collect a manuscript. I am sure she went up to the poor man's room, picked up the thread lying there, pulled out the slow fuse, lit it with a tinder and then came back down here.'

'Was she so certain Shallot would be roused?' Mandeville asked.

'Oh, if Roger hadn't woken, she always had me. After she returned, she could feign sleep and say she wanted to retire. I would go to my chamber on the same gallery as poor Cosmas and, of course, notice something was wrong.

'However,' Benjamin stared at Rachel, his face betraying his hurt at being used by her, 'only after examining the Templar chapel following Damien's death did I really begin to suspect Mistress Rachel. You see, in the chapel, near one of the windows, I noticed bits of wood from a ladder which had been left there. Only a member of the Santerre household would have access to such a ladder.

'Secondly, when I simulated what she had done, I found the window was rather narrow. Even I, slender as I am, found it difficult to squeeze through.' He paused. 'So it had to be someone young and supple and only Rachel fitted that description.

'Finally, there was something else. Did you notice, Sir Edmund, when we were trying to force the door of the church, how Rachel and her mother hurried along shouting for Damien through the window? At the time I thought it was strange but, on reflection, Rachel was simply checking that no trace of her departure from the church remained. Once we were inside, she was also most assiduous in accompanying us as we searched for any secret entrance or passageway. I recall her being near one of the windows. I am sure it was then she either brought the latch down or, if it had already fallen, made sure it was in place.'

'But the snow?' Mandeville interrupted. 'You said someone who had been travelling through snow stood at the back of the church.'

'No, that was just a clever ploy to tangle matters even further. Rachel could have brought the snow in and let it melt so as to distract attention from herself. She had ostensibly stayed in the manor house all day.'

Benjamin paused and we all stared at the young woman now sitting back in her chair looking up at the rafters, tapping the table top and humming a tune to herself. She was one of the most curious assassins I had ever met. Benjamin had levelled the most serious allegations against her, yet never once had she protested, objected or interrupted. Even my master seemed unnerved by her cool demeanour.

'Daughter,' Sir John grated, 'have you anything to say against this?'

'I am not your daughter,' she replied flatly. She then sat up straight and stared at my master. 'Where's your proof that I lit the slow fuse? Where is your proof that I garrotted two men, not to mention an old woman, in London? Where is the proof that I lurked in a church and killed Mandeville's servant with a crossbow bolt? Or that I killed and mutilated a half-mad witch?'

Benjamin pulled a face. 'Aye, Mistress, you are correct. Other people could have bought the scarlet cord. Other people could have committed these terrible crimes. But, think carefully. Someone at Templecombe knew where to get gunpowder, oil and a slow fuse. Someone at Templecombe knew where to hide both herself and a scaling ladder in the church, as well as how to use that poor hag; first to deliver messages and then, as a warning to the rest of us, as a victim.'

'The same is true of Bowyer and Southgate,' I interrupted. 'Their horses were fed a meal of oats and bran to make them more fiery. Who else but someone at Templecombe could manage that? And then you changed their stirrups and tainted their spurs with mercury?'

'So Bowyer's death was no accident?' Mandeville interrupted.

'Of course not!' Benjamin replied, and gave a short description of what we had found in the stables and in

215

Southgate's chamber. Rachel heard him out. She placed her elbows on the table, resting her face between her hands, nodding approvingly as if Benjamin was some favoured pupil who had learnt a poem by rote.

'But you have no proof,' she repeated.

'There's the proof!' I snarled, pointing to her white-faced mother and the haggard Sir John. 'They know! They suspect!'

The young woman shrugged.

'Then there's the servants,' I continued. 'Those who carried out your orders. You dragged down everyone with you.'

Rachel daintily arched one eyebrow as if I had mentioned inviting her servants to some feast or revelry. Benjamin watched her curiously.

'You are not afraid of death, Mistress?'

'Why should I be frightened of the inevitable?' she replied. 'And why threaten me with death? As I keep repeating, you have no proof.'

'The King's torturers in the Tower will find it!' Mandeville retorted.

Benjamin walked in front of Rachel and studied her carefully. I watched, fascinated, for this was the first time he had confronted a murderer with a plausible explanation but very little proof. The deaths of the agents, Cosmas and Damien, Bowyer and those terrible injuries inflicted on Southgate, would in a court of law puzzle any jury. They might declare there was a case to answer, but what proof? (Mind you, Mandeville was right! Henry VIII cared little about evidence or the finer points of law. I always remember him turning to Thomas Cromwell about the trial of an abbot who had refused to take the Oath of Supremacy. 'Give him a fair trial,' the fat bastard roared, 'and then hang him from his own gate!')

Benjamin beckoned Rachel. 'Mistress, a word by ourselves, please?'

She rose, tripping round the table as if Benjamin had asked her for a dance. They walked down the hall and stood near the fireplace. Benjamin whispered to her and I heard her hissed reply, followed by silence. She then spread her hands and Benjamin led her back to the table where she stood defiantly before Mandeville.

'Master Daunbey is correct,' she murmured. 'I am a member of the secret Order of the Templars. I am responsible for the deaths he has listed.' She smiled obliquely. 'I pay respect to his brilliance and subtle astuteness but I am proud of what I did. My Lord of Buckingham's death is avenged. Those responsible, except you, Sir Edmund, have received their just deserts.' She lowered her voice. 'But don't sleep easy, Mandeville, for your time will come. Beware of every alleyway, of every drink and bite you swallow, of every horse you mount, every stranger you meet, because in time, when you least expect it, other Templars will finish what I have begun!'

'And us?' I shouted.

(Isn't it strange? This mere slip of a girl responsible for at least seven deaths. A self-confessed killer who could, even on the brink of her own destruction, still hold us with a threat. And you know Old Shallot, I have a well-developed sense of my own preservation. Yes, I will be honest, Rachel Santerre, or more correctly Rachel Mortimer, chilled my soul to the marrow.)

The young woman stared at me. 'I like you, Shallot,' she murmured. 'No, for the moment you are safe. What happened last night should never have taken place.'

Now Mandeville got to his feet. 'Rachel Santerre,' he intoned, 'I arrest you for treason and the most horrible homicides. You will be taken to London and stand trial for your life before King's Bench at Westminster. Sir John, Lady Beatrice, you will accompany her.' Mandeville walked to the door and called for some of Bowyer's soldiers. 'Take this woman,' he ordered, pointing to her, 'to her chamber.

217

One man is to stay on guard in the room, two others outside! She is to be chained hand and foot. Do it!' he ordered the surprised soldier.

The fellow grasped the unresisting Rachel and pushed her out of the hall. Mandeville glared back at Santerre.

'I will now search this house,' he barked, 'beginning with your daughter's chamber!' And swept out of the room.

'Roger,' Benjamin whispered, 'come with me.'

He hurried out of the hall. The soldiers were already putting manacles around Rachel's wrists. Her face was marble-white, Even then I knew she was determined not to become the plaything of the London mob.

'Mistress Rachel,' Benjamin asked, ignoring Mandeville's protests, 'is there anything we can do?'

She forced a smile and shook her head. Mandeville pushed her further down the gallery.

'Sir,' Benjamin intervened, 'the woman is your prisoner, there is no need for such rudeness.'

Rachel shrugged off Mandeville's hand and looked once more at Benjamin.

'Ever the gentleman, Master Daunbey. I am sorry about last night. I was ordered not to touch you.' And without explaining that enigmatic remark further, she allowed the soldiers to lead her away.

Benjamin and I walked back into the hall. Lady Beatrice was sobbing hysterically. Sir John Santerre looked an old, beaten man.

'Master Daunbey,' he pleaded, 'what shall we do?'

Benjamin climbed on to the dais and leaned over the table.

'You have interests abroad, Sir John?'

Santerre nodded.

'And gold with the Antwerp bankers?'

Again the nod.

Benjamin looked at Lady Beatrice. 'You knew, didn't you?'

218

The woman's thin face was a mask of terror. 'I couldn't stop her,' she whispered hoarsely. 'When I married my husband, I knew the legends, the stories, the whispers.' She glanced round the deserted hall and glared at Santerre. 'I hate this place!' She spat out the words. 'I asked Sir John to burn it to the ground but Rachel played him like a piece of string around her finger. She could always do that! Templars, ghosts, curses – and now we shall answer for it with our lives!'

'Sir John,' Benjamin replied briskly, 'there are secret entrances and passageways out of Templecombe, are there not?'

Sir John nodded. 'Yes, yes,' he said absentmindedly.

'Then, sir,' Benjamin declared, 'I would collect up all that is valuable, leave immediately, get to the coast and put as much distance as you can between yourself and the King's fury. It's your only chance,' he persisted. 'Otherwise the King's lawyers will spin their web and have you hanged at Tyburn. You'd best go now.'

Benjamin straightened up as if he was listening carefully. 'Your servants are wise, Sir John. They have already gone. I suggest you do likewise.'

Chapter 14

We left the hall and I became aware of how true Benjamin's words were. We wandered into the scullery. The fires had been doused and only a half-witted spit boy sat smiling amongst the ashes. Outside in the cobbled yard the story was the same; ostlers, grooms, stable boys, all had fled. (Looking back there was nothing singular in that. I had been to enough great houses where the lord had fallen from royal favour and it's eerie how quickly the word spread. The effect was always the same: desertion and flight.) The only sounds were the soldiers hurrying along the corridors.

Sir John and Lady Beatrice left the hall and slipped like shadows up the stairs. Benjamin was right. For the moment Mandeville was concerned only with Rachel but, once more soldiers arrived, Sir John and Lady Beatrice would be arrested. Old Henry would have little compassion for them.

'Come,' Benjamin muttered, 'let us ride out the storm in your chamber.'

We walked up the stairs. The soldiers were already breaking into rooms, intent on full-scale pillaging. The chamber servants had also disappeared and I marvelled how quickly this stately mansion was collapsing in chaos. I was all agog with curiosity but Benjamin refused to say anything until I locked my chamber door behind us.

'Did you always know it was Rachel?' I asked.

'No, I had a number of suspects. They included

Mandeville and Southgate and Sir John Santerre and his wife. But I suppose murder has its own logic and everything pointed towards Rachel.' He ticked the points off on his fingers. 'The scarlet cords, the easy access to gunpowder in Templecombe's cellars, the litheness and suppleness of the assassin in the Templar church, as well as the young woman's movements both on the night Cosmas died and when we discovered Damien's body in the chapel.'

'But how did you make her confess?'

'Ah!' Benjamin lay down on the bed and stared up at the rafters. 'That, my dear Roger, will have to wait until our return to London. But for the moment, let us be patient and wait a while.'

He closed his eyes and I was left to twiddle my thumbs whilst all around us I could hear the sound of breaking doors and the running steps of soldiers. Mandeville came up to render grateful thanks, though he had the look of a vindictive hunter.

'I cannot find Sir John or Lady Beatrice,' he stated.

Benjamin hardly moved.

'Do you know where they are, Master Daunbey?'

'Oh, for God's sake, Sir Edmund, you have found your quarry and the King will have Templecombe and its estates. If the Santerres have fled, let them go!'

Mandeville shifted from foot to foot. 'The King will hear of this.'

'His Grace the King will also hear of our great industry in this matter,' I taunted back. 'If it had not been for Master Daunbey, who knows where this would have ended?'

'How is Mistress Rachel?' Benjamin asked.

'Cold, distant and unrepentant.'

Benjamin rolled over on the bed, resting his head on his hand. He looked up at Mandeville.

'She is not to be harmed. No brutality or violation.'

Mandeville looked away.

'Sir Edmund, I want your word on that, or I promise you this – the Lord Cardinal will get to hear of it! Sir Edmund,' Benjamin insisted, 'you owe me something.'

'You have my word,' Mandeville muttered. 'She will be given food and drink. Tomorrow morning she will be taken to London.' He moved to the door then suddenly turned back. 'Southgate will be left here with some of the soldiers until my return when I will root out this nest of traitors!' He left, slamming the door behind him.

We stayed in my chamber most of the day. A soldier brought up some badly cooked meat and a jug of wine after which I walked along the gallery. The cloths and tapestries had been wrenched from the walls whilst in the hall every precious object had been removed. The kitchens were pillaged, the soldiers were even defecating and relieving themselves in the corners of rooms, whilst some heartless bastard had shot two of the greyhounds. Templecombe now looked as if the French had landed and the manor been turned over to pillagers.

I wandered out into the chill night air, wondering if I should visit Rachel Santerre and ensure that Mandeville was keeping his word. Behind me I could hear the sound of breaking furniture, the shouts of soldiers and the stench of cooking fires. Even I, a professional thief, felt sickened at the wanton vandalism. I was half-way between Templecombe and the chapel, about to turn back, when a dark shape stepped out of the bushes.

'Master Shallot! Master Shallot! For the love of God!'

I looked round. No soldiers were present so I moved into the shadows to meet Mathilda.

'It is all over?' she asked.

'Yes. The Santerres have fled. Mistress Rachel is Mandeville's prisoner.'

The girl bit back a sob. I remembered the icy waters of the lake and seized her by the shoulders.

'You could have killed us!' I hissed.

She looked up fearfully. I could tell by her white face and staring eyes that she did not know what had happened.

'What do you mean?' she whispered.

'Nothing,' I replied. My hands fell away. 'Did you know that Rachel Santerre was the leader of the Templar coven?'

The girl shrugged.

'We suspected but nothing was proved. Sometimes we met on the island but the master was always hooded and cowled. Orders would be issued, instructions about what we had to do.' She licked her lips and stared fearfully over my shoulder towards the house.

'We were told you were not really our enemy, Master Shallot. I was asked to know you better.' She moved a little closer. 'What will happen to us?' she pleaded.

'By now,' I replied, 'Sir John and Lady Beatrice should be on board ship bound for foreign parts. Mistress Rachel is to be taken to London.'

'And us?'

'Tell your people to flee. Put as much distance between themselves and Templecombe as possible, your father especially.'

'Where can we go?' she wailed.

I glimpsed the terror in the poor girl's face and realised she had simply been a tool. They had all been used by Rachel Santerre for her ancient order. I loosened my money belt (oh, yes, where I went, it went) and counted out ten gold coins, a veritable fortune, then slipped a small jewelled ring off my finger and pushed it all into her hands.

'Take your child,' I said, 'and your father, and within a week follow Sir John and Lady Beatrice abroad. I cannot do more for you.'

I walked back to the house, feeling as brave and courageous as Hector.

'Roger!'

I turned and glimpsed Mathilda's white face in the shadows.

'You should go,' I repeated.

'They said you were a rogue but you have more honour than any of them. Goodbye, Roger Shallot!'

I saw the shadows move, Mathilda disappeared and I walked back into the house. Now, naturally, with so many light-fingered bastards about, I decided that the best course of action was to recoup my losses with Mathilda. I grabbed whatever took my fancy and walked back to my chamber with a jewel-encrusted cup plucked from the fingers of a drunken soldier. After all, the labourer deserves payment and I wanted to show a little profit.

Benjamin was lying on my bed snoring like a child so I walked back along the galleries. Mandeville was frenetically trying to re-impose order whilst at the same time preparing for a quick departure to London the following morning.

'Are you and Daunbey returning with us?' he snapped.

'Must we?' I asked.

He shrugged. 'That is a matter for you. It is important that I take my prisoner to London and report direct to the King.'

'May I see Mistress Rachel?'

'Why?'

'I wish to take my farewells.'

Mandeville looked at me suspiciously.

'My master has ordered me to,' I lied glibly.

(Do you know, when I was young, I looked my most innocent when I was lying through my teeth?)

'She has been moved from her own chamber,' Mandeville retorted, 'to one of the cellars beneath the hall. She is being well looked after.'

'My master is the Cardinal's nephew,' I added.

Mandeville pulled a face and shrugged. 'Come! I will take you there.'

The passageways beneath the hall were lit by torches and guarded by Bowyer's soldiers. We stopped before an iron-studded door.

'Open it!' Mandeville ordered.

Inside the cellar smelt musty though, even in that dark forbidding place, I still caught the tang of Rachel's perfume. The woman herself sat on a trestle bed: she looked composed, even serene, and smiled as I entered.

'Good evening, Master Shallot. You have come to gloat?'

Mandeville slammed the door behind me and turned the key.

'A place for a princess, eh, Shallot?'

I looked round the gaunt chamber. A cresset torch flickered high on the wall and tallow candles dripped their smelly wax on a shabby table.

'Stolen from the stables,' Rachel explained, catching my glance.

I took a stool from beneath the table and sat opposite her. Though pale and tired, she quickly assured me that she was being well looked after. She had been fed and was free from molestation. Mandeville had even withdrawn the guard from sitting in the cell with her.

'They check me every so often.' She laughed. 'But there is nothing I can do. The only embarrassment is when I go to the latrines but I think the soldiers are more concerned about their plunder than they are about me. I suppose Mother and Sir John have fled?'

I nodded.

'I thought as much.'

'Why did you do it?' I asked.

She shrugged and looked over my shoulder at the candle flame.

'The Templars have always existed,' she replied. 'And Templecombe is their home. In here now, Roger, I feel their ghosts pressing around me, applauding what I did.

Mandeville and those bastards murdered Buckingham, and that fat slob in Westminster wishes to put his greedy fingers on the most precious relics in Christendom.' She shrugged. 'It was just a matter of planning.'

'But all those murders?'

'They deserved to die. Your master is most astute. Warnham and Calcraft were easy: two drunken agents full to the gills with ale as well as the evil they had committed. Cosmas and Damien?' she smiled. 'They were cleverer than you think. They were the ones who forged the letters which purportedly came from Buckingham.'

'And Mistress Hopkins?'

She looked away.

'And the old witch?'

'She served her purpose. If I could buy her, then so could Mandeville. She had to be silenced.' Rachel giggled like a young girl who had carried out some childish prank. 'I tried to warn them. I really thought Mandeville would panic and leave. He didn't so Bowyer and Southgate came next.'

'And the Grail and Excalibur?'

She shook her head. 'God knows where they are.' She looked at me under lowered eyebrows. 'Perhaps your master will find them?' She grasped my hand. 'Whatever happens, Henry Tudor must not have them! Promise me that?'

What could I do? The girl looked so pleading, I forgot she was a malicious, cold-blooded killer and gave her my word that I would do what I could.

'What will happen to Templecombe?' Rachel murmured.

'Everything ends,' I replied. 'The King will seize the manor and give it to some favourite. Who knows? Sir John may return, buy himself a pardon.'

'I don't think so,' Rachel replied. 'They will not come back here.'

She swung her legs off the bed and sat so close to me our knees touched. I stared into those strange eyes and knew

227

that, despite her cool demeanour, her feminine wiles and cloying beauty, Rachel wasn't sane. I was soon to find out why.

'Neither Santerre nor my mother will come back here.' She caught my hand. 'I am not playing games. You see, Roger, my father was a Templar. He loved Templecombe and passed his secrets on to me. Sir John was his friend. He often visited us here and my mother, who feared Father's mysterious ways and his close relationship with me, plotted his murder.'

'How?'

'My father was killed in a riding accident. Don't you remember when Bowyer's body was brought back my mother became hysterical because my father had been killed in the same way? All I did was copy what she had done. The horses made more fiery, the spurs tinged with mercury . . . Your Master suspected that. It was one of the things he whispered to me when he led me away from the rest in the hall. He said that if I confessed, he would ensure that Lady Beatrice and Santerre paid for their crime.' She laughed and rubbed her hands together. 'Exile in foreign parts is punishment enough.'

'One other thing,' I queried. 'What else did my master say?'

'Ah!' Rachel propped herself back on the bed. 'That's for Master Daunbey to tell you.'

I rose and pushed the stool away. She looked up at me.

'What will they do with me in London?'

'Do you want the truth?' I asked harshly.

'The truth.'

'They will torture you to find out the names of the other Templars, to see if you have solved Hopkins's riddle, and above all to obtain the name of your Grand Master.'

'I don't know that. And after?'

I crouched beside her and stroked her gently on the

cheek. 'The King is a bully. You will be burnt at Smithfield.'

I saw the flicker of fear in her eyes but her gaze held mine.

'In which case I must pray,' she said. 'Please, Master Shallot, ask Sir Edmund if I may have my rosary beads? The soldiers will not have touched them. They are old and battered, a present from my father. Please, I must have them.'

I agreed and walked to the door.

'Roger.'

I looked over my shoulder and forced back the tears which pricked my eyes: Rachel looked so beautiful, so vulnerable. I could hardly believe that she was responsible for so many terrible crimes. In a way her mother was responsible, guilty of tipping her mind into sudden madness.

'Adieu, Master Shallot.'

I banged on the door and Mandeville let me out.

'What did she want?' he asked.

'Nothing,' I replied. 'She is reconciled to her fate. She wishes to pray and has asked for her rosary beads.'

Mandeville looked as if he was going to refuse.

'Oh, come on, man!' I insisted. 'Give her that at least.'

Sir Edmund rapped out an order and a soldier went scurrying off to Rachel's chamber, returning a few minutes later with a set of rosary beads wrapped round his fingers. Mandeville examined them carefully. The beads were battered, the chain weak copper.

'What are you frightened of?' I scoffed. 'She can hardly hang herself with them!'

Mandeville crunched the beads together, weighed them in his hand and looked at the guard.

'You watch her all the time?'

The guard pointed to the small squint hole high in the door.

'All the time, Sir Edmund,' he replied.

Mandeville tossed the beads to him. 'Let her have them but watch her closely.'

I returned to my chamber. Benjamin was still asleep so I made myself comfortable in a chair, wrapped a rug round me and dozed fitfully until he shook me awake just after dawn. We did not bother to shave or wash. The room had grown cold because the flight of the servants meant no fresh logs had been brought up and the water in the lavarium was now covered with a film of dirty ice. We went downstairs and I marvelled at how Mandeville had brought everything under control. He had worked the soldiers all night. Every chamber except ours had been stripped. All clothes, possessions, anything which could be moved – chests, chairs, mattresses, bolsters, canopies, drapes, cups and plate – had been piled in the hall and the doors sealed. Mandeville, satisfied with what he had done, led us into the buttery where we managed to find some stale bread and a jug of watery ale.

'Everything's ready,' he informed us, snatching mouthfuls of bread. 'Southgate will stay here under a small guard until the other soldiers arrive. When he is able, he will be moved to the infirmary at Glastonbury and then to London. All the moveables of this manor are now piled in the hall and the door sealed against further thievery. The King's Commissioners will arrive and make sure everything due to the crown is seized.'

(Too bloody straight, I thought. Henry VIII's Commissioners were the most heartless set of bastards. They would snatch a crust of bread from a dying child!)

'And Mistress Rachel?' my master asked.

'She has breakfasted and been allowed to wash and change. She and I will be on the road to London within the hour.'

Mandeville was as good as his word: a short while later we heard him shouting his farewells and going down to the main courtyard where the dead sheriff's soldiers, much the worse for drink, were saddling their horses. We glimpsed Mistress Rachel in the centre of them, cloaked and hooded, her hands tied to the saddle horn, another rope under the horse's belly securing her ankles. Sir Edmund mounted and, after a great deal of clattering and shouting, the party made its way out of the manor. Never once did Rachel stir, never once look to left or right or back at Templecombe which had cost her so much. God rest her, I never saw her again.

For a while Benjamin and I went round the manor house, now empty and quiet as a tomb. Only two or three soldiers remained under the command of a burly sergeant. We visited Southgate but he still lay swathed in bandages attended by the old hags who seemed impervious to the tumult around them, being well paid by Mandeville to look after his lieutenant.

It was like visiting a house of ghosts. So difficult to imagine how, only a few days earlier, Lady Beatrice had swept round as grand as a duchess; Sir John had acted the benevolent lord; and Mistress Rachel had watched and plotted behind a demeanour as serene as a nun's.

Now, as I have said, it's hard for you young people to imagine such terrors but during Fat Henry's reign such occurrences became common. Time and again the King's agents would swoop on some great houses – Thomas Moore's, Wolsey's, Cromwell's, Boleyn's, Rochford's, Howard's – and the effect was always the same. One day it was all gaiety and dancing and the next despair and ruin.

Ah, well, it was no different at Templecombe. Benjamin was lost in his thoughts. The only time he smiled was when I informed him about Rachel wanting her rosary beads. I also pressed him on how he had made the woman confess.

'Later,' he murmured. 'Everything in its due time, Roger.'

He seemed restless, wanting to make sure Mandeville

had left. Then, about noon, when the soldiers were busy broaching a new cask of ale, he borrowed a huge mallet from the cellar and bustled me out of the house, down to the Templar chapel. Now he became excited, his face flushed, and once inside the church, locked and barred the door, making sure the windows were also closed.

'What's the matter, Benjamin?'

He turned to me, the mallet gripped tightly between his two hands.

'Don't you remember Hopkins's verse? "Beneath Jordan's water Christ's cup does rest, and above Moses' Ark the sword that's best"?'

'You think the relics are here?'

Benjamin put down the mallet and walked up the church, under the rood screen and into the sanctuary. He pointed out the old stalls where the Templars had stood to sing the divine office, and the misericords, the intricately wooden carving on each upraised seat.

'What do you see there, Roger?'

I walked along the stalls, giving him a description of each misericord; a bull, a wife, a rabbit, etc. Then I stopped. On one of the stalls, men dressed in flowing gowns were carrying a small casket between them.

'What is that?' I asked.

Benjamin joined me. 'It's the Ark of the Covenant, Roger. The small box built by Moses at the foot of Mount Sinai to carry the tablets of stone on which the ten commandments were carved.'

'Moses' Ark!' I gasped. 'You mean the Sword Excalibur is there?'

'Well, Hopkins's verse says "the sword is above the Ark".' Benjamin looked up at the heavy beamed roof. 'At first I thought it might be there but I have been up into the choir loft and that's impossible. So let's look at the seat itself.'

He drew his dagger and walked along the stalls, tapping

each with the hilt. A dull thud answered every knock but, when he reached the stall depicting the Ark of Moses, the wood sounded hollow. Benjamin carefully inspected it.

'This panel seems to be pegged together, I can trace the joining line.' He sighed. 'Ah, well, there's no other way.'

And, taking the heavy mallet, he dealt the top of the seat a resounding blow. The wood was old and weathered and immediately splintered. Benjamin cleared a space big enough to put his hand down but, when he did, the smile of triumph faded from his face.

'Nothing!' he exclaimed. 'Nothing at all.'

Benjamin took a lighted torch from the wall. We both looked down into the empty recess but there was nothing there.

'Once there might have been,' he remarked. 'But perhaps the Templars thought differently and moved it.' He banged the top of the heavily carved seat with his fist. 'I suspect there's a hidden lever which would open this recess.' He sighed and let the mallet drop. 'Perhaps they took Excalibur and threw it into the lake, its true resting place.'

'And the Grail?' I asked.

Benjamin sat in one of the choir stalls and pointed down the church. 'Do you remember, Roger, I remarked how the water of baptism is often called Jordan's river? Now, there's a baptismal font in every village church. But why here, in a Templar chapel where no women or children were allowed?' Benjamin got to his feet. 'At the risk of more destruction, I suspect that baptismal font has never been used but was built simply to guard the Grail.' He walked wearily over and I followed him. I sensed his disappointment for, if the Templars had removed Excalibur from its hiding place, why not Christ's chalice?

We carefully examined the paving stones on which the baptismal font had been erected, poking with our daggers around the edges. However, the stones had apparently never been moved since they had first been laid so we shifted our attention to the font itself. This was a simple, very large rounded bowl resting on a small, stout pillar. We looked for some hidden lever or crack but the stone held firm and, when we tapped it with our daggers, it sounded solid. Then I looked at the fine layer of cement between the baptismal bowl and the stone plinth supporting it.

'Pass me the mallet.'

Benjamin grew excited as he realised what I had found.

'No, let's do it differently,' he said.

We spent an hour chipping away at the layer of hard cement, using our knives and chisels, until it began to crumble and the bowl worked loose. The Templar mason had been very cunning. When we finally removed the bowl, we discovered the stone plinth was at least six inches thick but with a small hollow cavity in the centre. Benjamin pushed his hand in and drew out a stained, black leather bag bound at the neck. We both crouched as he cut the cord loose.

The bag, which had begun to rot, fell away and, I tell you this – Benjamin and I knelt in reverence before the Holy Grail, the very chalice from which Christ had drunk at the Last Supper. I, Roger Shallot, have seen this cup. I have held it in my hands, the greatest relic in all Christendom!

We did not hear any angels sing nor silver trumpets blast from heaven. All we saw was a simple wooden cup, shallow-bowled, with a crude stem and stand. The wood had been polished by the hands which had held it over the last one and a half thousand years and, when I smelt it, the cup gave off a resinous fragrance as if its guardian had smeared it with some substance as a protection against decay.

We sat and looked at it. Benjamin held it, then passed it to me. Now, you know Old Shallot is a scoffer. I have seen so many pieces of the true cross that if you put them together you could build a fleet. I have seen feathers which are supposed to have fallen off Angel Gabriel's wings. I have been asked to kiss a piece of Jesus's swaddling clothes; a scrap of Mary's veil; St Joseph's hammer; not to mention a handkerchief used by Moses. I have always laughed out loud at such trickeries but the Grail was different.

When I held it I felt warm, a sense of power and if I closed my eyes, I was no longer in that icy Templar church but in the warm, sweet-scented hills of Galilee. A truly mystical cup! No wonder Arthur searched for it, the Templars guarded it, and that fat bastard Henry VIII would have killed for it!

We paid the Grail reverence, Benjamin wrapped it in his cloak and left, telling me to wait. My master returned with a mixture of cement and plaster and we restored the baptismal font so that, at least to the untrained eye, it would look as if it had never been tampered with.

'What about the choir stall?' I asked.

'Leave it,' Benjamin answered. 'Let the soldiers take the blame.'

We returned to the manor house to pack our belongings. The next morning we saddled our horses and slipped away from Templecombe, that house of horrible murders. We reached Glastonbury later the same day for, though the countryside was still in winter's icy grip, no snow had fallen and at last the clouds were beginning to break. Benjamin and I had already agreed on what to do. We met Brother Eadred in the guest house. Benjamin quickly described what had happened at Templecombe. Though Eadred tried to hide his pain, Rachel's arrest, the flight of the Santerres and the destruction of the manor house obviously came as a body blow to him. He slumped on to a stool, wrapping his arms round his belly, bending forward almost as if he was in pain.

'Oh, poor Rachel!' he breathed.

'You are one of them, aren't you, Brother?' I asked.

He looked up, dark eyes in an ashen face.

'You're a Templar?' I continued.

He nodded his head. 'As are some others here,' he replied softly. 'We are guardians of a great shrine, keepers of mysteries and, yes, in a sense, avengers of those Templars who were seized, imprisoned and killed.'

'Does that give you the right to murder?'

'To protect the mysteries and secrets, yes. But Rachel went too far. She nourished a personal revenge, perhaps even a murderous madness, against the likes of Mandeville and her own family.' He took a deep breath and stood up. 'What will happen to Templecombe?'

'It will be stripped of everything.'

I saw the fear in the monk's face.

'They won't find anything,' Benjamin smiled. 'They will never discover Excalibur or the Grail.'

Eadred shrugged. 'The relics were never at Templecombe.'

'But you suspect they were? After all, succeeding abbots of Glastonbury have established that such relics do not exist here.'

Eadred stared back.

'Excalibur's gone,' Benjamin explained, 'but the Grail . . .' He loosened one of his saddle bags, plucked out his cloak and laid the small cedar cup on the table. The change in Eadred was incredible. He fell on his knees, hands joined, and stared fixedly at the holy chalice.

'You found it!' he murmured.

'And brought it to its rightful home,' Benjamin concluded. He picked up his saddle bags, gestured with his head to me and walked up the stairs to our chamber, leaving Eadred to worship alone.

The next morning, after a short meeting with Eadred, we left Glastonbury for London. He escorted us to the main abbey gates. Only when we were on the very point of departure did he clasp Benjamin's hand and thank him with his eyes. My master leaned down.

'Never,' he whispered, 'say anything to anyone. We have not been here. We gave you nothing. We shall not return.'

Eadred stepped back, sketched a blessing in the air, the gates opened and we left for London.

We took eight days to return to the capital and found it still in the steel grip of winter. The Thames had frozen whilst the city's dirt and refuse were hidden under a carpet of ice which at least killed the offensive stench. We took lodgings at Baynards Castle near St Paul's, sending a message to Hampton Court where Henry and the Cardinal were lodged preparing for Christmas. We patiently waited to see what would happen.

Three days after our arrival dear Doctor Agrippa arrived. Swathed in black robes, he looked like some merry gnome except for those strange, colourless eyes. He stamped his feet and clapped his hands against the cold, shouting for mulled wine. Only when he was alone with us in our chamber did he drop all pretence.

'The King is not pleased,' he snapped. 'Nor is My Lord Cardinal.'

'Oh dear,' I retorted. 'Little thanks for a frozen arse, almost being killed, not to mention having to spend so much time in the company of bastards like Mandeville and Santerre.'

Agrippa smirked. 'Oh, the King is not angry with you. You have heard the news?' His eyes held mine. 'Rachel Santerre died on her return to London. Apparently her rosary was not what it seemed: two of the beads contained a poisonous substance which deals death in seconds. Her corpse has been left at the new hospital of Mary of Bethlehem just north of the city.' Agrippa pulled a face. 'The King is furious. She could have provided much information.'

Benjamin rubbed the side of his face. 'But His Grace

the King should be pleased. My Lord of Buckingham is destroyed, the woman responsible for so many deaths has received her just desserts and the King can seize all the treasures of Sir John Santerre and his wife. I do not mourn for them, for they richly deserved what they got. A Templar coven in Somerset has been broken. And finally,' Benjamin shot a warning glance at me, 'although Excalibur is missing and probably will remain so until the end of time, we have brought back the Grail.'

I schooled my features but, do you know, that was the only time I had seen Agrippa surprised. His cheeks flushed and his eyes glittered.

'Where is it?' he grated.

Benjamin went to his saddle bag, took out a battered silver goblet and thrust it into Agrippa's hands. The magus gazed at it carefully.

'Where did you find this?'

'At Templecombe.'

Agrippa peered at the ancient silver chalice, the paper thin silver of its bowl and the jewels encrusted along the stem. His eyes darted like those of a cat.

'This cup,' he began slowly, 'is ancient but I know the truth and I think you do, Master Daunbey. And perhaps, in time, even the King will.'

Benjamin grinned boyishly. 'But you will tell him it's the Grail,' he declared, 'because that's what he wants to believe, and that's what you want him to believe as well, eh, Doctor Agrippa?'

The magus looked squarely at us. 'What do you mean?' he whispered.

'Oh, come, Doctor Agrippa,' Benjamin replied. 'You are a Templar yourself, aren't you? More than that, I believe you are their Grand Master. You no more want the Grail to fall into Henry's hands than I do. You *must* be the Grand Master. You suspected Rachel Santerre even before we left London, that's why you gave us the watchword "*Age Circumspecte*", act carefully. At first we thought it was a piece of advice but, of course, it's the family motto of the Mortimers, Rachel's father's family. You were warning us. You knew she was a Templar, that the Mortimers of Templecombe had been Templars for the last two hundred years. The only person who would know such a secret would be the Grand Master himself. It's true, isn't it? The Templars exist in covens but only the Grand Master knows them all?'

Agrippa sat down on the edge of the bed, cradling the cup in his hands.

'Perhaps what you say is true, Master Daunbey.' He looked at us. 'Let us say this Grand Master did exist. Let us say he feared that King Henry was The Mouldwarp, The Dark Prince prophesied by the Templar magicians themselves as The Great Destroyer. And let us say that members of his secret Templar organisation, men such as Buckingham and Hopkins, defied the order of their Grand Master and began to search out relics which were best left hidden.'

Agrippa paused and chewed his lip. 'And let us also say, for sake of argument, that the Grand Master allowed these Templars to be punished by the due process of law. Perhaps the matter would have ended there but other Templars, desirous of revenge, muddied the waters even further. And so we come to Rachel Santerre. She had no right to execute Warnham and Calcraft or carry out her own private war against the likes of Mandeville and Southgate. She was ordered to cease this but made matters worse by attacking men like you, friends of the Grand Master. Ah, well.' He rolled the cup in his hands. 'Where is the real Grail?'

'In safe hands, as you will discover!'

Agrippa sighed, picked up the cup and walked to the door.

'Then let's hope it remains so.' He turned, one hand on

the latch. 'Rachel Santerre would never have lived to be questioned. I would have killed her as a disobedient servant as I did Buckingham and Hopkins.' He played with the cup. 'But I thank you for what you did. Believe me, the King and the Lord Cardinal will receive the most glowing reports!'

The magus slipped out of the room. Benjamin went across and locked the door behind him.

'That's what you told Rachel to make her confess, wasn't it?' I asked.

'Yes, I told her the Grand Master would not be pleased with her and that her continued obduracy might threaten other Templars. I even lied and told her that the Grand Master had given me her name before we left London.'

'And she believed you?'

'Yes, I think she did.'

'And the cup?'

'Agrippa is right. It's from the treasures of Glastonbury Abbey. Eadred gave it to me. I believe it once belonged to the Emperor Constantine's father who served as a general here.'

'Will the King suspect?'

'In time, when the cup does not release its magic, he will.' Benjamin gripped me by the shoulders. 'But we know the truth, Roger, and we must keep it a secret. If the King suspects, even for a second, we will go the same way as Buckingham. Now, come, before Uncle can think of any more tasks, let us pack, brave the weather and return to Ipswich.'

Oh, we did, to the most joyous Yuletide ever, leaving behind The Great Killer to sup wine from what he thought was the Grail. The Lord Cardinal sent us letters of the most fulsome praise and heavy purses of gold, but Henry never forgot and neither did the Templars. Sir Edmund Mandeville mysteriously died the following spring after attending a banquet at Sheen. I believe Agrippa was in attendance at the time. Southgate never recovered from his wounds and, although moved to the care of the nuns at Syon, died shortly afterwards. I am not too sure about the details but, the previous afternoon, Doctor Agrippa had come to enquire about his health. The Santerres waited a year and applied for a pardon, offering gold by the cupful, but strangely enough Henry refused to be bribed and I believe they died mysteriously in foreign parts.

Templecombe was seized and stripped of all its possessions, turned into a veritable ruin, but the King found nothing there. Years later, when he launched his great attack on the abbeys and monasteries, Glastonbury was singled out for special attention. Abbot Bere died in 1524 and was succeeded by Richard Whitting. Fat Henry sent special agents to seize Glastonbury's most precious treasures but Whitting was cunning and spirited these away and, for that, paid the supreme penalty. He was brought to London and tortured but would say nothing. Accordingly, he was taken back to Somerset and, after a mock trial, he and two of his monks, one of them being the scholarly Eadred, were dragged through Glastonbury on hurdles and then hanged on the summit of the Tor in November 1539. The secrets of Glastonbury died with them and only the good Lord knows the whereabouts of the Grail.

So this bloody tale is done. I stare through the window and watch the moon's silver light bathing the hard-packed snow in a shimmering light. All have gone. Sometimes I dream of Rachel, cool and serene in her cellar prison; Mandeville and Southgate, arrogant in their power, and those two sombre mutes, Cosmas and Damien, who served them so well and suffered so barbarously. The circle is complete. Mathilda's son has come back to return the ring I gave his mother an eternity ago in the dark shadows round Templecombe. Oh, for a cup of claret to warm the heart and hold back the tears about the past! Even my little clerk is sniffing.

I know he wants to stay, to lust after Phoebe's generous tits. He shakes his head, stands by the window and looks out at the winter sky.

'Do you think, sir,' he whines, 'that there really is a supreme intelligence above us? A wisdom guiding our affairs?'

'I sincerely hope so, because there's bugger all down here!'

Author's Note

I have just finished studying Sir Roger Shallot's next memoirs about his turbulent visit to Florence in sixteenth-century Italy. It's difficult to accept his almost incredible story but the same was true when I first edited his memoirs about the Grail Murders.

Sir Roger can be economical with the facts but there is a great deal of truth in these memoirs. Buckingham was executed for the reasons and in the manner described in this book, whilst the survival of the secret order of the Templars is a well-documented fact, referred to in Graham Hancock's recent book *The Sign and the Seal*.

The remnants of both Templecombe and Glastonbury can be visited today. At Templecombe in the 1960s a secret painting of Christ was discovered, copied perhaps from the shroud which the Templars once owned. This, in turn, gave rise to the spurious legends that the Templars adored a decapitated head, the source of great power.

Glastonbury did hold the remains of Arthur, and the site of his tomb at Glastonbury can still be visited. The origins and mysteries of that abbey, as described by Shallot, are well documented in various books. Excalibur has lain hidden for ever but the Grail was probably secretly guarded by the monks at Glastonbury which accounts for Henry VIII's vicious persecution of the abbot and his community when that abbey was dissolved in the 1530s. The abbot and certain

243

of his companions were barbarously executed on the summit of the Tor as Shallot describes. The Grail itself was probably spirited away to the abbey of Strata Florida in Wales. According to one source, it was last seen in the 1920s in a bank vault at Nanteos, three miles from Aberystwyth. Consequently, Sir Roger Shallot may not be the great liar we sometimes suspect him to be!